EVERYTHING BUT THE EARL

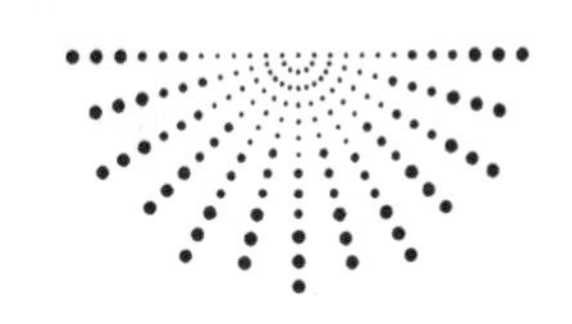

WILLA RAMSEY

EVERYTHING BUT THE EARL
Wayward & Willful, Book 1

CITY OWL PRESS
www.cityowlpress.com

Cover Design by Mibl Art and Tina Moss. All stock photos licensed appropriately.

Edited by Heather McCorkle.

For information on subsidiary rights, please contact the publisher at info@cityowlpress.com.

Print Edition ISBN: 978-1-944728-90-8

Digital Edition ISBN: 978-1-944728-89-2

Printed in the United States of America

For my family
Without your support, this book might never have been written.
(Although without you reading it, it might have been steamier.)

PRAISE FOR WILLA RAMSEY

"Miss Caroline Crispin, daughter to England's royal architect, speaks boldly and flirts audaciously...Ramsey's smooth prose and witty dialogue make for enjoyable reading."

- *Publisher's Weekly*

"Willa Ramsey is a delightful new voice in historical romance. Everything but the Earl is funny, fresh, and charming. I love the genuine partnership between Adam and Caro as he helps her fight the patriarchy and expands his own definition of gender roles."

- *Victoria De La O, 2017 RITA finalist for Tell Me How This Ends*

"Everything but the Earl has everything you could want in a Regency romp: a headstrong, forward-thinking heroine; a charming, homebody of a hero; and enough witty repartee to fill readers with delight. Willa Ramsey brings a refreshing new voice to Regency Romance."

- *Elizabeth Essex, Award Winning Author of the Highland Brides Series*

CHAPTER ONE

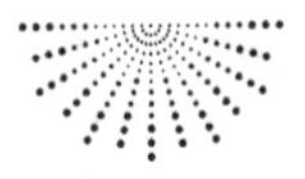

JULY 1819

Was there any greater satisfaction than the satisfaction of a party gone wonderfully well?

Miss Caroline Crispin didn't think so. Or if there was, she hadn't found it just yet.

She lifted her foot from the cool tile of the entry hall, curling her toes discreetly. She'd been on her feet nearly a whole day by then, and her soles were telling the tale. But as she recalled the sea of ruddy cheeks rolling across her parents' grand ballroom, the echoes of wildly stomping feet, and the sweet, summertime heaviness in the air, she smiled. The sleepy, achy, sated ending to a ball was always her favorite part.

It was nearing dawn, but rest could wait.

Lords Strayeth and Chumsley were next in the queue to make their goodbyes to her, each of them puffing out their chests as if they'd just discovered a new continent in the retiring room.

"My lords," she began in a low voice, returning their smirks. "Did everything meet with your approval this evening? Was the conversation stimulating? Were the ladies' bodices...stimulating?"

"Indeed," Chumsley replied, his mouth a tight line. He was short but sturdy-looking, with white-blond hair and striking blue eyes that some had compared to the waters of the West Indies. "Lovely evening, Miss Crispin."

She shifted from one sore foot to the other. *When had these gentlemen become so...straitlaced?* Certainly, it was racy to talk this way. But she'd danced and flirted with them at countless social events since her seventeenth birthday, four years earlier. She had even kissed Strayeth once, at a public ball, behind what was perhaps the largest potted ficus in all of England.

"The conversation and the bodices were just to our liking," Strayeth added, his eyes fixed elsewhere in the crowd. He was the lankier and more fashionable of the pair, with a floppy brown forelock he had to constantly shake back from his eyes.

"Both were rather deep then, I imagine?" she asked, trying to egg them on.

She no longer sought attention from men their age, really. They were beginning to look for wives, and the very thought of marrying sent a shiver all through her. She'd watched her mother toil silently beside her father her whole life; had seen her design the grand home in which they now gathered but give Papa all the credit; had heard her cry quietly in the studio when she thought everyone had gone to bed. Caro knew a husband of her own would expect her to leave her ideas unsaid, too; to give up her charitable schemes. And her ideas and schemes were like wildflowers: They were exuberant, plentiful, and deeply resistant to the forces of domestication.

But she *so* enjoyed a bit of good repartee! Couldn't she jest with these gentlemen anymore? They had been friends of a sort, once.

"Thank you, Miss Crispin," Strayeth replied, bowing and nudging Chumsley toward the door. "Your abilities as a hostess are...most remarkable."

They hadn't stepped more than a few feet away, however, when Chumsley leaned over and murmured something in his friend's ear. She wasn't certain, but it sounded a bit like, "*Even my pointer has learned to shake hands.*"

Now she was confused. And a little bit unsettled. But just as she was resolving to speak less of bosoms and bodices, a loud *clang* sounded from the ballroom followed by several whoops and whistles.

"*Lud*," Caro said to herself, looking at the ceiling. "I asked Mr. McNabbins not to juggle the serving bowls anymore. His new assistant is hardly a proficient."

Grinning now, Strayeth and Chumsley made a quick bow and trotted off toward the ballroom, in the direction of the clattering dishware (and in all likelihood, her guests from the Sadler's Wells theater). She was confronted at once by another departing guest, a stooped older man in an unfashionable powdered wig.

"Where is your father?" Lord Tilbeth demanded, his mottled complexion growing pinker by the second. "I had but one moment's conversation with him all evening."

"He's in the studio, my lord." She rubbed her temple, glancing behind him at the long queue of guests that still extended through the spacious entry hall and into the ballroom beyond, all waiting to speak with her. "You know how it is."

He looked at her blankly.

"You see, when a person is in trade, he often has to *work*. Rather hard. Sometimes even at night."

"But your father is the Prince Regent's favorite architect! Look at all of these...these *people*!" he fumed, gesturing at the assortment of aristocrats and merchants, entertainers and artists, professors and cabinet ministers, all drooping sleepily behind him. "Half of London wants him to build their next home or some such! The least he could do is make himself available."

"They're like fighters, my lord."

"I beg your pardon?"

"Champions must stay in top form, Lord Tilbeth! Other architects are waiting just outside the ropes, so to speak, eager to take my parents' place."

He scrunched up his face—possibly upon hearing the word "parents" when most people would expect to hear "father"—but just then his wife emerged from a group of ladies standing nearby. She gave Caro a curt nod, the feathers in her turban bobbing haughtily behind her. Then she tugged her husband forward with a lurch, through the open door, and into the earliest glimmers of dawn.

Caro turned back to her guests and was delighted to find her dearest friend awaiting her next.

"It always amuses me," Edie whispered as they shared a firm embrace, "to watch the Tilbeths pretend to have fun at your balls."

"They fear they'll break into hives if they accidentally rub elbows with a shopkeeper," she replied, her laugh fluttering Edie's straw-colored hair. "Heaven help them if they ever bump into my butcher. He never misses my parties."

She stepped back and watched as Edie bent down to pick up an enormous basket at her feet, its contents obscured by a piece of white linen.

"Dearest! What are you doing?" Caro asked.

"It's your apples. I thought I'd bring them to the orphanage for you. Well done, Caro. Wherever did you get the idea to ask everyone to harvest the ornamental trees in their gardens? This might be your cleverest scheme yet."

Just one basket? From three hundred guests? This was a disappointing result, indeed. "I suspect all the credit goes to a half-dozen servants," she replied over a sigh, "as they were the ones who did the harvesting."

"Actually, my brother picked all our apples," Edie replied, looking into her basket. "Although he had to steal them, I believe—"

"Edie!" Caro exclaimed, cuffing her lightly on the shoulder. "Your own brother is here, and you haven't introduced me?"

Edie cuffed her back, bobbling her basket a little. They'd spent many a year together at Mrs. Hellkirk's Seminary for Wayward and Willful Girls, and had taken rather well to the unusual set of manners taught there. Like fish to water.

"I'm not his keeper," Edie replied as she adjusted her heavy load. She nodded toward the ballroom. "He's the big one."

Caro whipped her head around and looked.

And then she looked some more.

That was Edie's brother?

"Thank you for a lovely time," Edie told her.

Caro had long been curious about Edie's mysterious older sibling. He wasn't a recluse, she'd explained, just a determined homebody with a preference for the country. Caro strained on her tiptoes, angling for a better look.

"I'm putting on my bonnet now," Edie added, waving a hand in front of her face. "And my cape. And sword."

Caro knew that Edie's brother—Adam Wexley, the Earl of Ryland—had some notoriety as a fighter. Everyone did. But in school Edie had described him as "oafish" and "insufferable." Caro had been left to imagine a lumbering, pasty sort of man. Weak-chinned, and prone to sneering at independent-minded ladies.

"And I'm taking your apples, Caro. I'm going to throw them into the River Thames, and dance a jig along the bank."

But Lord Ryland appeared to defy Caro's low expectations. He was standing rather far away from her, but she could see that he was indeed exceptionally tall and broad-shouldered. His hair was very dark—was it black?—and seemed shorter than most men were wont to wear it. Caro couldn't make out any other details, but one thing was certain: Lord Ryland was striking. Even from the next room.

And his chin seemed perfectly fine.

Caro settled back on her heels and pulled her friend close.

"Edie."

"She speaks."

"*Edie!*"

A gentleman farther back in the queue cleared his throat, and Caro knew she must hurry things along.

"Yes?"

"Nothing. Nothing of any consequence," Caro replied as she leaned in for a one-armed embrace. "Give my regards to your mother. I do hope she feels better soon! And put down that basket, Lady Edith Wexley! It looks heavy. I can manage it."

"Honestly, Caro," Edie replied, smiling as three or four apples tumbled from the basket as Caro took it. "If you're going to conduct all these schemes of yours, you're going to have to accept a hand every now and again."

* * *

Adam was struggling.

Struggling against the urge to let out a cracking-good laugh.

He was standing with one of the foremost Italian opera singers, and the poor soul was enduring a small torture of his own: that of having to pick apple peel from his lower front teeth.

"Does an Englishman always bring such gifts to a party?" the baritone asked, giving up on the remains of his first pilfered apple and moving on to a second, greener one.

Adam was accustomed to being the deepest-voiced person in a room, but he could swear he'd seen the candelabras tremble in the presence of the bushy-bearded performer's low and sonorous authority.

"No," he replied. "We're not often asked to bring a hostess something we've found on the ground."

The singer bowed and headed to the refreshments, so Adam was free to step into the loose queue of people waiting to leave the party. He wondered where his sister Edie had gotten off to, and lamented being torn away from the novel he'd begun earlier that day.

He glanced around the ballroom. *Criminy!* The view into Crispins' back garden was unbelievable. The ceiling soared, and the windows were positively enormous. The room must be bathed in sunlight all day long. Now he understood why the crème of society had lined up to kiss the hand of Mr. Crispin's only daughter and hostess: the architect's talents were extraordinary, and his home showed it. No wonder everyone admired him.

What would Father say, if he could see the state of his own beloved townhouse?

He rubbed hard at his forehead, trying to banish the unflattering thought.

Father wouldn't have neglected the place. And he wouldn't have allowed Edie to run about without an escort. And Mother wouldn't be recovering from a terrible injury.

The couple in front of him stepped forward a few paces, giving him a better view into the entrance hall. And for the first time Miss Caroline Crispin was in his view, too. He'd never seen the hostess before, but he could tell it was her by the way all of the heads in the vicinity oriented themselves toward her—watching her, hoping for a moment of her notice.

He could hardly blame them.

Edie had mentioned that her friend was confident and outspoken. Brash, even. She'd told him that she admired the architect's daughter for the quickness of her mind and tongue, her bottomless generosity; her relentless pursuit of the things she wanted to accomplish.

What his sister wouldn't have known, of course, was that such levels of confidence, when combined with an already-pretty countenance, tended to render a woman stunning. Unforgettable, even.

And Miss Caroline Crispin already had a pretty countenance.

Her hair was a dark brown—that was all Adam could tell of it, from a distance—and perhaps it was strange, but the next thing that struck him was her posture. She was of average height, but she carried herself more naturally than was fashionable. She gestured expressively with long, gloved arms, nodding and swaying, deep in debate with the gentleman standing before her.

The lucky devil.

Whomp—a man's hand landed hard between his shoulder blades, sending him forward a full step.

"Ryland, old man! When did you get here? Been hiding out in the hinterlands again, pruning those pretty little flowers of yours?"

Adam swallowed a frown and made a quick bow. "Strayeth, Chumsley. I arrived in town last week, actually." *I'm just very good at avoiding you.*

They hadn't changed a bit. Clearly. He'd met them at his club some years earlier, when they'd been drinking hard and wagering over something awful—an upcoming cock fight, perhaps? He hadn't wanted to know the details.

Strayeth grabbed and squeezed his shoulder, then gave him a light shake. "We need to get you brawling again, Ryland. Don't we, Chum?"

Adam's heart began tapping a little harder at his ribs. Father had often squeezed him on the shoulder, whenever Adam asked to stop sparring; when he craved the serenity of his small garden—the roses he could never get enough of, the shaded bench he could read on for hours. Father had been firm with him as a boy, but never rough; as if by placing a big, still hand on his shoulder he could infuse in him the drive not only to fight, but to win, and the mental fortitude to train for it. It never worked, though. Adam could not find the first of those traits within himself, though he could—and did—force himself to continue doing whatever Father had asked of him.

Adam both missed and dreaded that hand on his shoulder—and the memory of it—all at once.

"I have no plans to return to the ring," he replied as he wiped a bead of sweat from his brow.

"What, now? You wouldn't want to break the Ryland tradition, would you? Your father was a fine man, they say."

"The very best," Adam replied.

"Then why not honor him?" Strayeth continued, letting go of his shoulder and poking him instead, deep in the recess of his collarbone. "Besides, you can't break the Duke of Portson's arm and nose then retire to a life in the country, Ryland. Tell him, Chum."

Adam took a deep breath as the heat in his skin ticked up still further. He *so* hated to be poked and prodded. "Right now, gentlemen," he replied finally, turning back toward the entry hall for another look at Miss Crispin. "I'd just like to shake hands with our fair hostess and get back to the comforts of my own home."

"Who?" Strayeth asked. "Caro?"

Adam winced at the use of the young woman's given name.

"You know the lady?" he asked.

"Is that what we're calling the opinionated young miss from Marylebone these days?" Chumsley asked, looking at Strayeth with a snort. "That honor is conferred a bit too broadly, is it not?"

Now Adam had had enough. He could only assume that they disdained Miss Crispin on account of her birth, and his patience for their arrogance had been worn to a husk. "Do watch yourself, both of you!" he growled, snapping back to them. "You are guests in this home!"

Strayeth took a step back, his chuckle bloating rapidly into a full-throated laugh. "Oh ho ho, Ryland! Didn't realize you were such a friend of the lower orders! Want to take it outside, then? Is this how we finally get you brawling again?" He put up his fists and took a fighting stance, biting his lip and punching the air in front of Adam's face.

Adam closed his eyes and leaned away from the jabs, regretting his angry outburst. He opened his eyes and bid them farewell, exited the ballroom, and gestured to a footman for his hat and cane.

He knew it was terrible manners to leave without a proper farewell, but he'd become rather adept at withdrawing from the world, at avoiding obligations whenever it was convenient for him. So with his accoutrements in hand, he strode briskly down a darkened corridor toward the rear of the house, where he expected there would be a servants' staircase of some kind.

But as the voices faded behind him, he stopped. *No. Not this time.* He rapped his cane on the floor and recalled Father's dying words: *Be a gentleman, Adam. A true man. Always.*

He'd been just fifteen years old when he'd heard them, and they'd gone with him everywhere, ever since.

He might never forgive himself for abandoning the family's boxing legacy, but he could begin fulfilling other duties: He could fix the townhouse. He could better protect his family. He could step up his efforts to find a wife and get an heir. And he could stop avoiding people. Or at least, do so a little less often.

He was about to turn back when a familiar voice called out, "Ryland? A word?"

He turned to find an old schoolmate, Lord Quillen, approaching with Miss Crispin on his arm.

How does a person laugh without really laughing? Because that's what Miss Crispin seemed to be doing, her eyes the color of tea left out in the afternoon sun. And then she smiled at him, those strong-brew eyes growing wide—unnaturally wide, he thought—as if they could absorb all the light from the nearly extinguished candles along the walls.

It was an expression that seemed to say: *Finally, something exciting is going to happen.*

"Our hostess just informed me that if I didn't introduce her to the gentleman sneaking away from her party," Quillen began, "that I'd find myself seated between two Tilbeths at all future card parties." He gave an exaggerated grimace and performed the introductions.

"I beg your pardon, Miss Crispin," Adam began, pulling at the bottom edge of his coat. Why did his throat feel so dry? *Say your piece, Ryland. Look stern. Exit through door.* "But my mother is quite—"

"You cannot blame this on your mother," she interrupted.

He stilled. "I beg your pardon?"

"Your mother's injury *cannot* be the reason you're skulking through our portrait gallery, my lord! I saw Lady Ryland just yesterday, and she felt *so* well that she sang me the latest from Schubert. Loudly, and with feeling." Her lips twisted into a wry sort of expression, raising the hair on his forearms in tandem.

You were in my house just yesterday, and I missed it? Clearly, I haven't worked nearly hard enough at being a homebody.

Quillen glanced back and forth between them, a bemused expression stretching slowly across his face. Then he bid them farewell and headed back toward the entry hall. Adam was now quite alone with Miss Crispin, about a hundred feet from the nearest guests and servants.

"Do not vex yourself, Lord Ryland. I'm not going to check your pockets for silver," she continued, adjusting the tops of her gloves. "Your sister warned me about these peculiar manners of yours."

"She warned me about you, as well," he replied in a rush, straightening and re-straightening his shoulders.

"Did she, now?" Miss Crispin opened her fan with an exaggerated *crack,* fanning herself theatrically. "And what did my dear Edie say about me, my lord? I'm all anticipation."

"She said that you are—what was the word?" He stepped closer. He wasn't sure what had come over him, but all thoughts of leaving seemed to have evaporated.

"*Brash,* I believe. Edie said you were brash."

"Ah, yes. An American word. A good word."

"An apt word?"

"Most certainly."

He found himself eager to impress Miss Crispin, to keep her eyes on him, to keep her talking. He scratched at the hair above his ear. "She also told me you had a quick mind," he said softly, leaning down. He was now only a foot or so away from her.

"Oh, *stop*," she replied. "I'm blushing now."

"And a quick tongue."

And with that, the loquacious Miss Crispin went quiet, her loose posture suddenly quite still.

He stepped back. *Too bold, Ryland. Too bold by half!* He feared he'd offended her, though she continued to smile and look him straight in the eye. "And you clearly have little sympathy for gentlemen who feel entitled to sneak away from your party," he continued, more warily now. "Rightfully so, I might add. I must apologize."

"Ah, yes," she responded, her limbs suddenly fluid and easy again. She fanned herself some more. "What *is* it with you modern gentlemen, and your prodigious sense of entitlement? If only I could make a fuel from it, no one in London would so much as shiver, all winter long."

He laughed aloud—he couldn't help it—but she spoke again before he could think of a riposte.

"You are free to go, Lord Ryland. In return for your rather generous donation of apples this evening, I give you leave. *Sneak away*." Then she curtsied and turned, heading back to her guests in the entry hall.

As he bowed and watched her go, he felt utterly strange. On the one hand, their exchange had been a burst of pleasure he hadn't realized he'd been needing. Disappointment at the brevity of it coursed through him.

But he also knew that parting ways with Miss Crispin was for the best. He might not be well-practiced at moving in society, but even he knew better than to flirt unguardedly with a lady unless he intended to court her.

But then, what if he *did* intend to court Miss Crispin? He wanted to marry. His family wasn't concerned about her birth, and seemed to admire her for more than her impressive position in society. And couldn't everyone benefit from a few more bursts of pleasure in their lives?

Perhaps finding a wife would be one duty he could attempt with some ease.

* * *

"Toby, you're a true prince! Just don't tell ol' Prinny that I said it," Caro told the dog as they descended the stairs to the ground floor. She wanted to take him on a sunrise constitutional now that the last of her guests had departed, but they needed to see the housekeeper first. So she brought the beloved mongrel—half-bulldog, half-terrier—to a secluded nook off the entry hall where she could drop into a small chair and wait. Toby sank obediently to the floor, his foot landing hard on her slipper.

"You've a head like a small anvil," she cooed, leaning down and massaging his velvety ears. He yawned back at her. "And a mouth like a small lion."

A soft knock sounded on the wall. The tiny space was little more than a wrinkle at the edge of the room—the snuggest of snuggeries—and had a narrow opening that wasn't visible when looked at straight-on. "Miss Crispin, you wanted to see me?" asked Mrs. Meary in her familiar lilt.

"Yes!" Caro replied, holding out a sack of coins. "May I give you this now?"

"For splittin' amongst everyone, Miss?"

"That would be lovely, thank you. The evening went off so beautifully. And would you ask Stinson to take this beast on his walk?" Caro handed her the dog's leash. "I thought I could manage it, but I'm not sure I could keep pace this morning, after all."

As Mrs. Meary led Toby away, Caro leaned back and lifted her skirts, giving her feet a much-needed rubbing. She smiled at an assortment of pleasant memories from the ball: The pungent smell of the garden when the windows were opened at midnight. The shouting of witty parries over jubilant music. The refreshing tang of the lemonade after an especially brisk waltz.

And what about that exchange with Lord Ryland? *Lud!* Where was the oaf Edie had promised? The mythic fighter? He'd been positively timid with her—apologetic, even.

Perhaps he was simply good at play-acting. His words had eventually turned salacious, after all, and when her pulse had begun jumping and dancing in her veins she'd figured it must be her conscience, reminding her not to flirt with men of marrying age. She resolved, now, to make conversation that was a bit less personal—and not about bosoms or bodices—in future.

The sound of heavy boots clomping on the entry-hall tile roused her from her reverie. *Who could possibly still be in the house?* She stood up and brushed at her skirts but didn't move fast enough; she was still out of sight when two gentlemen started speaking.

"All right, then. I will see you later on."

Chumsley.

"Right, Chum. At White's, per usual."

And Strayeth, of course. Perhaps they expected Barclay to come forward with their hats and canes? They wouldn't know that the butler was already busy with the myriad extra tasks that awaited him after a ball. It was just like them to linger after giving their farewells, to claim the last of Cook's delicacies and have a laugh about the nude portraits and sculptures throughout the home.

"I don't understand it," Chumsley sighed.

"What is it, man?"

"I *do* understand that everyone is quite desperate to put Crispin to work for them. But there's got to be another way, without having to bow down to his whore daughter all of the time."

She felt as if she'd been kicked in the chest by a horse. She exploded with pain and dropped into her chair with a *shoosh*.

Strayeth cackled in response, a loud *crack* suggesting that he also slapped himself rather hard on the thigh.

"I cannot be the only gentleman who finds it tedious to have to keep pretending that she's respectable!" Chumsley went on. "Who on Earth does she think she is, with all that talk of bodices?"

"I don't know," Strayeth replied through his laughter. "Someone who hasn't realized that a lady doesn't speak of bare bosoms? But she's always been quite the coquette, Chum. You know that."

"True enough," Chumsley said, sounding exasperated. "It's as if a common whore has all of society wrapped around her little finger. I saw her with a bishop earlier, Stray. Do you suppose she spoke to *him* of stockings and petticoats?"

More laughter.

Caro burned behind the eyes, her chest still throbbing.

"She claims she doesn't want to marry, but it's just another one of her jokes, I'm sure," Chumsley went on. "Anyone can see she's set on marrying well. Can you imagine, Stray? Honestly, it's embarrassing."

The other lord snorted his agreement. "I make it a rule that once a woman's been compromised by three of the men in my circle, I no longer dance with her."

Compromised? Caro sat up again, suppressing a snort of her own. *What in Heaven's name are they referring to? That I've kissed a few men over the years?*

And three? She looked down at her fingers and did some quick accounting.

Fair enough. Three it was. Possibly four, depending on how one looked at things.

"Pish!" Chumsley continued. "I wouldn't hand that woman into a carriage!"

More laughter.

"She might not be suitable for proper courting," he went on. "But she might be useful for other...purposes."

His voice softened, and seemed to be moving closer to the nook. Caro stopped moving. Every bone, breath, and sinew, every hair and nail and thought and fiber—all of her stood as still and cool as a new headstone, gone fresh into the ground.

"I've long suspected she was mine for the taking," Strayeth whispered, his voice a low rasp. "She flutters over to me whenever I enter a room. And she sometimes puts a hand on my sleeve!"

"Pish! *You?* You've a gift when it comes to the debutantes, Strayeth. But while you've been worshiping at the finer doorsteps in town, I've entered into many an enjoyable apprenticeship with the daughters of shopkeepers and newspapermen."

"And what about the daughters of builders?"

"They might as well be next in my education."

More laughter.

Really, it was the snickering that sickened Caro most of all.

"Well then, Strayeth. We seem to be at odds on the issue. Perhaps we can make it a wager?"

"Always! What did you have in mind?"

"Let's do it this way: whichever of us gets under Miss Crispin's petticoats by the end of the season, wins."

"And what coin are you willing to put on it?"

Chumsley paused a moment. "The losing gentleman shall pay the other one hundred pounds."

Caro heard the hollow *clap* of two hands coming together, and knew they were shaking on it. The dull *click* of the front door soon followed, together with the familiar rattling of frames against the walls. At these sounds, she slid from her chair—and into a large urn—before hitting the floor, a pile of limbs and fabrics and shards of fine porcelain. Tears of mortification plummeted down her cheeks.

CHAPTER TWO

Half an hour later, Caro was still on the floor—every part of her numb with shock, her thoughts a thick sludge—when she heard the front door open, and with it the furious scratching of canine toenails. She brushed off her gown and stood, still wiping hot tears from her face.

Air—that's all I need. Some fresh air. She smoothed at her hair and emerged into the entry hall.

"Stinson, hello there!" she called out, extending her hand. "I'll take Toby now, thank you."

"He's had quite a good run, Miss," the footman replied.

"That's wonderful. I'm taking him out again anyway."

"Are you sure, Miss? He did himself in, just now. Chasing 'em squirrels he hates so much."

"Oh, but he likes them, Stinson! He just wants to kiss one or two," she replied, cringing as soon as the words had left her mouth. She hurried through the door just as the sun was extending its amber fingers between the rooftops along her street.

"But, Miss—"

"We'll be going now!" she interrupted, not turning back.

She bounded down the steps, Toby's leash in hand, and turned them down Upper Wimpole Street. It was one of their usual routes, and they charged toward Cavendish Square as if the fate of their world depended on it.

No one else was on the street at that crisp, early hour, which was perfect: She didn't want to see *anyone*. Everything about her felt loose, jumbled, and out of sorts. Everything she thought she knew had been pulled down from the cabinet of her mind and tossed up into the air, willy-nilly, like Mr. McNabbins with her very best serving bowls.

She didn't get very far in such a state, of course. After a few blocks, her breathing became so labored that she all but collapsed onto a low wall before a stately terrace home.

She shook her head and after several slow breaths—*one at a time, one at a time, one at a time*—sat up rigidly and looked down.

Lud! She was still wearing her ball gown!

And she'd left her gloves at home.

She clutched at her pink, low-cut bodice. What had she been thinking?

She'd been thinking: *I am not a whore. Why would those gentlemen, who as children had stomped and squealed with me in our garden, call me one?*

And: *What did Mrs. Hellkirk always say? 'There are many insidious ways to check a woman who speaks too loudly, or too often.'*

Footsteps sounded on the sidewalk, several doors down. She lifted her head and squinted into the first glare of morning. A well-dressed man with graying sideburns and a boldly patterned coat approached, looking a bit like a former pupil of her parents'—a Mr. Maplebaum. She clutched her bodice tighter and cursed herself for charging from the house in such a state. *How could I be so self-indulgent? What will Mr. Maplebaum say?*

Lord. Did he already think her a whore?

Did *all* the gentlemen she knew think of her that way? It was strange, but the next man who came to her mind was Edie's enigmatic brother, Lord Ryland. She felt a pang of something—guilt or regret, perhaps—as she considered whether he might think ill of her, too.

The man with the sideburns stopped three doors away from her, just close enough for her to conclude that he was *not* Mr. Maplebaum, thank goodness. *Whew!* Too young, too spry. Still, he was looking at her in a strange way, and she wound Toby's leash twice more around her pale and shaking hands, as tightly as she could. Toby whined and licked his lips, then looked up at her.

Oh, dear Lord. Had this man heard something about her? Had Strayeth and Chumsley been calling her terrible names at their club, telling exaggerated tales even before her ball?

Did gentlemen she'd never even met believe her to be...available?

Fear seized her chest. It was as if someone had plunged her favorite hairpin there, and she crumpled around the pain.

What had she done to find herself here? Improperly dressed, on the street at an unusual hour, and confident that the strange gentlemen approaching her would expect more from her than from other misses?

Devil take it. Am I a whore, then?

She allowed herself a quick sniffle then erected herself again, taking a moment to make herself taller, straighter, steadier. She even loosened her grip on Toby's leash, which had already made deep, ruddy grooves in her palms. A fortuneteller outside Covent Garden had once told her that the pattern there—this same delta of thick blue veins, now pulsing wildly under leather-burned skin—meant she would overturn a giant one day.

Was this to be her giant? The oafish and outsized claims of these gentlemen?

A loud *clank* and a *whoosh* sounded just behind her, nearly sending her out of her skin. She jumped off the wall, sending Toby skittering to his own feet with a start.

"Miss Caroline Crispin! Is that you?"

She breathed a sigh of relief and managed to eke out the words, "Mrs. Cavel, hello there. Pardon our intrusion on your threshold. My dog and I were just...just in need of a short rest." She glanced down the street. The man with the sideburns was gone.

"Linger all you want, my dear," Mrs. Cavel replied. Voluptuous and good-humored, she was old enough to be Caro's mother and wore a fanciful, peacock-blue dress, edged in black lace. She pushed up her bosom and fluffed at the curls underneath her bonnet, examining her reflection in her front door. "Tell me, how is your father? Perhaps you could mention to him that my façade is in need of some improvement, hmm?"

"Of course, Mrs. Cavel."

"And that my house needs some work, too," she added with a wink as she turned and descended the steps.

"I'll mention it to them."

She stopped half-way down. "'*Them*'? Who is 'them'?"

Caro sighed. Should she admit to Mrs. Cavel that "them" included Papa *and* Mama? But that many years ago a wealthy minister, after hearing Mama explain to him the engineering principles of stress and strain, asked Papa never to bring her to his building site again? That another patron insisted their meetings take place at a gaming hell, thereby ensuring Mama could not attend? That still another made a habit of pinching her derriere? And that these and other mortifications gradually nudged Mama's work—and her genius—into Papa's long shadow?

There are many insidious ways to check a woman who speaks too loudly, or too often.

No, she couldn't tell Mrs. Cavel any of these things. And she certainly couldn't admit that such things were the reason she would never do anything that put her *own* voice at risk—her own work and independence. She wouldn't gamble a single guinea of her inheritance, she wouldn't delegate any of her schemes, and she certainly could never marry. She was even more certain of this now that she'd discovered two men she'd considered her friends thought so ill of her. Who could she possibly trust?

"My father and his pupils," Caro replied, resignation in her tone. "I'll tell Papa and his pupils you'd like to speak with them."

"Good. Now what is *that*, child?" she asked, nodding at the hem of Caro's gown.

She looked down. "Dirt, I'd say. Looks a lot like dirt."

"Dirt, with a light coating of manure!"

Caro managed a laugh. "You should see me on market day, Mrs. Cavel. Blood and grease up to my knees."

Mrs. Cavel clucked her tongue. "Only you, Miss Caroline Crispin! You could roll around in the gutter and dump flour on your head, and all of society would pretend they didn't notice."

"All but you, it would seem."

"Humph! It must be nice to be the daughter of the Royal Architect."

Caro was about to reply when it struck her: Chumsley and Strayeth wouldn't dare speak ill of her at their club—or anywhere else, for that matter. Dukes and bishops and even the Prince Regent himself held Papa in the highest regard, and lesser aristos knew better than to risk rebuke from such powerful people.

In fact, all of society gave her a level of respect not normally due the daughter of a "builder," because all of them wanted Papa to build them their next home. They turned a blind eye to her dalliances, her love of bawdy talk, and any other "mud" that attached itself to her, as Mrs. Cavel had put it.

Other young misses were not so lucky, of course; their indiscretions led to their being snubbed and ignored, sometimes even pushed out of society. She had known all of this for as long as she'd known her own name. But earlier, in the confusion and pain of the nook, she'd somehow forgotten it.

"Good day, Miss Crispin," Mrs. Cavel said as she stepped off the final stair and turned away.

"Good day, Mrs. Cavel."

Caro loosened her grip on Toby's leash. She would move on. She would put Strayeth and Chumsley out of her mind, and she would continue to live life as it pleased her.

Mostly, anyway.

Standing ever so slightly taller, she turned Toby toward Cavendish Square again and charged on.

Her chest would stop aching eventually, she assumed.

CHAPTER THREE

It was nearing 11 o'clock when Caro stepped inside the front door following her walk with Toby. Once inside, she found Barclay, Mrs. Meary, and Stinson all waiting to address her. Mama and Papa always hired the friendliest servants they could find; they seemed to find the staff's chatty, informal company a relaxing tonic after their long and arduous days.

"Good morning, everyone. Have my parents been to breakfast yet?"

"Yes, Miss Crispin. They're in the studio," Mrs. Meary replied.

"All right, then." She unhooked Toby's leash, and he snuffled off in search of some upholstery in need of more dog fur.

But the servants stayed put.

"Is there something else?"

Mrs. Meary turned to the others, but when they didn't so much as blink she twisted the slim newspaper in her hands and turned back to Caro.

"It's just that..."

"Is this about the urn, Mrs. Meary? Because I can explain..."

"Not the urn, Miss. Some of us just feel that...Gah! I'm not sure how to go about this at all. Barclay?"

Caro gave them her most plaintive of looks: *I love our frank discussions, but now is not the best—*

"We're not gonna hide your paramours for you, Miss Crispin. We're not gonna hide your men from your parents."

Stinson. This lovely outburst was from Stinson.

"I beg your pardon," Caro began, "but did you just say 'paramours'?"

"What he means to say," Mrs. Meary replied, shooting the young footman a look, "is that your gentlemen friends...are becoming a bit of a problem."

Strayeth and Chumsley, of course. The two lords must have found time to disrupt the servants, sometime between drinking too much claret, insulting her, and flouncing their way to the front door—long after the other guests were home in their own beds, bothering their own servants. Friends, indeed.

"Listen, I didn't ask Strayeth and Chumsley to linger here so long this morning. Please understand that these are grown gentlemen, capable of being rude at their own initiative."

All three servants looked at her in horror, their eyes bulging.

"We haven't seen those gentlemen since dawn!" the housekeeper whispered in a rush. "Not here, Miss. Not in *person!*"

"Oh," she replied, her hands finding her hips. "What are we talking about, then?"

"Lord Chumsley's valet shoved this note at me when I was out with young Toby earlier," Stinson said, passing her a letter. "I tried to tell you, Miss. But you ran off."

"*What?*" Caro asked, her voice thin. The small bit of optimism she'd cobbled together upon speaking with Mrs. Cavel began to break apart again.

"And Lord Strayeth's footman came to the kitchen door this morning, not half an hour ago," Mrs. Meary added. "He grabbed poor Sophie by the arm and asked her about your plans for the day."

"This..." Caro whispered, "this is most unusual."

Stinson snorted. "I dunno if I'd call it 'unusual.'"

Everyone looked at him.

"Well, we've all *seen* it!" he cried, throwing up his hands. "She gets awful cozy with the gentlemen sometimes."

"That's quite enough!" the housekeeper snapped.

"No, no, Mrs. Meary—that's all right," Caro replied. "We all know that I've...consorted with my gentlemen friends over the years, and that society clucks its forked tongue at such things. But those encounters were fleeting! And private! And...mutual!" She turned the note over in disbelief. She'd been so consumed by the cruel names Strayeth and Chumsley had called her that she'd failed to consider how they might behave in their attempts to win their ridiculous wager. "This, on the other hand? Secret letters and back-door inquisitions? *This* I didn't ask for. *This* is something worse."

"Much worse," Stinson said with a nod.

Now Mrs. Meary grabbed three inches of the footman's arm and twisted them, hard. His *"Yowww!"* hit the double-height ceiling before bouncing off the walls of the corridors above.

"Begging your pardon, Miss," the butler said, speaking up for the first time. "But what you're saying isn't entirely true. You also received secret letters from Sir Grimbell for a while."

"Barclay—Sir Grimbell is a cabinet minister! And he wrote to me about dog fighting, after I cornered him at a ball and complained about the goings-on at Westminster Pit."

"But Miss—suppose Lord Chumsley and Lord Strayeth knew about those letters? They might have thought..."

"They might have thought *what*?" Her brows went sky-high, daring the butler to speak the words. "They might have thought that corresponding with the minister meant that I was...giving him special favors, of some kind?"

Mrs. Meary looked away, and Stinson examined his fingernails.

"And that I therefore owe *them* special favors, as well?"

She looked at the old butler, her sometimes-surrogate papa, the man with the ready smile and the sweet treats and the hands that had scooted her along after the bumps and frights of her childhood.

He shrugged.

"*Et tu,* Barclay?" she croaked.

Shoulders sagging, she glanced into each of their faces and then at the newspaper in Mrs. Meary's hands. The housekeeper was an inveterate gambler, and frequently sent Stinson to place bets for her on the latest brawls and horse races.

"What day is it, Mrs. Meary?"

"The thirteenth of July, Miss."

"And most of the *ton* leaves London for the country by the twelfth of August."

Mrs. Meary nodded.

"Excuse me," she said as she turned and made off for the staircase.

Strayeth and Chumsley had one month to seduce her. It wasn't a lot of time, and judging by the actions of their servants that morning, they were prepared to be rather aggressive about it. She shuddered as she recalled the stranger with the gray sideburns on the street earlier that morning, and how she'd feared what he might expect of her, when no one else was about.

Once at her desk, she dashed off a quick note to Edie. She requested her "calming, comforting presence" at the market, but didn't mention that something had happened. In fact, she was still so shocked and discomfited by it all—and even a bit ashamed—that she wasn't certain she could bring herself to tell Edie about it in letter *or* in person.

CHAPTER FOUR

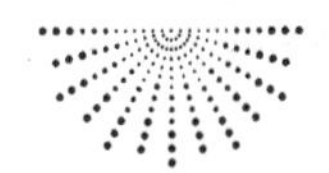

Adam stood in the window, holding a cup of coffee. He barely noticed the fashionable young beauties coming and going along the sidewalk, as he was too preoccupied with whether or not he could squeeze an apple tree into his miniscule front garden. And might a cherry tree do better there? What if it were potted?

He sipped his coffee and laughed gruffly at himself, thinking again about the woman who had planted, so to speak, the subject of flowering flora in his mind in the first place.

Miss Crispin had given him lots to wonder about, indeed.

He loved plants and planting. He'd spent countless hours moving dirt and rock at his estate over the years, digging trenches and building walls, planting and replanting. But he'd never thought it possible to grow much of anything in town.

Not until a certain hostess had suggested it.

"Have you found someone to mate with me yet?" a voice called out from behind.

He turned and watched his sister enter the dining room, an unusual bounce in her step. "Good morning, Edie. You're more chipper than usual today. And more vulgar."

She went to the sideboard and picked up a plate. "I refer to your husband-hunting duties, of course. Mother just informed me that if you hadn't come home from Caro's ball with a list of possible suitors, I should send you upstairs immediately for retribution."

He cringed at the mention of his bed-ridden mother. His last glimpse of Father had been in a bed in that same room, some years earlier. That had been before Adam had gone off to school with the promise of a speedy recovery from the physician, and before that promise had been broken.

He pushed the memory down and forced a smile. "And how is our beloved matriarch this morning?"

"I'm no physician, but I'm fairly certain this forced bed-rest will kill her," she replied flatly, filling her plate with eggs and toast. "It's been two weeks since that mare threw her, and you know that if Mama isn't thundering about and badgering people, she gets dithery and sore."

"Well, now that I'm here, I can be of more help. Tell me about this renovation that Mother started," he replied. He'd decided against taking rooms of his own when he'd arrived in town a week prior. He intended to help Mother however he could while she recovered, and indeed, foremost on her mind was getting him to take up the mantle of finding Edie some marriage prospects. The renovation was a close second. "That scoundrel she hired—how long was he here? A week? His workers seem to have left things even more dilapidated than before."

Edie looked at him askance as she took her place at the dining table. "Are we living in the same house, Adam? Truly, it's not so terrible. We've closed off the rooms they left in disrepair. The rest is just...*old*."

He turned again, and took in the wall of windows. Their Mayfair home was ninety-some years old, in fact, and required regular maintenance he had not kept up since Father's death. He'd always imagined—had romanticized, in fact—that his future wife would oversee the renovations for which it was due. Yet a month prior, Mother had decided she'd waited long enough for daughter-in-law and renovation alike, and had hired the first architect she'd found who could begin the work at once. But when she'd discovered the man was not an architect at all but a clever fraud, she'd relieved him of his duties. Her subsequent riding accident had delayed the resumption of the project, and she refused to remove herself and Edie to other accommodations.

He took a deep breath. Men like him weren't supposed to apologize. He'd never heard Father apologize, of course. But he had broken so many of his obligations to the man—what was one more? "I've been wanting to tell you that I'm sorry, Edie. I'm sorry you've had to live in a moldering home all this time."

"Adam, you exaggerate," she replied between bites of toast. "And I can't tell what's truly bothering you: that we live in a house that lacks modern features, or that the builders left Father's old rooms in a bit of a mess."

Both things. I hate both things. "I'm going to stop avoiding these projects, Edie. I promise."

She squinted at him, as if deciding whether to allay his guilt or rub salt in his wounds, like any decent sister would. "Fine, Adam. You are a terrible, negligent, mean-hearted landlord. Now go and find me a husband to make up for it."

He loved his sister—his strange, funny little sister with the unkempt hair and intense green eyes, set wide on sun-flecked cheekbones. But he sometimes felt that he barely knew her. They had spent only a couple of months a year together, as he'd gone to Eton and Cambridge while Edie had studied with the notorious Mrs. Hellkirk. Now he avoided big society events by remaining in the country while she remained fascinated by the gritty bustle of town, observing it from the edges of the *ton's* best ballrooms. Even when they *were* in the same vicinity, Edie spent a great deal of time sealed off in her rooms, drawing and scouring the newspapers and who knew what else, while he went off to tour the latest public squares and canal-building projects. "About this husband-hunting, then. It's not clear to me that you *want* to be married just yet."

"Allow me to make it plain: I do not want to be married just yet. Possibly at all."

Edie's pronouncement flummoxed him. Didn't she remember Mother and Father debating the latest from Parliament at breakfast? Issuing subtle glances to one another over their goblets? Perhaps not; Edie had been very young when Father became ill.

He, on the other hand, remembered all of his parents' sweet rapport. It had given him the hope—nay, the expectation—of marrying for love himself one day. He'd come into town a few weeks each season these past few years, hoping to meet a woman he could take back to the country, back to his books and his earth-moving.

But between his quiet nature and his insistence on a love match, his conversations with society's more demure young ladies went nowhere. It didn't help that he became irritable whenever someone brought up his family's fighting legacy, or assumed he was a bruiser.

But Miss Crispin, now! Miss Crispin, with her open and engaging demeanor, had piqued something in him that had never been piqued. He wondered how soon he could see her again—and if it might perhaps lead to a courtship.

Edie cleared her throat, yanking him back from these pleasant musings.

"If you don't want to marry, Edie, then why are you prompting me to find you a husband?"

"Because I want to watch you play matchmaker with all the mamas."

"Have you told our own mother that you don't want to be married?"

"Repeatedly. She says I will change my mind."

"She may be right, you know. But in the meantime, I see no reason to plunge forward when your heart's not in it."

"Oh, make no mistake, Adam: We will be plunging. Plunging will occur. I intend to accept every invitation I receive if it means you'll have to spend an entire evening propositioning young lords on my behalf, waxing at length about my many virtues. I'm certain you'll need to spend a great deal of time with Lady Tilbeth, as she's also trying to marry off a young relative this season. And secrets must be shared! Plans discussed! Fashions criticized!"

He smirked at her. "Be careful, Edie. You can pitch me to society's wolves if you like, but I can just as easily fill your dance card with bachelors of bad hygiene and even worse politics. London has quite a lot of them on offer."

She didn't even look up from her newspaper when she replied, "Do your worst, brother."

The door opened and Brandt, their butler, approached Edie with a silver tray. She lifted a small card from it, and upon recognizing the sender, tore into it with some haste.

"What is it?" Adam asked, sitting down.

She held the paper in front of her and read, ignoring his question.

"Has Mrs. Hellkirk finally been arrested?" he teased.

She dropped her hands to her lap, her prominent brows high and still.

"No need to fret. She can write you from the Tower."

She tossed him a light scowl as she scooted back her chair. "You're so...*brotherly*."

"It's my sacred duty. Edie, what is it? You're clearly troubled."

She gathered her skirts and stood. "I'm off to the market at Covent Garden."

"*What?* Why?" He stood up, too.

"If I tell you, will you stop with all these questions?"

He thought for a moment. "I can't promise you that."

"Caro has asked me to meet her there. It seems...urgent."

"But you cannot go there on your own," he replied. "It's not seemly. And don't look at me like that—it wasn't even a question." Now his mind was whirling, too. What could have perturbed the imperturbable Miss Crispin? He was struck with a sudden need to know, as if she were already someone in whom he had special interest, a special claim.

But Edie was already heading through the door. "Mrs. Hellkirk says that walking alone promotes self-sufficiency in a young lady. Caro goes everywhere alone."

"Edie, Mrs. Hellkirk has graduated a great many ladies who have fallen out of society," he said, following on her heels.

"I'll take Tildie then," she replied.

"That's a wonderful idea. There's room enough in the curricle for you *and* your tiny lady's maid."

"But...you never let me drive in town," Edie began, confused and excited at once. She looked up at him expectantly, almost beaming.

"I'm not. I'm coming with you."

She glared at him. "We'd better take the coach, then."

CHAPTER FIVE

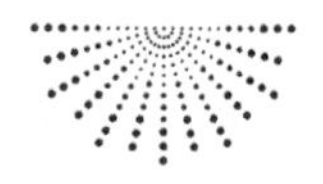

"*Supposed* gentlemen," Caro muttered, grabbing a beetroot and casting it roughly aside. "Pfft! Damn them all. Damn them all, and their pretty horses, too..."

It was mid-day at Covent Garden, and no gentlemen were about just yet (not coincidentally, neither were the prostitutes). There were horses, however, and plenty of other livestock, and lots of servants and costermongers, all of them jostling between stalls, wagons, and barrels, and hopscotching amongst steaming piles of produce, entrails, and dung.

She lingered over the beetroots awhile, where the one-eyed, one-toothed costermonger dipped his chin at her, unfazed by her strange mutterings. He was unfazed by her lack of a chaperone, too, as he'd likely seen far worse in his time, perched as he was atop an old keg that'd been blackened—much like his tooth—with the grime and rot of many a decade.

After several minutes, she moved on to the cucumbers at the next stall.

"'Compromised,' you say? I'll show you compromised! I don't believe you've really seen—"

"Have these cucumbers offended you, Miss Crispin?"

She whipped around. An exceptionally tall man stood next to her, his head dipped in greeting, his face hidden by a gloved hand and the brim of a fine black hat.

Her chest constricted as her thoughts raced back to the nook—to two other masculine voices and their cruel, ugly words.

"It's very nice to see you again. Tell me, are these vegetables bothering you?" The gentleman lifted his face, his lips releasing into a sly sort of smile.

Lord Ryland!

"I'm handling it," she replied, her voice somehow staying straight and true.

"Indeed."

She set the cucumber down. "Do forgive me, Lord Ryland. I am much...I am not..." She dipped a shallow curtsy and walked quickly to the next cart. "I must be on my way."

He followed.

"I was heading that way myself," he called out with a quick grunt of amusement. "Do you know, Miss Crispin? It's funny! But I'd forgotten they even sold vegetables here. Covent Garden is better known for...less savory fare."

"Good day, my lord!" she called back, lifting her skirts above some muck. She picked up her pace, too. She just couldn't bring herself to indulge the attentions of any gentlemen today. Today was different. Today, a gentleman who refused to listen to a polite refusal was anything but attractive.

"Crikey! That squirrel over there—do you see it, Miss Crispin? It has a lady's bonnet, and is running with it! What'll you wager he gets it to the top of that shed, there?" he continued.

Now she spun around and stepped up to him. "Lord Ryland, *please*. I do not desire anyone's company just now. Do go about your business."

He stopped smiling and took off his hat. "I apologize, Miss Crispin. I only meant to help, as I believe you are looking for my sister."

She crossed her arms. "I am, indeed. Is Edie here?"

Huh! Lord Ryland had just apologized to her for the second time in less than a full day. Gentlemen didn't do such things! She looked him over curiously. Their previous encounter had been brief, dim, and sleepy, but now she could examine him at length. He seemed to be doing the same of her, in fact, as if they were each meeting a character from a book they'd read over and over since childhood.

She could see that his pitch-black hair was too tidy for the day's fashion, for example. She could tell that his coat was of the highest quality, and very well cared-for. But she couldn't make out the color of his eyes—were they grayish, or blueish?—so she squinted up at him when he glanced aside at a sharp noise. Too late, she realized she'd leaned in a bit too close—close enough to detect that he smelled of rich coffee—and when he turned back again, his eyes and smile went wide—laughing in unison at her unexpected closeness.

"Oh, God!" she exclaimed, stepping back. "Do forgive me, Lord Ryland. I seem to have forgotten my manners entirely. I'm afraid it's been a...a rather unusual morning."

She reached out to touch his wrist—as it had always been her way to put a hand on a person's back or shoulder or such—but Lord Ryland appeared startled, so she caught herself, pulling her hand back sharply.

Lud! There she was, giving a marriageable man the impression she was interested in him again. She wasn't used to censoring herself, and doing so now felt jarring and unnatural.

So: no mention of bodices or bosoms, no more conversation of a personal nature. And no more casual touches. That ought to do it. *New leaf, Caro! New leaf!*

"No apology necessary. Please, allow me to escort you to my sister. She's waiting on the other side of St. Paul's." He held out his arm for her to take.

"Why? Is she unwell?" she asked. Edie wasn't terribly pious, she knew.

"She's fine. I asked her to wait there while I found you."

"Why?" she asked again, ignoring his arm.

Lord Ryland smiled. He glanced at the stalls around them and squinted into the sun. "I could tell you that I left Edie behind because I find it unseemly for a lady to come into such a place. But that wouldn't be the complete truth."

Her eyes narrowed. "What is the complete truth, then?"

"I also wanted to spend time with the infamous Miss Crispin. Alone."

Again, the pressure in her chest nearly felled her. Because she didn't know *which* "infamous Miss Crispin" Lord Ryland wished to be alone with: The one who devised audacious charity schemes, or the one who was reputed to give men "special favors," in dark corners?

Gathering every trace of bravado she had left in her wearied, trampled chest, she looked back at him and tossed up her chin. "Why is it you wish to spend time with me, my lord?"

His smile faded once more. "Miss Crispin, I would like to escort you to my sister."

"And I would like an answer to my question."

He stepped closer and lifted his cane to his chest, gripping it tightly with both hands. He twisted it slowly, his leather gloves straining and groaning against the polished wood. It was a sound of both resistance and strength, submission and control—and it numbed her in unforeseen places. It was a sensation that made her more curious about men than ever; about *this* man, in particular. And she suddenly hoped Lord Ryland *was* seeking her out for a rendezvous in a dark corner, because she suddenly wanted very much to be in one with him.

Alone.

She clenched her fists and flushed hot, a wave of shame washing over her. *What a foolish thing to think!* What had happened to the horror she'd felt at hearing Strayeth and Chumsley calling her a whore? She wanted *this* gentleman to think her "available," but not others? Had she lost her wits? She didn't know anymore. All she knew was that up felt like down, left seemed like right, and if dogs suddenly began mewing and purring in the streets, she wouldn't have been the least bit surprised.

"I only wanted to become better acquainted with the person Edie has told me so much about," he replied, glancing over every feature of her face. He lowered his cane and pulled out his pocket watch, his face softening into playful irritation. "But I haven't got all day, Miss Crispin. Edie will have my head if I don't deliver you soon."

"*'Deliver'* me? Sir, I am not a side of pork."

"Tell me, what shopping have you left? What other vegetables must we admonish?"

One thing was certain: He was definitely flirting with her.

* * *

Adam had been telling the truth: He'd gone into the market to fetch her, yes, but also to have her company to himself awhile. She was clearly skeptical of his attempts at escorting her to safety, however, so perhaps Edie had been right; perhaps something was troubling her.

"I'm off to the strawberries!" she announced as she walked off. "If you care to tell Edie my whereabouts, then you should know that I'm off to the strawberries."

"How fortunate! For I am also in need of some strawberries," he said as he reached her again. He glanced around at the assortment of carts. "And some turnips, of course. I cannot face my cook without a great many of those. So! What does one look for, in this case? What makes the elite strawberry?" he asked as he popped one into his mouth.

She looked at him with a frown—the kind that struggled to hold on to its downward curl, because every feeling seemed to want to reverse its course.

He liked that look on Miss Crispin, he found.

"I know what this is about, Lord Ryland."

"This is about fruit, I think. So many things with you are about fruit."

"No. You want me to stand here and tell you how all the best berries blush red, from tip to toe. Particularly once you've taken their tops off."

"I don't know what you're talking about, but do go on. That sounds interesting."

"Then we'll move on, and you'll want me to tell you that when a turnip gets big, it's wooden and hard. And that opinions vary as to the whether they are pleasant to the taste."

He coughed and spit his strawberry onto the ground, nearly doubling over in both shock and amusement.

"Lord Ryland, whatever is the matter?" she asked, all faux innocence.

"What are they teaching at Hellkirk's these days?" he asked between coughs.

They walked on to the next cart, but this time, instead of blustering forward in a single file, they strode more slowly—side by side. They settled into the pace of a country amble, and he found himself walking a little taller, his hands clasped behind his back, trying not to grin like a fool.

Miss Crispin was making him feel a strange way, indeed. This was not the sort of courting-type conversation he'd envisioned, but he was finding that few things with Miss Crispin went as expected. He didn't mind it. Indeed, it was uncommonly refreshing.

"Pray, Miss Crispin. Are you even *close* to being finished?"

"One cannot rush a good persimmon," she replied, putting an odd little fruit right up against her nostrils and inhaling deeply, eyes closed. He caught himself watching her bodice expand and contract and by the time she put the fruit down again, the turnips weren't the only things in the market too firm for their own good.

He needed to get them back into mixed company, as soon as possible.

"Persimmons, you say? That's what these little runts are?"

"Yes, my lord. Although I'm not sure you're ready for a lesson in persimmons. This isn't the place for fainting."

"All the persimmons, sir," he announced to the costermonger. "I will have all of your persimmons."

Miss Crispin looked at him agape. "Sirrah! You cannot have all of the persimmons!"

"Oh, but I can. And indeed, I *do*." The merchant began placing the last of his stock into three wooden bushels.

"But...how are you going to carry all of those?" she asked, palms out. "Throw them into your carriage, like it's a country wagon?"

"Miss Crispin, just recently, I was forced to carry an armful of apples to a party of yours. You can certainly carry some of *these* to my poor awaiting sister." He handed her the first of the wooden containers, to the horror of the costermonger and several onlookers, then picked up the others and marched off.

He didn't look back, but he could tell from the shadow wobbling at his feet that she was coming after him, with some effort.

* * *

Shock—and if she was being honest with herself, delight—coursed through her. "Do you often engage with young women in this way?" Caro asked as she struggled along.

They might as well be familiar with one another, she figured. Lord

Ryland had made her lug a heavy bushel, after all, and she had clearly abandoned her goal of avoiding bawdy conversation with men.

"What, now? I am not engaged, Miss Crispin. How forward of you to ask!"

"I did not ask if you were engaged, *my lord*. I asked if you speak to other young ladies in this...informal way," she repeated, catching up to him. She suspected he had heard her correctly the first time.

"No. I never subject ladies to such nonsense. Except for the ones I am related to, of course. They encounter it daily."

She smiled. Their conversation *had* been full of playful nonsense, hadn't it? It was her favorite kind of talk.

"'Tis a pity," he continued. "Perhaps if men and women were willing to be a bit sillier with one another, we'd see a few more love matches about."

Her tongue went fuzzy, her heart lurching every which direction. Was Lord Ryland suggesting they might be well-suited to one another?

And if so, why did that feel...fine? Good, even?

Her independence was precious to her, and any man known for sending one of his peers to the blacksmith for a gruesome bone-setting was precisely the sort of man who wouldn't honor such a thing.

Right?

"'Be sillier with one another'?" she replied. She knew she ought to change the subject, but she was far too stubborn and curious to do so. "You mean 'silly' as in foolish?"

"No, 'silly' in the old sense: Joyous, playful." He looked at her now, arching a brow. "You've never seen one, then?"

"Seen what, my lord?"

"A love match!"

She shook her head. "No. None that has lasted."

"Not your parents?"

"My parents..." she began before looking aside. She would never understand her mother's real feelings—not really. How wrenching it must have been to marry a loving husband and then discover a shared talent, only to spend the ensuing years watching that same husband receive sole acclaim for that talent. It was like something from one of those cruel fables she'd been forced to read as a child. "My parents' marriage is complicated," she answered finally.

"Forgive me, Miss Crispin. I should not have inquired on such a private matter."

"Oh! Not at all. I was going to ask the same of you."

"I am happy to talk of my parents. My father died many years ago, as you likely know. But I've remained very much in awe of his happiness with my mother."

"There was silliness, as you call it?"

"Quite a bit, yes. And since I have seen what a marriage can be like, where the affection and the laughter are both plentiful, I find I want to try for one of my own."

When she didn't respond, he continued. "Do you not have similar hopes, Miss Crispin? For your own marriage?"

She didn't know what to do with this man. One minute, he was making lewd suggestions over cucumbers. The next, he was speaking rather earnestly about love and marriage—a rare habit among aristocrats, especially the brutish ones. And the contrast between his light, teasing manner and that heavy, gravelly voice of his? It tickled her rather pleasantly, and her cheeks ached from all the smiling she'd been doing.

A current flickered through her, as she recalled him holding out his arm for her.

Perhaps she was not so entirely opposed to marriage. Perhaps she might consider it one day? Just a little? Potentially? Under the right circumstances?

No—absolutely not. The memory of Papa signing his own name to Mama's drawings made her cringe. The image of him *accepting praise* for them at a reception at the Royal Academy of Arts—while Mama stood calmly by—made her livid.

Her inheritance would protect her freedom; she needn't marry to support herself.

She smoothed at her gloves and collected herself. "Marriage is a risky undertaking for a woman, my lord. She is beholden to her husband's wishes. His work, his finances. Let's just say I've seen what a marriage can be like where there is...an *imbalance* of sorts."

He slowed, not taking his eyes off her. "That's...I am sorry, Miss

Crispin. I hope for all our sakes that we see more happy marriages than not in our lifetimes. More *balanced* marriages, if you like."

She looked over and met his eyes briefly, though she couldn't measure any of the angles on his face at that moment.

They walked quietly for several minutes. "Look, there's our squirrel again," he said with a nod toward an archway on the near-side of St. Paul's. "Last chance to put a coin on him reaching the top, ribbons and all."

She didn't lift her head when she replied, "Forgive me, Lord Ryland. But I'm not in the mood for any wagering today."

* * *

Ryland's spirits sank a bit. "Truly? But you must represent your sex, Miss Crispin! The ladies are depending on you."

She'd been looking at the ground for some time. Something about their discussion had quieted, even saddened her.

And she did not want to be courted, it seemed, by him or anyone else.

So Adam was feeling saddened, too.

He wanted to cheer her. And he itched to understand her cynicism about love and marriage. Why had she reacted so strangely when he'd brought up her parents?

"Miss Crispin, are you quite well?" he inquired after a moment.

She turned toward him, pushing a stray hair behind her ear. "Oh yes, quite. I just don't wish to risk any coin on my knowledge of rodents and flimsy headwear today. Another time, perhaps."

"As you wish, then. The ladies forfeit this particular bout. And the gentlemen take it."

Walking quietly, he had the opportunity to look at her more closely. He could tell that her long hair was a challenge for her. It hadn't decided if it wanted to be straight or curly, and some of the brown locks were near-ringlets while others fell to her shoulder with only a hint of a turn. She had tied a thin bandeau around the whole affair, giving her a resemblance to one of those Greek goddesses of yore: the kind with absurd amounts of power and a refreshing lack of timidity. They hadn't had time for perfection, either.

"Hold on a moment," she said, stopping abruptly and putting her hand out. This time she did make contact with his sleeve, and a surge of heat jumped from his arm to his torso with an intensity that shocked him. "What did you say, a moment ago?"

"Uh..." he began. "I believe I said, 'As you wish.'"

"No, before that." She was distracted now, and her hand dropped from his arm. He had to stop himself from dipping and leaning into it, as if he could chase it down and restore it to its place, his body moving instinctively to get more of that strange heat.

"Before that, I asked if you were well."

"You said something about other ladies depending on me. Mrs. Hellkirk told me that once, though I hadn't thought of it for some time."

"The lady radical herself? Heaven help me."

"Did you know that I was one of her first pupils?"

He shook his head.

"And she told me, many times, that I was more fortunate than my classmates, and I took this to mean that I should support them in their ambitions, their accomplishments," she continued. "But that wasn't all."

"What did she mean, then?"

"She meant that I have a...a special duty of sorts. Oh, Lord Ryland. *Thank you!* You have inspired something in me, and have therefore done me a great service. And look—here is Edie, at last! Hullo, dearest! I am here! Did you think me lost forever?"

She trotted off toward his sister, as best she could with the bushel of persimmons, so there was no opportunity for him to find out more about the mysterious epiphany that had restored her spirits.

When he reached them, he heard Edie inquiring about the pressing tone of her letter.

"What is the matter, Caro?"

"Nothing is the matter, dearest."

"Then why did you summon me here? You said you required comfort."

"I just meant that I wanted to see you, is all. You know that your company is my greatest comfort."

Edie crossed her arms at her.

"I'm sorry that I alarmed you, my love," Caro continued. "But now, your brother has entertained me *so* extensively that I'm afraid I am due back at home already. I must be off."

Edie turned and glared at him. "Will you at least walk me to our carriage, then?" she beseeched her friend, who responded by placing a hand gently on her shoulder.

Ah. Gentle touches were just Miss Crispin's way with people—not a sign of a particular interest in someone. He was...well, *silly* to have let it jolt him so.

'Silly' in the newer, more foolish sense.

"Now, let's be off!" Miss Crispin said, a new bounce in her step. "I've got a new scheme to conduct."

CHAPTER SIX

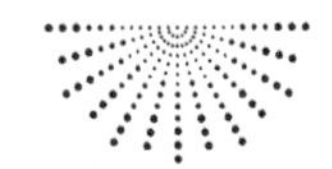

Hurrying home, Caro was so absorbed in her thoughts that she ran straight into the hitch of a carriage that had stopped for repairs on Regent Street.

"Oof!" she grunted as she doubled over. Then she pressed her bonnet to her head and righted herself, scurrying on.

Mrs. Hellkirk and Lord Ryland had been right: Other women were depending on her. She had to do something; she had to come up with a scheme.

A cunning, nefarious, diabolical scheme.

How many other women had Strayeth and Chumsley slandered? Were they spreading rumors that very moment, about some unsuspecting governess? Some young shopkeeper? She had seen them regale society crowds with tales of their more innocent shenanigans—of schoolyard pranks and athletic blunders. Who knew what they were revealing to their paid female companions, or at White's, their private men's club? Who knew what lies they told, what exaggerations?

She shivered: Had Strayeth and Chumsley recorded their wager in the betting book at White's?

Weaving through the crowds on the sidewalk, she ducked under the yoke of a milkmaid, causing her to bobble before regaining her balance.

"Begging your pardon, Miss!" she shouted back.

"*'Ey!*" the woman yelled, tossing out a few choice oaths.

If the wager was in the book at White's, it would be gossiped about. And if it was gossiped about, people would be watching Strayeth and Chumsley more closely—to see which ladies they gave their attentions to. It would make it far more likely that someone in society would discover that *she* was the lady in question.

And that would be a disaster.

She slung her sack of produce over her shoulder and picked up her pace. She reminded herself that women far and wide were depending on her to put a stop to Strayeth and Chumsley's awful behavior. Because if anyone could teach those two a lesson, it was she. She had fewer checks on her behavior—on account of her parents being so distracted—and the two gentlemen wouldn't expect any sort of resistance from her; they believed that she fancied them.

Ha! She would take a pin—nay, a lancet—to their swollen sense of significance.

She just had to keep her role in the wager a secret.

She kept her head down as she hopped onto the far sidewalk; she didn't stop for anything, not even a basket of wiggling puppies that reminded her of dear Toby. Having a new scheme had always put more bounce in her stride, sharpened her every idea. She enjoyed rolling a problem around in her mind and then finding, one by one, the tools to crack it open. But today, a dozen fuzzier thoughts pushed their way through her mind, competing for attention.

For example: How did one teach a gentleman a lesson he wouldn't forget? And how did one make the case that wagering about such things was wrong? These sorts of problems weren't at all like feeding orphans, or stopping those awful dog fights.

She took a handkerchief from her reticule and dabbed at her brow. In the heat of the afternoon sun, she regretted having refused Lord Ryland's offer of a ride in his carriage. At the time, she'd thought it unwise to remain in the company of that gentleman.

Goodness, what an unusual man he had turned out to be! Everything about Edie's brother had been a surprise, from his stronger-than-expected chin to his gentler-than-expected manners. And the effect he'd had on her insides? She already knew the thrill of a hand brushed lightly along her side, the rush of heat to her cheeks following a glance from a handsome gentleman. Indeed, her enthusiasm for such pleasures was what led to her current predicament in the first place.

But she had never felt her innards go all gelatinous until she had traded barbs in her portrait gallery with Lord Ryland. And it had happened again when he offered her a genuine apology, listened respectfully to her concerns about marriage, asked her to wager on a squirrel...

She squeezed her eyes shut tight, pushing away all thoughts of him. She couldn't allow herself to become distracted by superficial pleasures; she had scheming to do.

She stopped and waited as three men strained to move an enormous ox from the center of an intersection, where it was determined to continue cooling itself in a long shadow. As the ox lolled and rolled and its handlers tugged and struggled, she noticed a boy of perhaps eight or nine standing next to her. "Excuse me, young sir," she asked. "But what is the most ridiculous wager you've ever heard, and what was the outcome?"

The lad simply shrugged, as if this was the most normal question he had ever heard. He wore a cap with an over-large brim, and kept his eyes on the tussle in the street.

"There was some fellows carrying on one time," he began, chopping various letters from his words. "One saying that his piglets was pink with black spots, his friend saying no, they was black with pink spots. In the end, they put some coin on it."

"And how did they determine who won?"

"Couldn't say about the wager, Miss. But I know one of 'em shot the other in the knee the next day, so he came out on top, wouldn't you say?"

"Quite," she replied, looking ahead again.

She wasn't interested in shooting anyone in the knee. This was not about revenge; she only wanted to take the hurt Strayeth and Chumsley had caused her and turn it into something good. She had to stop these two men, at least, from feigning respect for women in society's drawing rooms only to slander them—and therefore damage them—in other company.

She reached the house and opened the door for herself. Stinson started to approach but she hurried past him, calling out, "Don't worry! I left all my paramours at the curb today."

"Yes, Miss," he replied with a sheepish nod.

Still carrying her bags, she scurried through the ballroom and out through the French windows. The sun was low in the sky, leaving the garden in cool shadows. She'd intended to remove her half-boots and stockings and walk barefoot in the low grass, as it always left her feeling newer, somehow.

But today she stopped at the edge of the terrace and looked around, wondering if someone might see her and judge her poorly for it.

Is it whoreish to walk barefoot in the garden?

When the absurdity of that question dawned, she plopped down on the spot and immediately unlaced her half-boots.

So: How to begin her new scheme?

First things first: she needed to confirm that Strayeth and Chumsley had recorded their wager in the betting book at White's, and find out precisely what it said. She needed to know how likely it was that her part in the wager would be revealed.

Her stomach curdled at the thought of Mama and Papa hearing of it.

Then another unpleasant detail occurred to her: What did those bastards intend to accept as proof of her having succumbed to their charms? She shuddered and forced herself to her feet.

When she found out what was written at White's, she would know.

She never asked others for help with her schemes, but in this case she would have to. She couldn't go into White's—no women were allowed—so her first step would be finding a man to go for her.

She stood up and stepped onto the grass, sighing deeply, savoring the tickling, scouring sensation of the coarse blades. Every part of her rebelled against asking another person—man or woman—for help. Time and time again, when she was just a girl, Mama would lean forward and look her straight in the eye, holding her gaze and her hands as she told her: *You can do this, Caroline. This is* your *endeavor, and you needn't anyone's help.*

But to get into White's? To the betting book? She had no other choice: she needed a helpmate.

And she already had a strong candidate in mind. A strong and tall one.

* * *

Adam's hands rested atop his cane, wobbling with the rocking of the carriage. Edie hadn't spoken since they'd left her friend behind at St. Paul's, and he wondered if she was displeased with him.

"I asked Miss Crispin if she wanted to ride with us," he said, nudging aside one of the bushels of persimmons at his elbow. "It was her choice to walk."

"You'll find that Caro refuses offers of all kinds," she replied, looking out the window with her usual dour expression. "She likes to do things on her own, and in her own way. She hasn't even a lady's maid."

He looked out the window, too, where the shadows of horses and men had grown long—the shadows of giants, now—in the late afternoon sun. "Your friend has a stubborn streak. It took some time to figure out how to trick her into following me out of there."

"And now you can't stop talking about her."

He jerked his head around and found her staring back at him.

"You've got me there, I suppose. I've been wondering what was bothering her," he admitted. "She was much like you'd described her: Outspoken. Energetic. Willfully independent. But she also grew quiet at times, as if she were suspicious of me and needed to be ready to attack at any moment."

"Indeed. There's something she's not saying, but I hadn't enough time to coax it from her."

"Well, for what it's worth, I am inclined to like her. Despite her being out of sorts."

Edie smiled now, as if she were lit from within by a slow burn that only coincided with certain rare moons. "I'm glad. She's wonderful. Stubborn to her bones, but wonderful."

They arrived at the house, its stately front façade evincing signs of the construction that had begun some weeks earlier.

"You know, Adam," she said as she accepted his hand and stepped down from the carriage, "I've just noticed: The bricks are falling out in places. Just there. And *there*." She pointed to the places in question.

"This morning, you didn't care if the entire house crumbled to the ground and we camped in the rubble like soldiers. Why the change of heart?"

"I didn't see it before. Now I think it's terrible, and I'm very embarrassed about it."

"Edie..."

"Humiliated."

"I don't believe you."

"Mortified!"

"The theater is *that* way..."

She sighed. "Fine. You're right: I don't care a whit what people think of the house. I'm just trying to convince you to hire Mr. and Mrs. Crispin."

He ignored her and continued up the front steps.

"Caro would come around here a *great deal*, you know, if her parents were to work for us," she added in a sing-song voice that got right under his skin.

He stepped into the house and stopped before a marble bust of Father, which somehow managed to convey his imposing athleticism despite having no arms. Or legs. Or torso.

"The Crispins are too busy," he answered finally, mimicking her grating tone. "And there's no sense in teasing me about Miss Crispin, Edie. Your friend isn't interested in marriage."

"She told you that? How interesting..."

He removed his hat, noting a slight tremor in his hand. He turned and looked at the stony likeness of Father. There was a similar one at Ardythe, and three different portraits throughout the home.

"Perhaps it isn't my place, but you should understand—"

"You do your friend a disservice," he said, interrupting Edie a little more gruffly than he'd intended. He turned away from the bust. "She knows her mind, and she does not want to marry."

Just then Brandt hurried into the room, muttering his apologies. Adam handed him his hat and cane, and Edie remained silent while the butler lingered close.

"Caro may never open her mind to marriage," she whispered when Brandt finally stepped away, still fussing with their things. "But do not dismiss the opportunity to work with her parents because you think they are too busy. I have known them a long time, and if my own dear brother were to write to them today, asking for a meeting on the subject of much-needed repairs, I know they would see us."

He straightened his cuffs, thinking: The work *did* need to be done. He had promised Edie he would begin fulfilling his duties. And he was certain that Mr. Crispin—or both he and his wife, or whomever he was meant to hire—would do an excellent job. Who was he to decline such an opportunity?

"Fine. I'll write the letter. But, even if they do meet with us, it's likely just a courtesy. Let's not get ourselves in a dither just yet."

"You're a wonder, brother. Thank you. Now, where are you going? We've just got home."

He had snapped his fingers for his hat and cane again, and was heading toward the door. "Royal Academy," he said curtly before stepping out.

"Ah, yes. You and your pretty landscapes. Wait—on *foot*?"

* * *

He swung his cane roughly, *thwapping* at the weeds along the curb. Taking up all these duties after avoiding them so many years—fixing the house, finding Edie a husband and himself a wife—made his head feel thick and electrified all at once. But taking them up under Father's ever-present marble gaze? That was just too much.

He didn't care about the distance. He knew that a long walk—and some masterful paintings—would clear the roiling clouds from his mind.

Edie had been right: His curiosity about Miss Crispin had grown stronger by the minute, and his decision to seek her parents' help had surely been influenced by his desire to see her again.

But, unlike Edie, he wasn't sure this was a desire he should indulge.

It could not be a good idea to become further attached to someone who was skeptical of marriage, and perhaps even of love itself. He'd be better off focusing on finding Edie a husband, and proceeding with a renovation of the house with a different architect.

But, he had never been so open, so comfortable with someone he didn't already know. Something about Miss Crispin had neutralized his fear of being judged for what he said and did. It had been exhilarating for him.

And yet, on their second meeting, he had discussed with her his hopes for marriage. Not the weather! His hopes for *marriage*.

Perhaps exhilaration was something he should take in smaller doses.

Turning down a narrower, less familiar street, he decided he would take one meeting with the Crispins and then move on. Because if he continued to spend time with their daughter, he might continue to admit things he ought not to admit. And he might continue to become more and more attached to her.

His swung his cane up and around and was about to strike a loose cobblestone when he heard shouting from an alley just ahead. He hurried forward and looked down at a crowd of men not fifty yards away, wearing everything from the tall beaver hats of society to the soiled aprons of the butchery. None of them noticed as he approached, their shouts and cheers growing louder.

Inside the circle of onlookers—Adam could easily see over them—was an unruly tangle of scraped knees and longish hair: two boys of perhaps ten or twelve, holding their fists aloft in a mimicry of real pugilists, took turns pummeling each other with messy blows. Adam stepped back, his heart thudding in his chest. He might be a grown man, and his body might be pressed against the wall of a London shop at that moment, but his heart and mind traveled back to Ardythe, and back to his boyhood. There, he was sparring with Father again, while a poison of one part boyish eagerness, one part deep reluctance, coursed through his veins.

He shook himself free of this unpleasant spell and stepped forward, toward a man standing nearby. He was a merchant of some kind, judging by his new-looking clothes and by the accent he revealed when he shouted his encouragement to the boys.

Both boys, Adam noticed.

"What's going on here?" he asked. Breaths had become harder to come by. "Are these your sons?"

"Yes, my lord," the man replied, his fingers hooked inside his lapels. He smiled broadly.

"What are they going on about?"

The man cocked his head at him. "I don't understand, my lord. We're just having some sport—"

A blood-thickening screech came from inside the circle, and Adam turned just in time to see the larger of the boys tackle the other about the waist. Both went thudding across the foul ground, knotted up in a frenzy of grasping, yelping, and biting.

Adam cringed and pressed himself against the wall again, gently palming the smooth stones. Father had shown him how to execute punishing combinations, to inflict crushing blows that would debilitate an opponent. He'd been able to give Father his attention, at least, but he'd never been able to summon the courage—or was it nerve?—to do such things to another person. Indeed, he'd never overcome the visceral disgust that bubbled within him at the very thought of harming another. So he'd never graduated from sparring—at least not before Father's fever worsened, not before Adam could rush home from school, not before a sudden and unexpected death shocked their entire household.

"It toughens 'em up," the man continued. "Makes a man outta 'em. Wouldn't you agree?"

"I do *not* agree," he replied.

"Beggin' your pardon? These are my boys, and there's no harm in—"

Adam didn't let the man finish. He turned and pushed aside several onlookers, eliciting an *"Ey!"* and a *"Watch it!"* before the speakers could turn and take in his size, his attire. He reached into the melee with both hands, his heart pumping wildly, and pulled the boys apart by their collars like a pair of snarling alley-cats. He lifted them off the ground, feet dangling, and brought them to their father. The men of the crowd had suddenly much less to shout about.

"H-h-how have we offended, my lord?" the man stammered in the newly quiet alley.

Adam ignored him, and looked at each boy in turn. "Do either of you like art?"

The boys looked at their father, his eyes wide and darting, then back to Adam. The younger one shrugged sheepishly, his face and neck stained with tears, and the older one trembled as he tried to pick the grit from the scrapes on his every extremity.

"Is this your place of business?" Adam asked with a toss of his head to a nearby storefront. "With your permission, I'll take these lads with me to the Royal Academy. I'll have them back before sundown."

The man nodded, and Adam let go of the boys' collars. Then he tugged downward on his waistcoat, tipped his hat, and moved on to his paintings, a pair of new companions in tow.

CHAPTER SEVEN

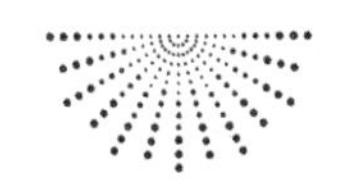

"*Dear Mr. and Mrs. Crispin,*

I write to you with a business proposal. My sister, Lady Edith Wexley, and I would like to discuss with you some repairs that are required at our London home. We began a renovation last month under the direction of another architect—who was in turn under the direction of my mother, Lady Ryland. When the architect broke his contract and Lady Ryland broke her leg (in incidents unrelated), the home was left in a state of half-repair. Bricks are falling. Stucco is peeling. I have been told that something must be done, and that you are the family to do it.

I understand that Lady Edith is already known to you through her friendship with your daughter, Miss Caroline Crispin, who is also a graduate of Mrs. Hellkirk's Seminary for Wayward and Willful Girls. One of these young women has already gotten it into her head that our collaboration would be a fine idea; if the other is to get wind of it, there will be no stopping it. I don't know what Mrs. Hellkirk does in her leisure, but I'm quite certain that our fine officers on the Peninsula could have benefited from her tactics, once upon a time. General Bonaparte would not have stood a chance.

If you are amenable, please advise me as to your availability.

Yours truly,
Ryland

"What do you make of it?" Papa asked, smoothing his beard.

"May I see it?" Caro replied, snatching the letter and walking closer to the window. "When did it arrive?"

"Just now. Stinson brought it upstairs at once."

"Humph. It would have languished in your correspondence a long time if he hadn't," she muttered, grudgingly giving Stinson some credit.

"A few weeks, at least!" Papa replied, fanning a folded newspaper before his face. Even with the best air circulation in London, their third-floor drawing studio could be sweltering by midday. "That's how far behind we are in the letters, Caro. We need more of your help in that regard, I'm afraid."

"Indeed," Mama added. "Papa and I seem to become especially busy with other things when it comes time to write the most powerful men in England, denying their requests."

"Especially those who are known brutes!" Papa added. "They say he almost killed a man, you know. In the ring, when they were just sixteen."

Mama tossed him an affectionate frown, then walked over to Caro and put her arm around her waist. "He has an odd sense of humor," Caro said, still engrossed in the letter.

"Who? Ryland?" Papa had returned to his stool and was leaning over a drawing.

"Is that what you call him, Papa?"

"I've never met the man. But his peers do, yes."

She stopped now to picture Lord Ryland as Ryland; as a man alone, apart from his aristocratic bona fides. *Lord Ryland...Ryland... Rye...Adam...My—*

"Caro," Mama interrupted softly, "are you listening?"

"Mmmm?"

"Can you do that for us?"

"Do what?"

"Write a polite refusal to Lord Ryland," Papa replied, frustration edging softly into his tone. "That's why we called you up here."

"But his project—shouldn't we consider it?"

He removed his spectacles and massaged the bridge of his nose. Noticing his discomfort, Mama passed him her handkerchief and watched as he dabbed at his brow. As usual, smudges of ink and graphite blackened the heels of his hands and the undersides of his forearms. And as usual, Mama was even messier. She nearly always wore black, to hide the traces of paint that inevitably made their way to her dresses, coats, and gloves.

Both her parents looked much older than their years. They were in their early fifties and their health was fine; they were spritely on building sites, and could sit for long hours atop hard wooden stools. But the deep grooves in their hands and foreheads had created the cruel illusion of years, as did the abundance of whites and greys in their hair.

"My dearest Caroline," Papa began again. "We cannot accept any new commissions. You know this. And we have a great deal to do in preparing the balloon for our next land survey. We should refer Lord Ryland to another architect—one who needs the work, and who could use it to build up his name."

Mama looked at the floor. It was a subtle expression, and it came precisely when Papa said the words "his name."

It was obvious to Caro—and to anyone who spent time with her parents—that Mama was utterly devoted to Papa's work. What wasn't known beyond their small family (and Edie, and their various pupils, past and present) was that Mama didn't show her devotion by keeping the books or by mothering said pupils, but rather by contributing an equal share of design ideas and by drawing more drawings than anyone else in the studio.

Caro walked over and put her arm around her Mama's waist, nuzzling the crown of her head into her neck. Mama responded by leaning back against her, allowing Caro to support her, her head resting against the pile of soft curls. A small sigh swelled and crested through each of them, one then the other. And when Caro lifted her head, Mama smiled and touched the pendant on Caro's necklace—a silver locket that every young woman received upon graduating from Mrs. Hellkirk's.

It had been Mama who insisted on sending her to that controversial school, where strange notions were taught and where it was expected that, one day, the lives of women would be different. Where it was taken on faith that the hearts and minds of women had always been far more than they were credited to be.

"I noticed that Ryland addressed his letter to both of you," Caro added, planting a kiss on Mama's cheek before walking over to Papa. "That's unusual. It must be Edie's doing."

"You mustn't call him Ryland, dear," Papa replied.

"You did."

"Yes, but only to the two of you. You're likely to do it to his face."

She smiled and placed a hand on Papa's forearm. She did not blame him for silencing Mama; she knew that in private, they consulted over every expenditure and every cornice-line, and that it was society that demanded they hide Mama's contributions. Indeed, it was marrying Papa —then a fledgling pupil to a hard-drinking master architect, who needed all the help he could get—that gave Mama the chance to learn architecture in the first place.

"I think we should meet with them," she replied.

"*Caroline...*" he droned, shaking his head slowly.

"His letter is so polite."

"*This isn't up for debate...*"

"And it's just one meeting...a tour of their home, as a favor to our beloved Edie. While we're there, I'll call him Ryland and he'll run us out of the building in horror."

He looked up at her and smiled.

"I'd call him Adam, but I fear that'd be a touch too far."

"*Dearest, if only—*"

"We should do it," Mama said suddenly, speaking up for the first time in several minutes.

Papa tilted his head and stared into her eyes for some time. Neither of them flinched, and the exchange seemed to communicate more than a simple disagreement on whether or not to accept Lord Ryland's invitation. Their expressions seemed to contain within them the clashes and compromises of many decades—the incremental dismantling of individual hopes, and the building up of new, different, shared ones. "Darling...I—"

"It's like Caro said, Mr. Crispin: It's just one meeting. If the work doesn't contain any interesting new challenge, we can simply decline it."

Papa sat hunched on his stool, bending lower every second, looking more and more defeated as he went.

"And won't it be pleasant to socialize with such a charming pair of siblings, Mr. Crispin? Amusing people, whom our daughter is so clearly attached to."

"Well," Caro replied over a cough, "I'm attached to Edie, of course..."

Papa sighed. His head was practically resting on his desk now. "I believe I am outnumbered."

Caro bounced on her toes at his concession, stopping just short of clapping her hands. It often worked out this way: Mama wanted Caro to do as she pleased, and Papa wanted to exercise caution. As Caro ran out the door she called back, "And we *like* you, Papa. Just think how Monsieur Bonaparte would feel!"

* * *

She descended a flight of stairs and scuttled down the hallway to her rooms. She was happy, for the sake of Edie's entire family, that her parents had agreed to meet with them. But that wasn't her only reason for feeling pleased: She needed the meeting for her own benefit.

She needed to see Lord Ryland again.

The night before she had paced her bedroom, considering whether Lord Ryland would be amenable to going to White's for her. She was now certain that he was her best, and perhaps only, hope.

Situated at her writing desk, she drafted her response:

> *Dear Lord Ryland,*
>
> *Thank you for your letter. We would be happy to meet with you and Lady Edith to discuss the architectural needs of your home. And by "we," I refer of course to Mr. Crispin, Mrs. Crispin, and myself...*

In her many years of helping Mama and Papa with their letters, she had never referred to her parents as if they were equals—partners, in a way. But Lord Ryland had done it; why couldn't she? That he had addressed them both endeared him to her, and it suggested a sensitivity in him that bolstered her hopes that he would grant her favor.

> *...Our ability to work on your home will depend on several factors, which we will discuss at our meeting. We have an opening tomorrow and can be at your home for a tour around 10 o'clock. Are men of your station up and about by then?...*

There was no one else she could ask, really. She hadn't any gentlemen friends; Strayeth and Chumsley had made that painfully clear at the time of their wager. She did have a few acquaintances among the artisans who collaborated with her parents, but those men kept quite busy and were unlikely to be members of an aristocratic-leaning club. Papa and Mama's current London pupils—a Mr. Dalton, a Mr. Davies, and a whiskerless fellow named Mr. Darrin—were amiable enough, but she'd have to ask them to keep the favor a secret from her parents. And that wouldn't be fair at all.

> *...You are probably concerned—though not surprised—that I have already taken over your project. But do not fret. I only write to you (and other potential patrons) because it allows my parents to devote more of their attention to design matters. I promise to leave the architecture to them. Or most of it, at any rate...*

Lord Ryland, on the other hand, could waltz right into White's if he wanted to. He was probably a member. And he had good reason to accept her strange request, and to be discreet about it: She and Edie were as thick as peas in a shell, and the society mavens who knew them practically thought of them as one. If the respectability of one were to take a steep tumble, it would surely dint the respectability of the other on its way down. A woman's reputation never belonged to her alone, she had learned; many other people had a stake in it, and an influence upon it.

...Please be prepared to furnish all prior plans, elevations, sections, and other drawings of your home upon our arrival.

Yours truly,
Miss Caroline Crispin

She set down her quill and looked out the window. Her desk faced the street, and at that time of day there was always a parade of fashionable people coming and going along the sidewalk.

A woman dressed in a scarlet frock caught her eye, and Caro recognized her at once as a Miss Greer, a prostitute who seemed to find steady customers on the streets of Marylebone and Mayfair. Visible even from a second-floor window, the ruby-red paint on her cheeks was a telltale sign of her profession.

Suddenly Miss Greer looked up, and Caro ducked swiftly beneath the windowsill. She rose after a few seconds, holding a thick burgundy drape in front of her, and watched as Miss Greer continued down the far sidewalk. She held her head high, even as a finely-dressed couple crossed the street in a clear attempt to avoid her.

And to Caro's surprise, she felt a pang of guilt at having taken such umbrage at being compared to her. She had long regarded prostitutes as just another set of cogs in the rigid social machinery of London. How strange, then, that it had stung her—had pained her to the point of distraction—to be compared to one.

She recoiled into the hard, wooden chair. *Does Lord Ryland enjoy the charms of a prostitute? Or two, or three?*

She hugged herself tightly, surprised by her fidgety, dyspeptic response. She had obviously adopted a tolerant outlook on the pursuit of libidinal pleasures. But she had not considered until then that Lord Ryland might take a tolerant outlook on Strayeth and Chumsley's libidinal pursuit of *her*.

Edie's brother might be a sentimentalist when it came to marriage, but he was unlikely to be spending his remaining days as a bachelor in a chaste manner. Mrs. Hellkirk had furnished her students with plenty of information on the relations of men and women. And one didn't become friends with the members of a theater troupe without knowing the ins and outs of the act, as it were. She knew that men were more inclined to indulge in their carnal appetites, or so it was commonly believed. Why should Lord Ryland be any different?

She watched now as Miss Greer turned the corner, out of sight. Finding no other familiar faces on the street, she went downstairs and gave Stinson her letter for delivery. She asked him to wait for a response, knowing from experience that even earls did not dally when responding to the best architect—nay, *architects*—in all of England.

* * *

An hour later, she was still in the entrance hall, her arms crossed, toes tapping, gazing intently at the dozen or so paintings that adorned the high walls. It was as good a place as any to fizz with anticipation over Lord Ryland's response.

Suddenly, the door opened and Stinson entered. Her heart found its way to her throat, and took refuge there as he handed her the following letter:

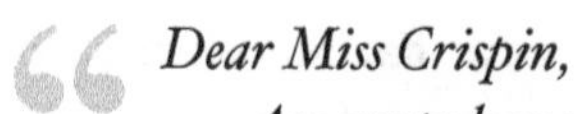

> *Dear Miss Crispin,*
>
> *Are we to have a correspondence? How shocking! What's next, then—a friendship? Please do not relay this possibility to my mother, or I might be cast out of the house and the project will be off entirely.*
>
> *Edie and I will greet you and your esteemed parents at ten o'clock tomorrow morning, as requested. Our cook informs me that an apple and persimmon galette will be served with coffee in the drawing room to start us off. We'll need sustenance for the grand tour, and besides, we have quite a lot of the stuff to be rid of.*
>
> *Until then,*
> *Ryland*

She beamed, her smile testing the limits of her cheeks.

She would see him again. Soon. And she would see her smile reflected back at her in his bemused features, and she would meet him, parry for parry—

No. No—enough with the frivolity, Caro. She forced herself to remember the task before her, to consider how she would feel when she looked Lord Ryland in the eye and related the sordid details of her predicament. *You see, my lord, 'tis true, I have long been in the habit of dallying with men. Yes, yes, potted plants and all that. Now, two of your peers have put one hundred pounds on which of them will be first to prove me no better than a common whore. And as we all know, whores are...bad?*

Perhaps it would be best if she didn't put it quite like that.

She inhaled deeply, preparing herself for the possibility that he would reject her request. All that really mattered was finding a way to teach Strayeth and Chumsley the error of their ways, and that the lesson would haunt them so intensely that they would never bother another woman because of it. Appealing to Lord Ryland was simply an obstacle on her journey. A *handsome* obstacle—and one she suspected was far more gentle and yielding than was widely known—but an obstacle nonetheless.

Nothing more.

"Miss?" Barclay said, making her jump. She hadn't realized he was with her in the hall.

"Yes, Barclay?"

"I'm not sure if this is of interest, but I've seen Lord Chumsley walking down our street twice today, and it's not yet noon."

She held her breath, folding and unfolding the letter from Lord Ryland. "Thank you." He started to head off when she added, "I wish it wasn't of interest, Barclay. But for now, it is. Thank you for letting me know."

He nodded, and was gone.

CHAPTER EIGHT

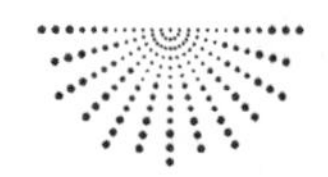

"Miss Crispin! How dare you *do* this to me?" Lady Ryland proclaimed.

Adam winced. Why must his mother address their guests—Miss Crispin and her parents—as if she were their general and they were the worst soldiers ever to don regimentals? He tried not to dissolve into a pool of embarrassment on his drawing room floor as she continued to play the scold.

"Young lady, you have finally brought me your mother and father," she went on, as imposing as ever in her rolling chair, her injured leg propped high on a gold-tasseled pillow. "But you have not given me the opportunity to prepare a full dinner for you all! How could you *do* such a thing?"

Miss Crispin curtsied deeply. She wore a sunny yellow dress, and had smiled so warmly upon greeting him a few moments earlier that he'd nearly turned the wrong way as he guided them inside, so dazzled were his wits. "My lady, I do you grievous harm. Perhaps one day, God willing, you can forgive me."

There. Good. Miss Crispin understood Mother's strange and aggressive sense of humor.

"Humph," Mother replied. "I do not know that I *can* forgive you,

Miss Caroline. Only time will tell! Good thing for you that I am so resilient. Now, come closer and give me a kiss."

Miss Crispin complied at once, and her parents came forward a half-step, too. Adam knew that the couple had many patrons among the *ton*, but he could tell by their manner that they had not been born into such circles. They clasped their hands in front of them like servants, and kept back even when their daughter took a low stool between Mother and Edie.

"Do not trouble yourself, my lady," Mr. Crispin began. "We will be honored to join you for a meal when you are well."

"You will do no such thing."

"No?"

"No."

Mr. Crispin looked bluish. "I beg your pardon, my lady. I thought—"

"You must come within a fortnight, sir! I insist! Nothing waits for this fool leg." She rapped on her cast with the ruler she had taken to carrying around like a scepter. "Brandt! Where is that handsome butler of ours? *Brandt!* Ah, there you are: Tell Cook to prepare a luncheon for next week. I want to stuff the Crispins full of duck and turtle soup, if you please."

Adam had to hand it to his mother: She might push everyone around for her own ends, but she had a way of making them feel important, too.

"Mother," he said gently, "we should not delay our tour any longer, as the Crispins have many other clients making demands on their time. And sanity."

He looked at Miss Crispin as he said it, and felt a thrill bubble through him when she smiled back, feeling for a brief moment that he was possibly the most charming (and in all likelihood, most handsome) man in all of England. He was relieved that she seemed in the same good spirits in which she had left him at the market.

So much for avoiding attachments with the skeptical, disinterested Miss Crispin.

"Yes, yes—be off with you, all of you!" Mother barked with a shooing motion. "But do take your time! Do look in all the cracks and crevices, my dears! And above all else, be sure to tell Adam and Edie everything you really think. No holding back!"

"What Mama means is that we need an architect who isn't afraid to tell us, for instance, that all of this dark paneling is hideous," Edie said, gesturing toward the walls.

"Precisely!" Mother chimed in, snapping her fingers and pointing to Edie for emphasis. "And that the dining room is far too small—"

"As are the mews," Adam interrupted.

"And the saloon is too stuffy, and the windows too few."

"Yes, it is entirely too dark in here. And I would love a proper garden," he added. "Would that be possible? The grooms were apoplectic when I tried to plant a tree in their area yesterday."

Mother guffawed. "Goodness, Adam! Must you really dig in the dirt here in town? I thought we agreed you would keep that habit of yours in the country."

Caro's head whipped around toward Mother, and he thought it must be surprise—or was it disapproval?—that had put the slight crinkle in her nose.

"Even so, Mother," Edie chimed in, "I think we can agree that there's too little room for the servants. In the garden, the mews, and everywhere else, really."

"And with that—let us proceed," Adam replied, trying for his most commanding tone. The Crispins rose and wished Mother goodbye, then reiterated their promises to share a rich, excessive meal with her very soon, and to relate to her offspring the many ways in which their home was cramped, tasteless, and in poor repair. Then they moved on with their tour.

* * *

Edie and Mama led the way, ambling arm in arm through the top-floor corridor, pointing at things, chatting at length. They were kindred spirits, both of them prone to sullenness and withdrawal. Papa followed close behind, joining in their observations and measuring the occasional doorway or window.

So Caro had Lord Ryland to herself.

I can do this. It is just one small favor, and the rest I can do alone.

She thought she was being discreet in her efforts to lag behind with him when he looked at her suddenly and said, "Miss Crispin, if I am not mistaken, you are purposely trying to dally with me."

She looked back at him in horror. "Sir!" His use of the word "dally" nearly gave her the vapors.

"Do not worry, Miss Crispin. I will not judge you for it. I simply find it amusing that my company is so delightful to you today, when you quite literally ran from me at the market just two days past. Has my conversation improved so markedly in so short a time?"

"I cannot tell yet, my lord," she replied, relaxing a bit. "Why don't you tell me something of your interests, and I will have more of an opportunity to assess your information, wit, and syntax."

Lud! Could she ever get used to seeing Lord Ryland smile at her like that. She could find a thousand witty things to say if he would just keep looking at her like that for the rest of the season. She might even be able to forget about teaching Strayeth and Chumsley a lesson.

No—that wouldn't do at all. She needed to focus on her task, and be careful not to misrepresent her interests: She remained resolute in her intention never to marry. Perhaps she and Lord Ryland could flirt for fun —but only a little, and not as part of a courtship.

"Right. Well, at present, my main occupations are fixing this house and finding a husband for Edie."

"Ah, yes! And who better for the job than the great hopeless romantic of Mayfair?"

"You mock me, Miss Crispin, but I assure you I am quite sincere in my enthusiasm for marriages of affection."

"I apologize, my lord. I did not mean to mock you. I just cannot resist an opportunity to *tease* you."

"Ah! You are forgiven, then, as teasing is entirely different from mocking."

"Is it? And here I thought I was grasping at straws."

"Indeed. Mocking is done with an intention to wound. Teasing is done with love."

Caro went red-hot beneath her skin. "I—I simply meant to point out one of the many ways in which you are unfashionable, sir. Firstly, you are a romantic. Secondly, there is your hair—"

"I beg your pardon!" he interrupted, lifting a hand to his cropped black locks. "What, pray tell, is your concern with my hair?"

Where to begin, my lord? She had first thought of sifting her fingers through his hair—and mussing it up a little—when she met him at her ball. The instinct had only increased over cucumbers in Covent Garden. And today, she had to clasp her hands behind her back to keep from reaching out and indulging herself.

"Tell me, sir. What other unfashionable traits are you keeping from me? Next, you'll be telling me that you take your seat in Parliament, and pay attention to the speeches."

He reached into the inside pocket of his coat and pulled out a red silk sleeve. He held it upside down and out fell a pair of spectacles. They looked tiny in his hands as he lifted them up, unfolded them, and put them on.

Lud.

"How is *this* for unfashionable?"

She tried to swallow without being terribly obvious about it, as her throat was suddenly rather parched.

"You...you look tolerable," she muttered finally. Though *tolerable* did not seem the right word for Lord Ryland's attractiveness to her at that moment.

He laughed and removed the spectacles, returning them to his pocket. "Lying is not one of your accomplishments, I see."

"Indeed."

She looked ahead and noticed that the others had turned a corner and disappeared, likely down a servants' staircase. They were alone.

"The most unfashionable thing about me," he continued, his throat busier than normal, "is that...well, I hesitate to admit it—"

"Lord Ryland," she interrupted, "you know I am being ridiculous, right? Do not believe a word I say. I—"

"Indeed," he replied. "Do not make yourself uneasy, Miss Crispin. I know you only tease, and in truth I enjoy it. Tremendously."

There was that demon feeling again—the one that tried to possess her hand and lead it to his arm, his hair, or to his own expressive and enormous hands. She wrestled it down.

"What is it, then? Is it about your spectacles?" She gasped and lowered her voice. "Do you wear them as a *disguise*?"

"No," he laughed, patting at his pocket. "No, it's just that—well, I have an unfashionable opinion about athletic competitions. That is, that I *despise* them. All of them, but boxing most of all." He shrugged.

She shrugged back, and waited for him to continue.

"I once beat a man very badly, Miss Crispin, and although I stopped fighting afterwards, society still lauds me as a fearsome fighter. But the truth is that combative sports make me *ill*."

She waved a hand at him. "I know that you are no brute, my lord. I had only just met you when I realized all that was nonsense."

"The desire to harm another?" He went on. "I cannot understand it, Miss Crispin. It's been years since I've gone near a gymnasium—or the fencing club, or any such places. I avoid hells and pits entirely. Instead, I can be found touring the latest public square, or garden, or canal-building project. Or at a lecture on landscape painting at the Royal Academy."

"I'm sorry you can't be more forthcoming about your dislike of sport, my lord. But you can certainly be proud that you are a scholar-gardener at heart," she replied. She did not regard his dislike of athletic competitions as a detriment, but she suspected it was difficult for a gentleman of such interests—and disinterests—to fit in amongst the aggressive, sporting males of the *ton*. It troubled him deeply, she could tell, and she now understood why he spent so much time in the country.

He shook his head. "Most people do not regard such interests as the domain of men."

She sighed. "I forget, sometimes, that not everyone gets to move among artists, professors, builders, and other lively and open people, as I do. I forget that people like yourself are largely restricted to the banalities of the *ton*."

"You're the first person I have admitted all of that to, Miss Crispin. You have power over me now." He held his hands out to the side, as if he had made himself an open book for her, and was waiting to see what she would make of the first passage.

And she didn't know what to make of it at all. What was he saying to her?

Whenever she felt confused and nervous together, she began talking and didn't stop until she had bluffed her way through whatever storm of uncertainty she had sailed into. "Do not be embarrassed, Lord Ryland. I think it's lovely that you enjoy everything that pertains to our beautiful English landscapes. In fact, from here on I'll expect to see you at all of my father's lectures—"

"Yes, but—pardon the intrusion—but what do you make of my inability to fight, and compete? My lack of courage in those areas?"

She snorted and crossed her arms. "*Sir,* it isn't cowardice to be wary of hurting another person. And it took courage for you to trust me with your secret, did it not? Besides, it takes a rare sort of confidence to allow women to speak plainly at every turn, as you have done with me from our very first meeting. And I value that still more."

He glanced away then, and if she wasn't mistaken, she thought she saw him change color.

"Furthermore," she continued, "you had my utmost support the moment you said you didn't go to those God-awful pits. You are already among the finest men I know."

"So tell me about these lectures of yours," he replied, his voice suddenly ragged.

"Despite all evidence to the contrary, it is not *me* who gives public lectures but my *father*."

"Right—your father's lectures. Will I need to bring a bushel of apples?"

"How right of you to ask! Not apples this time, but books. For his engagement next week, I'll be collecting books that I intend to distribute between Mrs. Hellkirk's and an orphanage for boys in the Almonry. Please gather all your unwanted novels, atlases, histories, essay collections, scientific treatises, and assorted volumes of poetry. Any condition will do."

She sighed. She would never have anticipated it, but there was a real comfort in sharing vulnerabilities with the same gentleman who made her positively squirmy with every glance. Her reluctance to share her secret and ask for his help had shrunk considerably, and she chastised herself for losing sight of what mattered the most: her scheme, and holding tight to the life that she loved. *Be careful, Caro. Share just this one secret; ask just this one favor.*

* * *

"When will we know if your parents can accept our commission, Miss Crispin?" he asked when they'd continued their tour.

He had begun to hurry them a little, stopping less and walking more swiftly, as he didn't think he could stand to be alone with Miss Crispin much longer. Not if she was going to say such wonderful things to him. Not if it was going to feel so bloody relieving to confide in her. If they continued in this manner, he was liable to admit that he was struggling not to reach out and take her hand. That he was trying but failing to respect her opposition to marriage. That in spite of that opposition, she certainly treated everyone she knew—himself included—with the kindness and humor that suggested an enormous capacity for affection.

And that it made her all the more appealing.

"We will have to see what Papa and Mama say, at the end of our tour."

"It was kind of you to meet with us," he said as he opened the servants' stair and waved her through ahead of him.

As they made their way to the lowest floor of the house and into a narrow corridor, she went quiet. And for the first time all day she resembled the woman he had first come upon at the market: withdrawn, tense. Possibly even afraid.

"Miss Crispin, is something the matter?"

She looked up at him. "I have a favor to ask. And if you can help me with it, I promise I will do everything in my power to convince my parents to work on your home."

"What is it?" He could not bring himself to jest with her, for she looked more forlorn with every second.

"I need you to go to White's, my lord."

What followed was a story that made him sick to his stomach: *Strayeth and Chumsley had done what? They had said what?* He tried not to interrupt her as she relayed what had happened to her on the morning after her last ball. He also tried to cool the outrage that simmered in his limbs, as it was the sort of thing that led a man to put a fist through the wall if allowed to boil over.

"It's all true, I'm afraid." She looked him in the eye, all through the telling of what was surely a painful story. He admired Miss Crispin then, for far more than her charitable schemes and her wit and her beauty. He knew that he was looking at someone who was unafraid to reveal something about herself, even if it might bring shame on her. Who was unafraid to be who she was, damn the consequences.

I could learn a lot from such a person.

"What will you do, if you find out the wager is in the book?" he asked, stroking his chin and leaning against the wall, trying to digest what she'd said.

She didn't answer him right away. Instead, her eyes went back and forth, back and forth—searching for something in his face.

Then he realized: She must be wondering if he thought poorly of her, now that he knew she was involved in such a thing. *Oh, dear creature. How wrong you are to even wonder.* All he wanted to do was take her in his arms and hold her there until those red-desert eyes of hers had gone dry again, and when he considered what it was taking for him to refrain from doing just that, he felt that he knew the strength in a team of ten.

"I'm not certain yet," she replied finally. "There's one thing I'm unclear about: If I were pursuing a woman in such a fashion, I'd be worried that the lady might mistake my intentions. I'd worry she would accuse me of jilting her when she realized I had no plan to offer her my hand. Society condemns men for such behavior, and rather harshly."

"I suspect they will not allow you to mistake their attentions for courtship, Miss Crispin. I suspect their pursuit of you will be conducted as much as possible in dark corners, and through whispers. They will probably be bold with you whenever they have you alone. *Very* bold."

"I see," she replied over a false smile. She hadn't stopped wringing her hands since they'd descended the stairs. "I can handle such things."

Adam banged the side of his fist against the wall; not with any real violence, but with a *thud* that reverberated into the next room. The scowling face of a young kitchen maid appeared around the corner, but disappeared again as it became clear who was responsible for the racket.

"Well," said Miss Crispin, looking at him expectantly. "What do you say?"

"I'll do it."

"You will?"

"Of course! Why would you suppose otherwise?"

She exhaled, relief gushing out of her. "Since that awful morning, I've found myself uncertain about so many things—things that I never doubted before. I've even begun to wonder what other people think of me."

"The horror!" he replied, warmed to his core when she smiled for the first time in many minutes. "Please promise me, Miss Crispin, that you will not do such things. Those men are utter bastards."

"You have no idea how relieved I am to hear you say that."

"Don't be. Remember? You aren't to care a fig what I think."

She smiled again, then reached toward the wall and covered his fist with her hand, a pale starfish atop a darker, rounded stone.

He went still, lips parted, anticipation pulsing through him. Should he pull her close? He was desperate to do so but he stopped himself; she had just confided in him, after all, that two longtime acquaintances found her easy and available. He didn't want to suggest that he shared their abhorrent views.

He closed his mouth and exhaled through his nostrils, every part of him settling in and battening down for whatever Miss Crispin might do next.

She pulled his fist from the wall and turned it over in front of her, then pulled his thumb away from his hand—slowly and deliberately—and did the same with his index finger. Fingertip by fingertip, knuckle by knuckle, she gently unclenched the fierce grip he had held onto so tightly, and for so long. By the time she finished, the warmth that had seeped through him earlier had grown hot.

And far more than his fist had become undone.

She turned his hand onto its side and slid her own into it, grasping it tightly. When he grasped back, she shook it as any gentleman might do.

"I believe we have a deal, then," she said softly.

He collected himself, thanking the stars that he had waited to see what she would do. "I have one additional request," he said, his voice sounding strained again.

"What is that?" she asked, a quick flutter of her eyelids betraying an otherwise calm demeanor.

"If we're to be in cahoots with one another, would you please call me Adam?"

"I thought everyone called you Ryland."

"You aren't everyone."

Her mouth went taut. "I will. But only if you'll call me Caro."

CHAPTER NINE

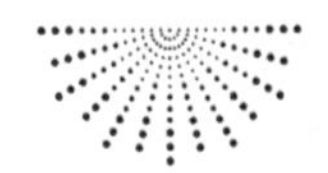

When a chit gets well-known for her teasin'
What man can maintain his good reason?
She'll be my chère-amie
Or that fellow's, may-be
Says our blunt, by the end o' the season.

Good God.

The imbeciles had put their wager in the betting book, all right. They had written it in the form of one of those newfangled children's rhymes. What were they called? The Irish ones?

A limerick—that was the thing.

Damn it.

Adam put his hand on his forehead and rubbed hard, thinking. He didn't know whether to be horrified or impressed that Strayeth and Chumsley had managed to come up with something moderately clever—just clever enough to catch the attention of the gentlemen who came through White's, browsing the betting book in search of something diverting.

He had not expected so much of them.

What he *had* expected was a quick, dashed-off line, stating little more than their names and the amount of the wager. That had been recorded too, of course, but the damned fools had gotten cute with the rest of it.

Not that he thought their horrendous behavior was "cute"; it was just that Strayeth and Chumsley hadn't treated the task as a simple matter of accounting, as he'd anticipated. They had treated it like a game.

Caro was a game to them.

He paced about the hall. An older member with a stiff gait and a monocle passed by, and Adam was relieved when he appeared not to notice him. He flagged a servant and asked for a table somewhere out of the way, and was led to a spot at the edge of the morning room. Preparing to sit, he noticed that the portrait hanging above the chair and small table was of Father.

He stared at it a moment. It depicted Father when he was about Adam's age, and while Adam had become the taller of the two many years ago, they still shared an astonishing resemblance—the same glossy black hair, the same focused blue gaze. It was uncanny.

He sat with his back to the wall—and the portrait—and rifled through the latest papers. He tried to scan for news of upcoming talks and exhibitions but realized after some minutes that he had read the same sentence at least a dozen times. He was wound up like a pocket watch, tense and ticking, and he couldn't stop ruminating over what he had read in the book.

Many of his peers would take a special interest in Strayeth and Chumsley's wager; the rich men who came in and stood over it, laughing with a cheroot and a glass of claret, would be fooled by its lilting lines, thinking it nothing more than some harmless fun. They would fail to see that it carried with it a terrible sting—the pain of which was headed straight for an innocent third party—a young woman who could not be in this place to defend herself, and who was not protected by a title.

He asked for a coffee and palmed a small book in the outer pocket of his coat, the way he often did when anxious.

He supposed he ought to be glad the damned fools hadn't put Caro's name in the book. Thankfully, she had been right when she explained to him that they wouldn't dare; Stray and Chum would find themselves shunned, she'd explained, and they valued their social life far too much to risk such an outcome.

But what if her identity were revealed by someone else? Someone might solve the mystery and her name would leak out, perhaps by word of mouth, or perhaps in a popular gossip column. Society would shun her then, as they couldn't allow anyone in their midst to be a proven participant in a type of relationship they professed to despise.

"Ryland! What brings you here, you old Corinthian? Trying to get civilized?"

Adam fumed. Monocle Man was back. He should have done a better job feigning interest in his papers. "Good morning, Sutcliffe."

"What's the latest from ol' Luke's, then?"

"I have no information to impart about the world of boxing, sir. My apologies."

"What? Come, now. Tell me all the news."

Adam sighed. People believed what they wanted to believe, didn't they? About himself, Caro—whomever!

Sutcliffe was harmless enough, but right now he just wanted to think about Caro. So he lifted the broadest newspaper in his pile and held it in front of his face, trying to give the man a hint.

"How about the racing, then?" he heard over the pages.

"I can't speak to that, either," Adam replied without lowering it.

"Fencing?"

"No, sir."

"Cock fights?"

"No."

"Dogs, then."

Adam lowered his paper. "Most definitely not."

When he raised it again, Sutcliffe appeared to get the hint. The man settled into the chair opposite him with a coffee and a paper of his own, and Adam was able to turn his thoughts back to Caro.

He balled up his fist, recalling the way she'd laid her hand over his. And right then and there he felt it again—that frisson of pure joy, all the way from his fist up through his arm, and somewhere in his middle, too. Just from thinking about it! He had known from their first encounter that he found her unusually appealing. But this had gotten to be something else entirely. He was hauling fruit, practicing witty remarks in his looking glass, and fretting over the betting book at White's.

Their encounters altered him on the most fundamental of levels. To wit: When he thought of what she'd told him in the servant's corridor? How she'd seemed to pull from some unseen reserve of strength, just to say the words to him? He wanted to overturn the table next to him—and that was entirely unlike him.

They called me a whore. They implied that I was too base to socialize with, then wagered over which of them could make me their lover by season's end.

Clearly, neither of those men knew "base" when it stared back at him from the looking glass.

He wondered why they had singled Caro out in such a way. Why select a woman of lower birth to pick on? Were today's young men so desperate for some new sport?

He thought back to his last interaction with Strayeth and Chumsley, the night of Caro's ball. Had there been any clue then of what they were up to? He tried to remember the gist of their exchange, but as usual it had been so banal that he struggled to recall even a snippet.

He remembered that Strayeth had poked him in the shoulder, and they had probably mentioned boxing, because they always did. They had called Caro "opinionated," which had struck him as the sort of thing only a half-wit would find fault with.

What else had they said?

Ah yes: They had also suggested she did not deserve to be called a "lady."

At the time, he'd assumed they were being snobbish about Caro's birth. But now he wondered: had Caro done something to bring on such a remark?

He stood up abruptly, sending his papers to the floor in a noisy flutter. Sutcliffe looked up, but Adam held out his palm to stop him from speaking. Then he marched toward the door, scolding himself under his breath.

He loathed it when he succumbed to believing what was said about someone, instead of what they showed him of themselves. He of all men should know better, as that was precisely what had led to his own predicament. Many years back, his classmates had talked widely of the only real bout he'd ever taken part in. They had told and retold the story until it became many different stories, and eventually those stories were told and retold until the groundwork had been laid for a legend that reached far beyond their schoolyard.

It didn't help that the story involved a duke. And his beating a duke, very badly.

And when the town gossips had got hold of it? They quickly convinced wide swaths of the *ton*—and anyone else who followed the fancy—that the new Earl of Ryland was *savage*. The remainder simply thought him an informal champion of sorts—and the rightful heir to his father's boxing legacy. He quickly lost sight of who believed what of him, finding the very thought of such erroneous distinctions disturbing and exhausting.

Perhaps, like him, Caro was not what her reputation suggested. It was unlikely that she'd behaved any differently than any other young lady who enjoyed dancing, parties, and flirtations. And even if she had, what could he possibly say to it? *I am sorry, Caro, but I believe you earned this wager when you chose pink as a favorite color for your gowns, and also when you pressed yourself against that gentleman. Shame on you. Now enjoy your punishment.*

No, he scolded himself. *That won't do at all.*

He found a man and asked for his hat and cane.

He would have to find a way to be patient until he could see Caro again, and come to know her further. And he would have to get to know her further if his mind were to be settled at all.

That decided it: He resolved that at their next meeting—at her father's lecture, the following evening—he would tell her he wanted to spend time with her, and inquire about ways he might do so.

He'd never wanted to spend time with someone so badly in his life. He couldn't ignore the compulsion any longer, not if it was possible that his feelings were reciprocated.

He would need to be forthright about such intentions and what led to them, then gauge her reaction. Perhaps she, too, felt there was something extraordinary happening between them. The possibility left him breathless. Perhaps knowing that he felt similarly would soften her beliefs in marriage. If it didn't, he would honor those feelings.

He took a deep breath and descended the steps of White's, into a gray noon.

A portly gentleman holding a tiny, hairless dog, both of them dressed in deep purples from head to toe, stepped down from a carriage and greeted him. "What's the latest on the racing, Ryland? What's the best bit of horseflesh these days?"

Adam didn't even know the man. But he was so widely recognized on account of his father's achievements, so plagued by stories of his own fighting ability, that gentlemen sometimes broke the rules of etiquette to engage with him. He gave the fellow the swiftest of nods and kept walking. "Put all your coin on...Twiddling My Gobble-Cock," he blurted out.

It was the most absurd thing he could think of on the spot.

"What's this? You recommend Twiddling My Gobble-Cock?"

"Yes, sir."

"'Struth? Twiddling My Gobble-Cock is a sure thing, then?"

"The *surest*. Tell all your friends."

There were only a few weeks left in the Season. Strayeth and Chumsley would be chasing Caro, and the *ton* would be watching.

Moving in society was about to get especially thorny for her. And while he suspected she could handle herself in whatever bramble the world threw her into, he intended to be around anyway, to help her take a hatchet to it.

CHAPTER TEN

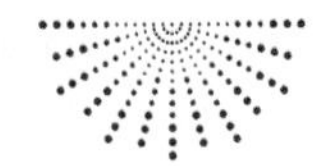

"Goodness! That's a lot of snakes," Caro said.

The woman straightened and looked at her defiantly. "Your advertisement said that all subjects were welcome, Miss Crispin. This is six volumes on the snakes of the central Americas, and I want *in*."

"I am only teasing you, Mrs. Moss. I love a unique passion when I see one. But why are you giving up your snakes, then?"

The woman lowered her voice and leaned in. She was dressed in a drab brown dress and clasped her reticule tightly. "I am only giving up on *one* snake," she whispered, nodding behind her, where her husband could be seen just outside. They were in the reception area of the society for the Encouragement of Arts, Manufactures, and Commerce, where Caro was welcoming guests and accepting their books, and where she could see those entering from the street. She could see that Mr. Moss, for example, was conversing with a pair of Cyprians. They were probably passing by in search of wayward academics who could be persuaded that a lecture on the History of Classical Forms in Britain was far less intriguing than a tour of their own lovely forms, in the present. And it looked like they had found one.

"And don't worry," Mrs. Moss added with a tremor. "They may be my husband's books, but he knows I brought them."

Caro shook her hand and watched her head upstairs to the great room, where Papa was set to speak. When she turned back, hoping for a glance outside at the lovely twilight, she saw none other than Lord Strayeth entering the building.

She forced a smile as the pain gripped her chest. "Good evening, Lord Strayeth."

He bounded up to her and bowed, then grinned at her as he sifted his fingers through his forelock. "Good evening, Miss Crispin. How lovely to see you this evening."

She did not know how to behave. It was the first time she had seen him since that terrible morning, and she had not anticipated him coming to her father's lecture. He had never shown any interest in the intellectual aspects of their work.

"Did you bring me any books, my lord?" she blurted out, eager to stab at the silence.

He glanced at the stacks of books on the tables that surrounded her on three sides. But he quickly lost interest. "No, but I brought *you* my most fervent admiration."

She suppressed a groan. *This was going to be a long few weeks.*

He leaned in. "In fact, I must insist that you sit with me for the lecture. I desperately need your explanation of things, as I am a terrible student of both history and the arts."

She felt her heart calm a little, and her skin cool. It was much easier, it turned out, to be in the company of one's enemy when one's enemy was being profoundly ridiculous.

"Not even I can make up for years of poor school performance, my lord."

"Oh—I bet you could teach me many things, Miss Crispin." He leaned in still further, his usual scent of leather and cloves more prominent than ever.

"Not when I do not plan to attend the lecture."

He cocked his head at her. "You will not hear your father speak?"

"I'm afraid not, sir. I must..." She tried to think of a place where

Strayeth would be loath to go. "I must bring these books to...to...Bott's House. Right away," she lied.

"*Bott's?* Truly? Isn't that where they treat people with the spotted fever?" He took a small step back.

"Yes, my lord." *Why are not more people coming in just now?* There was a lull in the stream of people arriving to the lecture, at just the wrong time. She picked up a pile of books and turned to take them to the adjoining room for temporary storage, trying to give Strayeth a hint.

"Here...allow me to help," he said, reaching out. His hands clasped onto hers beneath the pile of books, and he gave her a knowing grin. "You should not be doing this work on your own. And perhaps you can... show me what you've got in there," he said, nodding to the room.

She let go of the pile and began trembling again. *Here it is: the pursuit in dark corners.* "Of...of course," she replied, moving slowly. Then she had an idea. "That pile, Lord Strayeth? The one you so kindly took from me? It was donated by a recent patient from Bott's. Can you imagine? Just a week ago he was covered in red lesions. Now he's out and about, mixing in society!"

"Indeed?"

"Indeed. He even carried the books himself. Here, have another stack from him."

"Miss Crispin, I must apologize!" he said, dropping the books on a table. "I've just remembered a dinner engagement with my dear aunt." He put his hat on and stepped backward, stumbling on a loose tile. "Were I late, Aunt Fanny would be *most* upset."

"We cannot disappoint Aunt Fanny."

"Until next time, Miss Crispin."

As he left, she took a deep breath and chastised herself for not being more prepared for seeing him and Chumsley. Perhaps at their next encounter, it would be easier? No—as the end of the season drew nearer, they would only become more and more aggressive.

She made a note to bring some of the books to Bott's House, and moved several more stacks to the closet. When she paused for a rest, she saw Adam bounding toward the building in a nutmeg-colored coat and pale nankeen breeches. He had just removed his hat and was reaching up to smooth his hair down as he dipped his head and entered the building.

He still hadn't seen her, and she relished the opportunity to take him in for a moment.

She thought about what he had told her—that he hadn't any interest, and not much experience, in athletics. She could see why so many people made the mistake of thinking otherwise. Once, when she and her parents had visited Oxford, she'd asked for permission to watch the students compete in a bumping race. Her mother had agreed to accompany her to the bank of the river—rather eagerly, as she recalled—where they'd both been mesmerized by the relentless synchronization of the rowers. And, once a few of the men had disposed of their coats and shirts, and splashed and dunked one another? They were equally mesmerized by their fine, muscled backs. Although Adam avoided that sort of organized training and whatnot, seeing him transported her back to the Thames, to those physiques, to that fascination.

"Lord Ryland," she called out. "I'm sorry, but I see you have no books for me. I cannot let you pass." She was only teasing, though part of her was indeed disappointed that this gentleman, who had recently been so sensitive and thoughtful, would show up to her event without books.

He approached her with an impish smile. "It's true, Miss Crispin. I haven't any books." He lifted his hat and cane as if to emphasize his overall lack of books, then stood there quietly, as if waiting for her next move.

There were gentlemen waiting behind him, so she reluctantly stepped aside. As he passed by, however, he leaned toward her and whispered, "I didn't bring any books because it was *so* much easier to have them delivered."

She started to gasp but caught herself—just in time to turn it into an irritated snort. "*How many?*" She put her hands on her hips.

"As many as would fit in my carriage. A couple hundred, I should think."

She leaned back from him, taking in his satisfied expression. "Half to the orphanage, half to Mrs. Hellkirk's?"

"Edie provided the addresses."

"You're incorrigible."

He shrugged. "Or lazy."

She shook her head and whispered, "*Hardly*." She glanced at the men waiting behind him, then moved closer. "Thank you, Lord Ryland. Now save me a seat, will you? I'll be in shortly."

"We need a place where we can talk," he replied softly.

"How about we stand behind the last row of chairs?" she replied. "I don't want to miss the lecture."

* * *

"I did just inform you that I was lazy," he whispered, shifting from foot to foot. He was standing next to her at the back of the dimly lit hall and pretending to listen to her father. "I wish you would take me at my word."

"Consider it my retribution for your teasing me about the books," she replied. He didn't turn to look at her, but he could tell from the notes in her voice that she was smiling. "And besides, I do believe you're all talk."

He turned to her now—he couldn't resist—and asked, "I beg your pardon?"

"I believe you exaggerate, Lord Ryland, with all your talk of laziness."

"I assure you, Miss Crispin, I want nothing to do with athletics, and do no training whatsoever." *Really!* He had thought Caro was different—that she would regard him as he regarded himself, and be fine with his lack of sporting credentials.

He was beginning to feel a little sore when she responded, "Sir, I understand how the human body works. Perhaps it's not athletics that engages you, but I don't think you would look the way you do if you were loafing about your study all day."

"You've been thinking about...the way I look?" Too bad it was so dim where they were standing; he would have given half his fortune to see if she was turning crimson at that moment.

"I know it's scandalous, Lord Ryland—"

"Adam."

"*Adam.* My observation might seem scandalous, but *you* are the one who keeps emphasizing—three times now—that you are not the least bit industrious. I simply point out the obvious evidence to the contrary."

"Miss Crispin—"

"Caro."

"*Caro.* This seems like an excellent time to tell you that I wish to spend more time with you in future."

He watched her throat move as she turned back to him, and found he wanted to plant a kiss there, where a deep indentation ran the length of her lovely neck. Anywhere to the left of middle would do nicely. There was room enough in it for many, many kisses, in fact, and he wanted to be the one to deposit them there, very slowly if possible—and soon.

"Sir?"

"Adam."

"*Sir.* What are you saying to me, precisely?"

"I'm asking if I may call on you, Caro. I know you do not wish to be courted, but I enjoy your company and wish to see more of you. I might find an opportunity to prove to you my lack of athleticism, but if nothing else, we might get to know one another better."

"Are you quite serious?"

He stepped back. "Caro, I would not tease you about this, knowing what you have been through these past several days."

She turned back to face the room, and he moved his eyes lower, to the skin exposed at the top of her golden gown. He questioned why he had delayed moving his gaze there sooner, though he quickly forced himself to look up again. He didn't want her to catch him slavering over her, or she would never believe that underneath his obvious desire, he was entirely sincere about wanting to court her.

She eventually looked back. "That would be...fine. I've decided that that would be fine."

He smiled. "Good. Now that we've settled that, I have something to report to you from White's."

"Yes, let's get to business. Just tell me, please—quickly. What did it say?"

He took a deep breath and exhaled, wanting to comply with her request but fearing that she would be hurt when she heard the news. "You were right: the wager is in the book."

She nodded at him and crossed her arms. "And?"

He recited the limerick for her, and told her that only the men's names had been recorded. "And it said one other thing that might concern us: they agreed that proof would need to come in the form of a letter from the lady, and that it must state, to the other's satisfaction, that...that..."

"That the deed has been done," Caro finished.

"Yes."

She looked away, tapping a finger against her arm. "Couldn't a letter be fabricated?"

He shrugged. "I suppose. But these wagers are dependent on a strict honor system. And it's rather well adhered to, I must say. Despite the number of scoundrels who take part in them."

"So some proof is required, but its authenticity is accepted on the man's word alone?"

"Precisely."

"I would like to go into the other room, now. Will you accompany me?"

He followed her through the reception area, down the stairs, and into a small room where she'd been piling the donated books. Under better circumstances, he would have been thrilled to find himself in such a private space with her, but her face was grim, her posture rigid.

"I have a new scheme to conduct," she began. "Would you like to hear about it?"

"Of course."

She stood taller and put her shoulders back. "I am going to teach Strayeth and Chumsley a lesson."

Something in her tone caused his heartbeat to pick up a little. "What do you mean, 'a lesson?'"

"I'm going to teach them that their behavior toward me was insupportable."

He laughed nervously. "They know as much, Caro. They just care more for their own amusement than they do for your well-being."

She made a dismissive gesture, a wave of her hand. "I apologize, Adam—I've been unclear. I plan to teach them that they mustn't do such a thing—slander another woman—ever again."

He scratched behind his ear. "How would you accomplish such a thing, Caro? How would *anyone* accomplish such a thing?"

"They will make me a promise."

"Of what value is a promise from those two?" Incredulity seeped into his tone, and he smoothed his jaw with his hand. He was beginning to have a very bad feeling about this scheme. "Any man who wagers on a woman's virtue can't be trusted to keep a promise to one."

She shrugged. "A moment ago, you assured me that gentlemen's wagers are based on honor. Let's give Strayeth and Chumsley the benefit of the doubt, and assume that their promise to me will be equally honorable." Despite her calm tone, the hairs on his arm stood up. What was she saying? Was this the same Caro from Covent Garden? From the servants' corridor of his home?

"Caro—"

"I thought you would have a little more confidence in me, Adam," she interrupted, her eyes searching him. "I do have a plan, after all."

He forced himself to breathe deeply, and began again. "You are right. And I do, Caro. Please. Tell me about your plan."

"I'm still working out the details—"

"Does it require you to spend time with Strayeth and Chumsley, in public?"

"Yes," she replied, crossing her arms, perhaps annoyed at the interruption. "That much is certain."

He ran his hands through his hair, searching for calm, searching for patience. How did she not see that going after Strayeth and Chumsley would be a waste of time at best, and ruinous to her, at worst? "Caro—people will be watching Strayeth and Chumsley like hawks for the rest of the season, looking to identify the mystery woman from the wager. Any time you spend with those buffoons will put you at risk of being revealed as their object. We should seek to reduce the risk of your being revealed—not to increase it."

She scoffed. "Before, you said that they would pursue me 'in dark corners'—weren't those your very words? If that's true, then their attentions to me won't be terribly obvious. And besides, those two are beastly flirts. They've yet to be in the same room with a woman without batting their eyelashes nearly off their faces. Society's detectives will have quite a time sorting out which of the ladies they fawn over is the one worth a hundred pounds to them."

"You underestimate the sleuthing abilities of the *ton*, Caro. They will find you out, and when they do, they will shun you. Daughter of the Royal Architect or no, society will not accept you being involved in a scandalous public wager. It is a bridge too far."

She fussed with the ends of her gloves, her face pinker than usual, her eyes cast downward. "If society would shun me for being wagered about—without my knowledge and with no provocation—then I don't care to have society's good opinion."

He scratched roughly at his head. "You would not be invited anywhere, Caro! No more parties, no more balls. And Edie could not see you..."

"Edie would never shun me!"

"No, no—you are right. Edie would never shun you. It's just that... many other people...couldn't be as close to you as they would like to be."

"We would make do. People who care about each other make do."

"It's not that simple—"

"I believe it is."

He raised his hands to his temples, his pulse thundering beneath his fingertips. She didn't seem to be listening to him, and she certainly wasn't grasping his meaning: if she were shunned by society, *he* would not be able to see her. Edie—her longtime friend—might sneak in and visit her now and again, but there would be no future acquaintance with him.

He pulled at his hair. "The season is almost over, Caro. The wager could be all but forgotten by Michaelmas, if you just took pains to alter your behavior..."

He thought her eyes might bore a hole right through him. "*Alter my behavior?* In what fashion? You'd like me to stop bantering with unmarried gentlemen, I imagine? Should I also decline every invitation I receive? After that, perhaps you'd have me take up residence in a convent."

"You exaggerate, Caro. I only suggest that you blend in with the debutantes for a time."

A warm breeze came in from the street, fluttering a book that lay open on her table. He glanced over at it and when he looked back, something in Caro had been snuffed out. Her shoulders sagged, and her eyes glistened. Her arms hung limply at her sides.

"I want to change the men who hurt me, Adam," she said softly. "But you? You would rather change *me*."

"What is this need of yours to play the queen of the coquettes?" he pleaded, raising his voice still louder. "Please know that I wouldn't change a thing about you, but if it saves your reputation and keeps you from harm, then I would see you put on a disguise for a time, yes."

She turned for the door.

"What is it? What have I said?"

She stopped in the doorway and spun on her heels and faced him. "I withdraw my permission for you to accompany Edie on her visits, my lord."

Then she turned again and entered the reception area, and he followed. It was empty—everyone was in the lecture—but the door to the street remained open, letting in another gust of hot, gritty wind, and with it the groaning of carriages, the clacking of hooves, and the echoes of the rawest sorts of laughter.

"And you can expect a refusal from my parents," she said over her shoulder as she began picking up stacks of books and moving them with a *thud,* "when it comes to architectural services for your home." *Thud.*

He stepped back. "Are you so stubborn as this? Why do the words of two men matter so much to you? This can't just be about protecting other women, Caro."

Thud. She was going to ignore him, apparently. *Thud. Thud. THUD.*

"Caro—" he bellowed over the din, reaching for her elbow. "What is really going on here? Is this about revenge?"

She yanked her arm from his reach. "You would not understand."

"Please—help me to do so," he said in a softer voice.

She spun around. "When you are a woman, and you have been wronged by a man, and you have been told to alter something about yourself in response to that wrong, then you might begin to understand the depth of my anger."

"Caro—"

"And when such a thing happens to you many times over, always with the same pattern—you change yourself, but the man goes about his life, hurting another woman soon after, then another—*then* Adam, then you will know why I need to do what I am doing."

As he tried to put all of this together, he watched her raise her arm, summoning a constable from the street.

She was having him ejected from the lecture.

CHAPTER ELEVEN

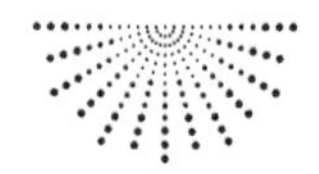

"What do you think, Mama?" Caro asked, pulling her brush from the bucket of thick, glutinous rubber and spreading it across the silk in firm strokes. "Am I as good a painter as you?"

"Yes, my darling. You are the Michelangelo of rubber," Mama replied, kneeling next to her. She put her own brush back into the bucket and stood. "Since you've got this well in hand, Caro, I'll go help Mr. Davies with the casks." She walked off with her skirts held several inches off the ground, revealing the heavy men's boots she wore on construction sites.

But they were not on a construction site. They were in Hyde Park, and it was not quite dawn. They'd been there for several hours, in fact, making repairs to the balloon that they owned. Papa and Mama claimed it was for surveying land, but Caro knew from the sparks it brought to their eyes and the fervor she heard in their voices that it was more of a pleasing diversion than a real investment in their business.

Caro just hoped that helping with the repair work would keep her mind off a certain gentleman, whose name began with an *A*, and who had set up her bristles two days earlier when he suggested that she "alter her behavior."

"When's the next launch?" she called to her parents as she moved on hand and knee, wearing thick leather gloves and her oldest dress. It had taken their whole family, all three pupils, and a half-dozen workmen to spread the massive silk "envelope" of the balloon—the part that would hold the hydrogen gas—across a large, level area of the park.

"*Bertie II* won't be ready to survey for some time," Papa called back. "But we'll test him here in the park in a week or so, if the conditions are right."

She had named both of their balloons Bertie. *Bertie I* had met a sad but spectacular end on a steeple just outside the park, and to this day, none of them could pass by that house of worship without wincing. "Will you keep him tethered during the test?"

"Caroline," Mama called, interrupting them. "Where are we on the decision to work for Lord Ryland?"

Damn it. Just like that, he was back in her head.

She sat up and pushed the hair from her forehead with the back of her wrist. "I don't know what to say about Lord Ryland," she replied.

It was the truth.

She steeled herself for the anger that had seethed up in her at the very mention of Adam's name since the lecture. But instead, with blobs of rubber dotting her dress and hair, armies of insects chirping indignantly at her from their hiding places all around, she felt some other feeling, gurgling deep in her gut.

Queasiness.

She got back to her sealing. "I was thinking, Papa, Mama. We could raise a great deal of money if we invited the public to the launch, and sold tickets," she called out. "We could sell subscriptions, and attract quite the crush—"

"We will do no such thing," Papa interrupted.

"Too true, Papa. Too true. We'll need refreshments and *at least a* four-piece ensemble if we're to expect a single soul. And decent chairs, and perhaps I could hold a contest—"

"*No*, Caroline—you know I support your work, but these launches are unnerving to me as it is. An audience would make it worse."

"I would love to see that, Caro!" Mama called to them from farther off. "Do not let Papa talk you out of exercising your talents!"

Papa grumbled something about the tyranny of democracies and went back to coiling his ropes.

Caro got up and walked off the envelope to fetch another bucket of rubber. She passed by piles of metal braces—for the casks in which the gas would be made—and other balloon-repair necessities, all of them heaped inside the carts they had brought to the park from their warehouse.

Adam had bought his persimmons from a cart just like these, she recalled as a swoony smile made its way across her face.

She shook her head vigorously.

Anger, queasiness, and now swoony smiles? Am I suffering some new sort of vertigo?

It would make sense, really. On the night of the lecture—in the space of a single evening—she had all but abandoned her resistance to courtship, flirted with a man who made her buckle in all sorts of places, had a terrible row with him, resumed her resistance to courtship—or perhaps just a portion of it?—then hid in a closet because she could not catch her breath, find her wits, or cool her temper.

It might have been the shortest, most fraught courtship in history—so perhaps some dizziness was to be expected.

She returned to the envelope with a new bucket. "We could also charge rich aristos to go aloft. That would really make us some blunt."

"We already have a partner," Papa replied. "We needn't any more cooks in the kitchen, so to speak."

"I'm not suggesting you get a partner," she replied gruffly. "Partners want you to 'alter your behavior.' Partners want you to *'blend in with the debutantes.'*"

"What was that, dear?"

"Nothing. Look—this is for charity, Papa. I know gentlemen who would pay a great sum to go up in *Bertie II*. Those young bucks are always looking for something new and dangerous to try, so they can best each other's stories over claret at their clubs."

"Have you inspected the car, dear? Please go inspect the car."

"It's just an idea, Papa," she replied as she brushed off her skirt and headed toward the car. "I'll bet our patrons would love it."

She knew she had more important things to think about than ballooning for charity. Her efforts to devise a scheme for dealing with Strayeth and Chumsley had not progressed, as every time she thought of it she was reminded of Adam. And when she thought of Adam, she fell back into the same confusing muddle.

It was unlike her to be distracted from her goals. Had she lost her enthusiasm for teaching those awful gentlemen a lesson?

She stepped inside the small wicker car and began looking for weaknesses or separation in the weaves. She started at the bottom of the small door and knelt low, so that she could push carefully at every seam.

Making her way around, she swept aside some leaves and a sheet of newspaper that had been left on the floor, probably by one of the workmen. The familiar font of a popular gossip page—the *Gabster* —caught her eye, so she tucked a lock of hair behind her ear and leaned back against the wall to have a look.

> *We are told that a certain lady scientist will soon set sail for Bombay on the H.M.S. Orca...*

She sat up straight. She knew a "lady scientist!" Her classmate at Mrs. Hellkirk's, a Lady Mariah Asperton, had enjoyed dissecting creatures so much that she had sometimes done so in one of the closets, in secret. Since leaving school, she had immersed herself in scientific pursuits—also primarily in secret—but Caro and Edie still saw her on occasion. *This must be about the recent paper she published, under a pseudonym in a journal of herpetology.*

> *...We can only wonder why she would choose to* confine *herself in such cramped quarters...*

The heat began at the top of Caro's dress and moved rapidly up her neck and face.

The use of the word "confine" was the paper's way of suggesting her old schoolmate was...with child.

And Mariah was not married.

> *...We know, however, from her many unsuccessful attempts at joining a certain scientific society, that she longs for the company of gentlemen...*

Perspiration formed on Caro's upper lip, her forehead, and under her arms. Was no woman safe from slander? And why did the paper choose to print *this*, instead of the fact that Mariah had found success with a finely written paper?

> *...and we wish her well with her little* bundle *of adventure.*

She crumpled the sheet into a ball and clambered to her feet. Then she threw it onto the floor of the car and stomped on it—and stomped and stomped and stomped on it—all the while letting out a savage *yawp* and grabbing onto the side of the car so that she could jump on it still further, this time with both feet simultaneously.

She realized, eventually, that she was making a great spectacle and stopped. She looked up, her hair tumbling from its pins in wild, sticky sections, and saw that the workmen and her parents were all staring at her.

But the good news was, her enthusiasm for her scheme had returned.

CHAPTER TWELVE

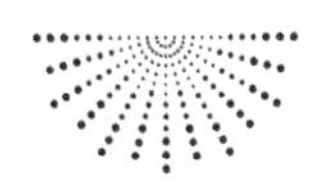

"Miss Crispin, you are a vision," Chumsley began, barely suppressing a yawn. "Why more ladies do not wear such an immoderate shade of purple is beyond me. But perhaps other ladies do not share your complexion? You are rather pale, I believe."

Oh dear me, Caro thought. *No wonder he called me foul names—he cannot put together a proper compliment.* "Why, Lord Chumsley. I had no idea you approved of ladies wearing such bold colors. But then, we have not established if you approve of such ladies on the street, or perhaps only in the bedroom."

He drew back and put a hand on his chest. "I cannot know what you mean, Miss Crispin. I only wanted to convey how lovely you look this evening."

He grabbed her hand and held it tightly, and before she realized his intention he brought it to his lips and gave it a languid kiss.

She glanced around, forcing herself to remain calm. It was late afternoon, and only a few other guests had arrived at the Tilbeths' famous, French-style garden. Why was Chumsley one of them? Few other bucks were so eager to attend the anniversary festivities of a grouchy baron and his standoffish baroness.

Perhaps he is here to find time alone with me?

"Miss Crispin?" he snapped. "You seem unwell."

"I am a little feverish," she replied, fluttering her fan. "Would you be so kind as to fetch me some refreshment? I can only be improved by...by the juice of a persimmon. Do remember."

He bowed deeply and turned away.

She went in the opposite direction, toward a series of gravel pathways that wound around some boxwood *parterres*. Behind her, gentlemen and ladies were beginning to filter into the garden from the back of the home.

Conversing with Strayeth and Chumsley was going to be more difficult than she'd realized. Seeing the latter had brought the pain of ten daggers to her chest, but she had to welcome his attentions—and Strayeth's—or risk letting on that she knew about their wager. She couldn't seem *too* eager to see them, either, or she'd raise suspicions among other guests who had heard about the wager.

Because Adam had been right on that point.

Fine. Adam had been right about several things. She could admit that now, as she paced slowly back and forth against a tall hedge, near the entrance to the pathways.

And since she was admitting things now, difficult things, she might as well confess why she had accepted Lady Tilbeth's invitation in the first place: She'd thought Adam was likely to be here. No true landscape enthusiast could resist an opportunity to visit such a spectacular garden. And she needed to tell him that she was sorry—that he had been right—but that she would never, ever hide herself, or be quiet, as he had asked.

"Miss Crispin?"

She turned and saw a thin man, just taller than her, with a thick wave of red-gold hair rising from his crown. Beyond him, ladies and gentlemen were streaming into the garden now, from large doors on the back of the home. "Yes?"

"My name is Mr. Perkins, from the Huffridge School for Boys," he replied, removing his hat and holding it in front of him. "Please excuse the impertinence of my introduction—I couldn't pass up the opportunity to thank you in person for your recent donation of books."

"Oh, you are quite welcome, Mr. Perkins. Tell me—what are your pupils' favorite volumes? Or don't they know just yet?"

He laughed and scratched at his unruly sideburns. He kept them quite long, which seemed to be the fashion among some young men. "The little ones fight over anything with pictures of insects. The older ones are looking for passages that pertain to—well, to adult matters of any kind."

The man blushed a little as he said it, and Caro returned his smile. "I was like that myself at that age," she replied. "So you won't find any judgment from me on that quarter."

"Indeed?" Now Mr. Perkins was really listening, looking nervously over her shoulder and back again, folding the brim of his hat back most harmfully.

She saw that she had alarmed the poor man, and reached out to touch his arm.

"Come, Mr. Perkins. I'd like to tell you about some other ideas I have."

But just as she said it, she saw Adam from the corner of her eye, stepping toward them and away from a cluster of gentlemen behind her. He seemed to have left the group mid-sentence. Their eyes all followed him, darting and furrowed, as he joined her and Mr. Perkins.

"Miss Crispin," Adam said as he bowed to her. "I don't believe I have the pleasure of knowing your friend."

He was speaking in a lower octave than he normally did. It was almost as if he was trying to intimidate poor Mr. Perkins, who was now crunching his hat to the point of being unrecognizable.

She introduced them, and they bowed. "What business have you with Miss Crispin?" Adam asked.

"I—"

"Lord Ryland, that is none of your concern," she interrupted.

Mr. Perkins gaped at her. "My lord, we were talking of Miss Crispin's charity. She has given my school so many gifts over the years, I have quite lost count."

"Ah! See there, Miss Crispin? I am always interested in charitable schemes of yours. Do tell me, what will you next be leeching from the men of good society?"

She could not read him at all. Was this cheek? Was he angry with her? He wasn't smiling the way he had done at the market, or during the tour of his home, or at the lecture, when he asked her if he could get to know her better. Now, his jaw moved under the taut skin of his face, and he focused his penetrating gaze on poor Mr. Perkins.

Ah. He wanted him to leave.

And in all honesty, she wouldn't mind it if Mr. Perkins left, either.

"Let me think," she said after a long sigh. "I suppose I shall ask the men of society for the one thing they guard most carefully of all—the thing they are wont to keep entirely to themselves."

"Coin?" Adam asked, turning to look at her for the first time.

Her heart flared as he did so, releasing a single pulse of something that diffused all through her, long after he'd looked away. "No. Their *ears*."

"How very interesting, Miss Crispin. How very violent."

"Not at all, Lord Ryland. I should only like to find a gentleman or two who are willing to *listen*, without prejudice, to those who were not born to the same advantages they were."

He smiled at her now. "That would be an impressive feat, indeed. Your magnum opus, perhaps."

"Indeed. Although clearly, I have yet to work out the details."

Mr. Perkins looked from one of them to the other, and put his hat back on. "If you'll excuse me, then..." He trailed off, and wandered off, but neither she nor Adam broke their gaze to acknowledge it.

Adam fought the urge to offer her his arm. That's all he wanted right then: for her to put her small, soft hand into the crook of his elbow and turn with him into the crowd—announcing to him and everyone else that she was his.

Well, that wasn't *all* he wanted. But it would certainly be a good start.

"Lord Ryland," she said finally. Was that a tremor in her voice, or had he imagined it? "A pleasure to see you, as always."

She started to curtsy, and he felt himself go cold at the thought that he might have to endure another evening without clearing the air, without her knowing that he was sorry and that he would do anything to have her stick her chin in his face again.

"Miss Crispin—please. Let us walk awhile. I would very much like to continue our conversation from the night of your father's lecture."

"Of course," she replied a little too quickly, then cleared her throat and glanced around. "Here. This path looks interesting."

They turned toward it and were walking side by side when Caro stumbled on a misplaced stone. He reached behind her, thinking only to steady her, but ended up squeezing the far side of her waist as if his hand were a vise and her torso was something he'd very much like to work on. She jerked and turned her head, revealing cheeks that had bloomed brighter than his favorite Ardythe peonies. She righted herself and he released her, turning forward again.

He cleared his throat and clasped his hands behind his back. He had never felt such an urge before—the need, deep in his bones, to have another person respond to him so definitively, and exclusively. When he had seen Caro standing with that wheat-haired Mr. Perkins, he had wanted to insert himself between them and shout it to the Heavens that he would be the only one entertaining her ideas, thank you very much.

Good thing he had recently learned to behave otherwise.

"Was Mr. Perkins the next man on your list?" he blurted nervously.

She looked at him, open-mouthed. "I—I—What do you take me for, Lord Ryland?"

"The invitation to call me Adam remains."

"I—*Oh.*" She had started to point a finger at him but something had dawned on her, and she lowered it. "You meant the next man I plan to confide in, about my scheme?"

"Yes. What did you think I meant?"

"Nothing."

"What other role do I play in your life, Caro?"

She stopped walking and spun around to face him. "Adam, you cannot play the constable when it comes to my conversations with other people," she announced, breathing heavily, her fists clenched.

He stopped, too, and though he was confused, he thought it a good sign that she was stepping up to him again, and calling him Adam. "What do you mean?"

"I mean that I will speak with whomever I wish, and it's none of your concern. Whether it's for charity, or for teaching gentlemen a lesson—it doesn't matter. I have schemes to conduct, and I shall conduct them."

"You are right, Caro," he replied, raising his hands to emphasize his *mea culpa*. "You owe me no explanations, and no changes to the way you go about things. I came here tonight to apologize to you for suggesting otherwise."

She looked him up and down. "You understand, then? Why I feel the way I do?"

"Perhaps a person in my situation *can't* entirely understand. But I believe you when you tell me those bastards harmed you, and that they're getting away with it. And I understand now that it isn't right to expect you to behave more demurely as a result." He looked at his feet for a second. He wanted to get the words precisely right. "If you have a need of it, Caro, I offer you my ongoing help with your scheme."

The sky was a spectrum of pinks, tinged black around the edges, and the summertime insects had begun to emerge for their evening's work. He shifted, and the movement of the gravel underneath his feet scraped at the quiet gulf between them. The calls and titters of couples in other parts of the garden had softened, as everyone but they had moved back to the heart of the party, for toasts and cake. They were more and more alone, with every second.

She unclenched her fists. "I accept your apology. And I am sorry, too. You were trying to help me, and I wouldn't listen."

He stepped toward her. "Caro, I want to ask you again: What other role do I play in your life, beyond this scheme of yours? My interest in getting to know you remains. Indeed, it's stronger than ever. May I still come see you, as you said at your father's lecture?"

She looked into his chest, now; she was so much shorter than he. Not ideal for kissing, but there were ways around this. He took another step closer.

She looked up at him.

"If I'm to help you, we'll need to meet," he continued.

He risked another step closer, but watched as her gaze lowered to his chest and her fists clenched again.

Damn it. He had misread that.

They were now but a foot apart from one another. Behind her, the soft sherbet of the sky was nearly consumed by blues and blacks. The sprays of individual conversations had disappeared entirely, replaced by the occasional applause of a single crowd—far away from them.

The outline of her form was increasingly difficult to discern, but Adam had memorized it, before the light had faded: the way she stood like a wrestler with one foot slightly forward, loose and ready to fight, shoulders squared at him, chest heaving. He watched her face, half-wishing she would look up and into his eyes again, and half-hoping that her decision to look straight into him was a sign that she was noticing something about *his* form—something that she liked half so well as he did hers. He studied her eyes, and waited.

She stepped forward, the gravel crunching beneath her soft slippers. "Accompany Edie on her visits if you wish, and see me when my parents work on your home. But Adam—we had better stick to my scheme as much as possible. We have a great deal to do."

Before he could ask her to clarify this statement, she lifted a hand and placed it against his neck, making a small dome against his skin. A fluttering sensation inside it startled him, but he held very still as her fingertips trailed gently, hotly, down his neck and she pulled her hand away, lightly closed. She turned it over and opened it into a pedestal of sorts, for a grand and shimmering moth—its wings a mosaic of browns and golds. Apparently, the thing had landed on his cravat without his noticing.

The insect turned this way and that, its antennae whirling as if it were assessing the pair of them and the absurdity with which they stood there staring at it—particularly when there was enough energy coursing between them to light the garden afire, were one of them to but graze a dry branch.

When it finally flew off, Caro said, "Meet me at my parents' studio tomorrow morning, and we'll get started."

He turned and watched her walk off, wondering how on Earth he was going to keep performing these Herculean feats of self-control.

Then she turned back. "Strayeth will be the first."

"The first?"

"To first to receive his lesson."

CHAPTER THIRTEEN

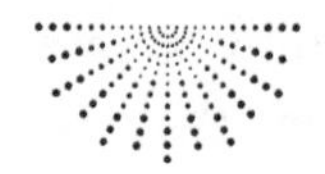

"P*ARAMOUR! Paramour, on the premises!"* Caro shouted into the entrance hall, her hands cupped around her mouth for effect. *"Do be advised!"*

Then she closed the front door behind Adam, and watched as Stinson's eyes and mouth formed a trio of perfect O's.

Adam looked bemused as he handed his hat and cane to the stunned footman.

"Right this way," she said with a wave of her arm. They were halfway up the first flight of stairs when she turned back and called out, "We'll be in the studio, Stinson. Coffee and cakes would be most appreciated, but you had better knock before entering!"

When they rounded the corner of the first landing, Adam turned to her, a smile playing on his lips. "What was that about, then?"

"Oh—I'm just having a little fun at Stinson's expense. The morning of the wager, I discovered that he and a few of the other servants think I'm a trollop, too."

"How nice," he replied through gritted teeth.

"Mmm. Apparently, when two gentlemen are too foxed to find their way out of our home after a ball, it is my own moral decay that is to blame."

She led him up two more flights and into the sun-washed studio, where two of the pupils, Mr. Davies and Mr. Darrin, were bent over their desks on the far-right side of the long room.

"Your parents are away? On one of their sites?" Adam asked, smoothing at his hair.

"Yes, at Carlton House. But I thought I could show you drawings of their other residential work. They might give you some ideas for your own home." She led him to a drawing table near the window.

"I thought we were here to discuss your scheme," he whispered.

"We are," she whispered back. "This is just a pretext, should anyone question why you are here."

"Ah, good."

"You see?" she replied, gesturing to herself. "The scheming trollop has a plan for everything."

"You do not really believe that," he replied, sitting on a stool with a quick flick of his coattails.

He glanced around the cluttered room, taking in the rolls of paper toppling out of giant barrels, stacks of books littering every windowsill, cups full of reed pens in various sizes, and enormous framed maps leaning like dominoes against the walls. As he took it all in, Caro looked *him* up and down. His breeches were worn tight—in this, he was fashionable—and she could make out the outlines of his muscles beneath them as he raised a leg and perched it on the lowest bar of his stool. His boots were dusty from the walk, and his hands were calloused, dry, and tanned, just as they had been when she shook one on their tour of his home. It had been one more sign that, beyond his dislike of athletic competitions, Adam was not like a normal earl.

"No, I do not really believe myself a trollop. I just say flippant things about my reputation in order to mock what other, less enlightened persons say behind my back." She rested her hands on the drawing table, around the corner from where he sat. "Or to my face, in the case of the servants."

Mr. Davies cleared his throat from across the room.

She leaned in and pointed to a drawing of a house they were renovating in Bath. "As you see here, Lord Ryland, we have reconfigured many a home to improve lighting in both the drawing and morning rooms." She inched closer to the corner of the table—closer to Adam—and lowered her voice. "We ought not to disturb the pupils."

He nodded, then reached into a pocket for his spectacles. After putting them on, he lifted one of the drawings and glanced at several more underneath it. One was a painting, actually—soft watercolors with the initials *B.C.* in the bottom-right corner. "I've noticed that you and Edie always refer to this work as being done by *both* your parents. Does your mother contribute as a partner might?"

"You seem to have figured out Mama and Papa's great secret," she said, smiling weakly at the work on the table. "Yes; my parents have the same set of skills. They were married just as my father began his pupilage, and my mother was already very accomplished in drawing and painting. She was phenomenal, really, even in those early days—it's astonishing to look at her work from before she met Papa."

He leaned closer, still gazing intently at the drawing. "Do go on."

She sighed. "Well, they went to live with Papa's master, who was a tippling and somewhat negligent fellow. His pupils took on a great deal of the work, and Mama was permitted to be at Papa's side through the whole of it. So she learned to be an architect, too. When they returned from their travels on the continent and the pupilage ended, they began their own practice. They advertised for patrons using Mama's drawings of classical antiquities in Rome and elsewhere. Yet still, they decided it would be best if Mama's role was kept a secret."

"So your father is the only one with his full name on the drawings, and the only one who gives lectures," he replied, looking back at the watercolor.

She nodded. "We once had a patron—a very large man, and a very rich one—who suffered terribly from gout. So Mama told him about the "moving rooms" she and Papa had seen on their travels, years before. Her idea—it was a revelation, really—was that a contraption that his servants could hoist between the floors of his home would alleviate the discomfort he felt using the stairs. And one would think he'd be at least *tolerant* of such a suggestion, even if he wasn't interested. But no! He threw a tantrum fit for a child of three, raving about how he had paid for an architect, not some *dilettante*."

Adam looked downright offended. "Not some *woman*, is what he surely meant."

"You should have seen it, Adam. Spittle flew, jowls shook. His wig went all askew. And I normally laugh at such displays, but *this*? This I couldn't bear. It pained me to see Mama abused in that way."

She paused and fidgeted, remembering that Adam, too, was a very rich aristo, and a patron. Through gritted teeth, she added, "If you desire Papa's input exclusively, that could be arranged."

He tilted his head back and belly-laughed at her. "Of course not! I'm simply curious about your parent's marriage, as you once spoke to me of not understanding it. It occurs to me now that even a love match could become quite complicated, if one not only shares a bed with their spouse, but also a trade," he said, leaning an elbow on the table and setting his head in his hand.

She didn't think she could stand another conversation with Adam about love matches, let alone one about marital beds. Things seemed as cordial and easy between them as ever, but they had gone from partners to near-enemies to partners again in the space of a few days, and she was certain she would struggle to maintain her sanity if the nature of their involvement continued to shift about at such a pace. Or if he continued to chip away at her long-held beliefs, like the importance of pursuing one's endeavors on one's own.

"I had not thought of it that way," she replied finally. "What I do know is that Mama has always been keen on my being allowed to speak, go about, and work as freely as possible."

They talked like that—Adam sitting on his stool with one leg up, rubbing his hand along his thigh with considerable force, her standing just around the corner from him, leaning in. Their heads were but a couple of feet from one another, discussing everything from Mrs. Hellkirk's unusual teachings to the care and upkeep of Hyde Park, pausing only when Mrs. Meary brought in a tray and left it on the far side of their table.

"Do you suppose she thinks less or better of me now?" Caro asked as they welcomed themselves to the refreshments.

"Less—most definitely less. Standing a few feet from a gentleman? With two chaperones in the room? A grievous offense, indeed."

She picked up a macaroon and broke it in half, leaning her elbows onto the table. "I have...kissed some men, you know."

She didn't know why she said it. She'd told herself that gentlemen's opinions didn't matter—that hers was the only one that *did*—but part of her still wanted Adam, at least, to have a full accounting of why Strayeth and Chumsley thought so ill of her.

She put half the macaroon into her mouth, and felt the pressure of Adam's eyes on her. She finished chewing and continued. "This is about more than my wearing colorful gowns on occasion. And it's about more than dancing and flirting, too."

"This is about a handful of ignorant ne'er-do-wells not liking that an architect's daughter has power over them in society." His voice was low, in both volume and tone; that it could be so harsh and yet so soothing entranced her. It was like a wash of gravel, capable of scouring some of the roughness from her distress.

"It is," she said, nearly in a whisper. "I just wanted you to know that I'm not trying to claim...I would never say that I am...that I am some *innocent*."

"Caro, there's no need—" Adam began, reaching out and putting his hand in the crook of her elbow, where it rested on the table. He squeezed it, hard. "There's no need to explain anything. I was wrong to question your speaking to Mr. Perkins—"

"I mean—" she spoke quickly, cutting him off. "I'm not...I'm not..." She looked at him now, and felt that old burning behind her eyes, that same internal maelstrom—of fear, uncertainty, and even a touch of regret—that she'd endured when she'd overheard the men's wager. She covered her eyes with her free hand. Adam kept his own clenched to the inside of her elbow.

He looked away then, as if checking to see that the pupils were minding their own business.

"Do you regret your actions?" he asked, his voice steady.

"I don't know," she replied. "I don't think so."

He exhaled. "You certainly needn't."

She straightened herself and lifted her elbows off the table—forcing Adam's hand to slip away from her.

How much did she want him to know? How could she tell a man she admired—more than admired, perhaps—that she had dallied with young men just enough for it to be noticed and speculated about, but not nearly enough to know true pleasure with one?

And why did she need him to know it?

"I haven't..." Her words trailed off. She sighed. She couldn't say it—and felt ridiculous suddenly for even trying.

"Would you feel better if we talked about your scheme instead?" he asked, rubbing his hand along his thigh again. They both looked at the end of the room, where the pupils had just stood up, and appeared to be packing up to leave.

She smiled weakly. "Normally, asking for someone's help on a scheme would be the most painful thing I did on a given day. But nothing these past several days has been normal, has it? Let us get to it then, and get done with it."

* * *

He couldn't watch Caro struggle like this. Not with two of her parents' pupils mere yards away. And not when she'd insisted that they "keep to their scheme." If she was going to confess things him to him, things that mattered her, or shed tears about any subject whatsoever, he was going to have to pull her to him and encircle her in everything he had. Or at least, to confess to her that that was very much what he wanted.

So he changed the subject, to her scheme.

"Here is what we will do," she began.

What followed was the most dangerous, outrageous, and implausible plan he had ever heard.

"I beg your pardon?"

Before, she had claimed that she wanted to teach Strayeth and Chumsley a lesson. He'd assumed this would involve a conversation or two. Something civilized. Something that sought out common ground between Caro and the two offending gentlemen.

But this? This was *medieval*.

"Are you...quite certain?" he asked, breaking the last macaroon in two pieces and handing one to her. He had learned a valuable lesson at the lecture: he'd learned to do more listening, to set aside his own reactions until he'd heard her piece in full.

"I am quite certain. It's perfect, really. Oh—and I plan to limit my social outings over the next few weeks. So that I won't be seen with Strayeth and Chumsley any more than I need to, just as you advised."

"Excellent," he replied. He smiled at her. One might even say that he *beamed* at her, so pleased was he that she'd taken his concerns into account, just as he had been moved by hers. They were subtle adaptations, but good ones. "And what is my role in all of this?"

She was smiling at him, too, and he was glad for it. When she'd finished telling him what she required of him, he added, "I am glad to see you happy, Caro. Not that you aren't entitled to be angry, of course. I just—it pleases me to be party to improving your mood in some small way."

"Look at us—we've become so earnest! And to think we started off with bawdy jokes over cucumbers. Tsk, tsk," she teased.

He smiled back at her. "With any luck, our conversation will be back in the gutter as soon as this is all over."

"Lud, I hope so." Her eyes stretched open a bit, as if her quick acquiescence to such a suggestion surprised even her.

His smile stretched, too, though he tried to hide it for propriety's sake. "May I ask you something?"

Her eyes darted across his cravat, then back up to his. "Of course."

He shifted in his chair—lowering one leg and raising the other. He felt warm all of a sudden, in spite of the steady cross-breeze through the studio.

Damn propriety to Hell. He had to know. "Earlier, you seemed to want to tell me something of your past. Your experiences with men."

She stared back at him.

"When I inquired if I could join Edie on her visits, I was thrilled when you said yes. And I believe you have forgiven my ignorant words there. So if you feel..." He ran his hands through his hair and began again. "I don't know what it is you are loath to tell me, Caro. But if you're hesitant to socialize with me and it is because of something from your past, I want to assure you that I could not care less. And let me be clear: I wish to *court* you on such visits, if you'll allow it."

A small smile struggled to upend the pain weighing heavily on her features. "Adam, you are a prince to say as much. But you and I both know that is not something you can promise."

"Do not call me a liar, if you please! Perhaps you'd like to tell me, so I can prove it to you?"

She sighed, letting her chin fall to her chest. "I have no great admission for you, Adam. Indeed, part of me wishes I could confess to you that I have been a frequent, generous, and untiring lover to many a man!" She laughed, lifting her head again. "At least then, I would have had the pleasure to go with the charges Strayeth and Chumsley have levied against me. But unfortunately, that is not the case. I have merely been too flirtatious with too many men; I have pressed myself up against some prominent young bucks, lips and all, and had the bad taste to be the daughter of a tradesman whilst I did so."

"I suspect that in their eyes, your sins have more to do with stating your opinions a bit too confidently, or too often. You needn't be embarrassed of that, Caro, nor punish yourself by refusing the attentions of someone who would get to know you better." He stood then, looming over her, wanting to reach out for her.

"Adam, it's only that I am overwhelmed—"

There was a knock on the door and Barclay entered. "Miss, your parents are home. They asked me to tell you that they will be retiring for a short while before luncheon."

Caro thanked the butler, who turned and left.

Adam just stood there, pulling at his coat and straightening his cuffs.

"Perhaps I've taken the wrong approach here," he said as they turned and headed for the door. "Perhaps I should tell you what's in *my* mind, so you can sort for yourself whether you think I ought to be ashamed."

She opened the door for herself and scowled at him. "You know it is expected for a man to have...baser inclinations."

"That is what they tell me, at least. But doesn't it signify that we might be suited for one another, if we share such an inclination? Particularly if such inclinations are about the other."

"Sir, I thought you wanted a love match," she said, stepping through and leading them toward the stairs.

"I do. What of it?"

"You seem to want a great deal in a match."

"Also true. What of *that*?" They were on the first landing now, and he stopped and gripped the carved handrail until his knuckles turned white. Caro watched—she always watched what his hands did, how his chest moved. He thought he had caught her looking at his lower half awhile, too, back in the studio.

"Adam, I think it's best if you—"

"Caro, I am no poet. But let me tell you what some of my inclinations are. I can barely stand to be near you, because of this intense need I have to seek out some patch of bare skin on you, and to find some excuse to place it up against some of my own. It's excruciating. And that is only the beginning."

"Do lower your voice, please!" She looked over the rail to see if anyone was in the entrance hall and muttered, "*Mr. Keats* would not do this to me."

He continued anyway. "I want to put all of myself around all of you, until there is no part of me that isn't next to some part of you..."

"Sir—you must leave now. My parents will be down shortly, and they haven't a taste for such...modern verse."

"Tell me you don't feel the same, and I will leave you be."

She turned and descended the stairs at a pace, and he felt his heart draw in on itself, a hastening implosion toward some deep corner of his chest. He followed her, watching with growing helplessness as she stopped on the second-to-last stair.

"That will be all!" she said, dismissing the servant who brought his hat and cane to her. Her words hit the walls of the entrance hall with more force than usual, but a hint of uncertainty trailed behind them, too—as if she was trying to be firm but something, somewhere inside her, was in revolt.

When he reached her, she was looking down at his things.

He stepped past her and onto the tile floor—berating himself again for pushing her too hard. What did it say about him, as a gentleman, that he continued to say such things when she'd already told him she was overwhelmed? That she didn't care for marriage? That the two of them had more pressing things to attend to?

He drew in breath and turned toward her, accepting his hat and cane and preparing to apologize—yet again!—for his untoward behavior, when she looked up at him with those tea-stained eyes, darker than usual in spite of the powerful, mid-day sunlight. Then a slight part appeared between her lips, and before he knew what was happening, she reached out and gripped his upper arms, pulling him toward her until his head was mere inches from her own.

So this was why she had stopped on the second-to-last step.

She was looking straight into his mouth when she whispered, "They frown upon women becoming poets. *So.*" And that was when she kissed him.

* * *

His arms were around her waist in an instant, crushing her against him. It was all the permission he needed, it seemed, to give himself what he wanted. And indeed, it felt to Caro that nearly all of him was around all of her.

And still, it wasn't nearly enough.

He let go of his hat and cane at once, and the two of them pulled their lips back in spontaneous smiles at the clattering and soft *clunks* the items made as they hit the wooden stairs, then the tiles. They pressed their foreheads together, an urgent back-and-forth motion—an exchanging of scents. And she loosened her grip on his arms so that she could circle her own around his neck, taking from him the same possession he had claimed to her waist. Then once again his mouth was on hers, harder and bolder and more furiously than before.

This was not like Caro's other kisses, in alcoves, behind giant indoor flora. This was a different thing entirely. Before, men had been tentative with her—exploratory, as if they were in search of the nearest route to her bosom, and were using her kiss as a means to that end.

But Adam kissed her like it was a paradise unto itself, like it was all he had ever needed, like he couldn't get enough of her lips alone. His arms literally encircled her—all the way around her back and around the front again, like some frightening, serpentine beast from one of Mrs. Moss's unwanted books, stilling their prey before consuming it whole. Caro had never felt so small, so light, and so full of power all at once. It was like there was something in her kiss—something coming from her, through her kiss—that this powerful man needed to get by. It was heady, and she wanted it never to end. Indeed, she felt as though she would give up the rest of everything, if she never had to leave his arms, or this second-to-last stair that she had never thought to like so well before.

A door sounded from the floor above—her parents emerging for luncheon, perhaps—and the two of them withdrew, simultaneously but slowly, reluctantly, from each other's kiss.

"Why are your hands so rough, Adam?" she whispered in a low rasp.

The question seemed to have surprised him, and he leaned back—his hands still locked on her waist.

"Not from boxing, I know that much," she teased.

He leaned in and nuzzled her nose with his own—then the cushions of her cheeks, her fluttering eyelashes, her still-parted lips.

"I must go," he replied. "But you can have access to my hands—in whatever manner you wish—another time."

He tore himself away but soon muttered a terrible oath and spun back, yanking her against him once again. She laughed as she crashed into him, then found the back of his head with her hands and cradled it gently to her, for one last, lingering kiss.

Then he spun around again, cursed again, collected his things, and strode off.

CHAPTER FOURTEEN

Caro had not thought it possible she could find Strayeth and Chumsley more unappealing than she already did.

She had been wrong.

They stood a couple of hundred yards away from where she walked on Rotten Row, guffawing with a group of young bucks. She tightened her grip on Toby's leash, wrapping and unwrapping it from her hands, partly to busy them and partly to prepare for the event that he spotted some small vermin he wanted to chase.

The very sight of the two lords quickened her breath, and studded her chest with pain.

It was for all the usual reasons, of course. And also because every moment she spent with them—or anyone else who wasn't Adam—was a moment that left her jumpy and peevish.

He had questioned her opinions from their earliest conversations, had made her look at things differently. He had pointed out her stubborn tendencies and encouraged her to accept the help of others. But their kiss on the stairs had left a new kind of mark on her—a wash of something permanent, something that would not be easily removed. When she thought of him, she could feel him all over.

And Strayeth and Chumsley suffered mightily in comparison.

She forced herself to smile and nod at a pair of matrons coming her way on the promenade. Like many people, they increased their distance from her when they got a good look at Toby. "Please don't be alarmed," she said, trying to force some brightness into her tone. "He's an overgrown pussycat, only with more drool."

They smiled and passed by without comment.

She looked back at Strayeth and Chumsley. They were looking her way now; they had spotted her.

It was time to put her scheme in motion.

She shook away all thoughts of Adam, and put on her most inviting smile. Then she called out to Strayeth, who was approaching her by himself. *Perfect.*

"Lord Strayeth, so lovely to see you again. And how is your dear Aunt Fanny?"

"Aunt Fanny? I haven't—*Oh!* Of course! Quite well, thank you. Quite well."

"I'm so glad to hear it."

He stepped in front of her and blocked her, causing Toby to whimper and yawn.

"Sit," she told the dog. He complied and licked his lips, more anxious even than she. She reached down and scratched his ears. *"You are the best dog! Yes you are! Yes you are!"* she cooed. His stump of a tail twirled wildly at her affectionate tone, though his eyes, ears, and posture all suggested that he remained suspicious of Strayeth, and vigilant.

"It's been entirely too long, Miss Crispin, since I've had the pleasure of your company. Tell me, are you well? It is so hot this afternoon, I thought perhaps you could use a rest in the shade. Perhaps over in those trees, just there?" He pointed to a nearby stand of oaks.

"How very inviting, my lord. I could think of nothing more pleasant—"

He turned to stand beside her, and crooked his arm for her to take.

"—but I'm afraid I have an appointment just now, and was about to leave the park."

"Oh, what a pity! I will escort you, then. Tell me, where are we off to?

The mantua-maker? I hear they make many interesting things besides gowns and bonnets. Things of silk and lace. *Hidden* things."

She laughed uneasily. "You are too kind, my lord. But I already have an escort," she replied, glancing at Toby, who released another uncomfortable whine. She reached down again. *Easy, friend. Easy.* "But perhaps you would be so kind as to...rendezvous with me tomorrow?"

Strayeth looked over at her, surprise and victory wrestling for room on his face.

"My parents are testing some improvements to our balloon, just before dawn, in the northwest corner of the park." She nodded her head in the direction.

He drooped a little, probably upon hearing that she was not inviting him to a private tryst. "Do not look so forlorn, my lord! It will be a fascinating sight. And there will be plenty of opportunity for slipping behind oak trees, in the dark." She gave him her sultriest smile, every muscle in her face rebelling against the effort. "There is...always so much to do at such things."

She must have convinced him that her intentions were amorous, because he looked puffed up suddenly, full of breath and arrogance and perhaps even a pinch of invincibility.

"Don't be late," she added in her huskiest whisper, turning to walk away. She glanced over her shoulder and looked him up and down, her eyes half-closed. "I have the *most* exciting plan for us."

And with that, she walked off, her heart racing, praying he would let her go without further discussion. She didn't know if she had the resolve to remain sweet and gentle if he came after her.

She made her way down the crowded promenade, trying not to look hurried. After a minute or two she breathed a bit easier; he had left her alone.

The first step in her scheme was complete.

"Miss Crispin!" Boots pounded the gravel behind her, and she closed her eyes and stopped. She knew the voice; it was Chumsley, trotting toward her. He must have seen her with his friend, and felt impelled to make an impression of his own before she left the park.

"Lord Chumsley, I must apologize, but I am late for an appointment—"

"I require but a moment," he replied, short of breath and short of manners, per usual.

"I do apologize, sir. I would love nothing more than to stay and chat, but I simply must go, I am—"

He reached for her hand. "Nonsense. You can give me a moment of your precious time, I am sure."

It would be so easy to slap him. He is well within arm's reach. She pulled her hand away as gently as possible, and willed herself to remain pleasant. It was not Chumsley's turn for his lesson just yet. She needed him to be patient while she dealt with Strayeth.

"You are right, of course," she replied, shifting from foot to foot. "What can I do for you, my lord?"

"You can ride with me tomorrow, in my phaeton."

"How exciting! And how kind of you. But I am engaged to work with my parents tomorrow, I'm afraid."

"What about the next day?"

"The next day is my day for volunteering at Bott's."

He tossed his head and rolled his eyes. "They will not miss you for one day," he snapped.

"Perhaps not, but I will miss them."

He smacked his hat against his thigh, surprising her. "I will see you at Tawbridge's, then. I will find you."

"I cannot attend Lady Tawbridge's, my lord. But I will save you a dance at my own party, in a fortnight. Don't forget: I've asked everyone to donate a candle—"

"But that is too far off!"

"That is all I can promise you, my lord," she replied as she curtsied. She did not like his tone at all. Unlike Strayeth, whose manner was light and easy, Chumsley could be churlish.

He stepped closer and glared at her with those watery eyes of his, his cheek twitching on one side. "I know just where to find you, Miss Crispin, if you do not keep your promise. Center window, third floor. Am I right?"

She blinked back at him, too shocked to answer. He knew the window to her bedroom? And was threatening to come through it, without invitation?

Lawks.

She was still looking dumbly at everything around her when Toby spotted a squirrel and yanked her away, abruptly and forcefully, toward the edge of the park. She held onto her bonnet and let him drag her, her legs and mind both reeling.

Oh, how I wish that Adam were here!

It was a fairly new feeling for her, one that had been creeping up on her. She had always been a lone wolf—a general, an army, and a corps of engineers all wrapped up together in a single, average-sized package. But now she wanted Adam around, no matter the time of day. Even when she imagined him slowing or disrupting one of her schemes, she found she *still* wanted him there, making her laugh and giving her a hand when she faltered.

Being her "second" when someone challenged her to a fight.

She slowed Toby to a walk as they she reached the entrance to the park, and was just catching her breath when they passed an elegant older couple, strutting arm in arm in the midst of a spirited conversation. She gave them a hopeful but awkward smile.

She could not reconcile her longing for Adam's company with her longstanding fear of marriage.

But she couldn't deny that her want of him was powerful—and exceptional—and impossible to ignore.

* * *

Adam tried not to tap his foot. "She will be here any moment, Edie. Do hurry."

"I don't know why it concerns you," she called out from across the entrance hall. She was standing with one of the Crispins' pupils, a Mr. Dalton, giving him instructions for the measurements he was taking throughout the home.

"I'm coming with you. That's why."

She finally turned and walked toward him, putting on her bonnet and gloves. "Is there some new menace in Berkeley Square? Something with a taste for independent-minded ladies?"

He went to the window again, and this time, unlike the previous six times, he spotted Caro. That muscular dog of hers pulled her along like a small, hornless ox.

He itched for her. It had been three days since their moment on the stairs—and three days too long. Had it been a full moment, even? It had felt like a lifetime and an instant all at once; the summation of every day of his life, and a bright, hot flash that was gone too soon.

He also itched to know where they stood in terms of a courtship, but he'd resolved to put her scheme first.

When that was all over, he would ask.

Now, he was just glad to see her—even if there would be his sister and a crooked-toothed dog between them.

Brandt opened the door and Adam gestured at Edie with a big, underhanded swoop, as if he could will her through the door at long last.

She trudged by, and he followed.

"Hullo, dearest!" Caro called out to them. If he wasn't mistaken, the usual gaiety in her voice was laced with something more tremulous—something like worry.

"You've brought me the beast," Edie replied, embracing her friend and the dog in turn. "I've brought one, too," she muttered, gesturing to Adam.

He approached them and bowed, trying to seem gentlemanly but disinterested. "Miss Crispin."

"Lord Ryland."

"He doesn't think we can walk to the park without stumbling into scandal."

Caro laughed—nervously, he thought. Then she glanced at him, a quick skim of his features before looking at the ground. "I suppose we can't be too careful."

"Humph," Edie replied, passing Toby's leash to him.

He took his place at the curb, walking apart from the ladies and focusing on keeping the dog out of the street.

He only needed a moment with Caro, to find out if her scheme was moving forward. He would love to have *more* with her, of course—more smiles, more saucy retorts, more time to plan their next outing—but he would settle for finding out if he needed to be in Hyde Park the next day, at a certain balloon test, just before dawn.

* * *

"There. That should keep him occupied awhile," Edie said after throwing a large stick in the direction of a host of swallows, resting in an expanse of grass. Toby went thundering toward them, Adam in tow.

"Are you sure that's all right?" Caro asked. "Does your brother even like dogs?"

Edie waved her hand. "I haven't seen you in *days*, and we were never to be rid of him otherwise. The man is a parasite lately."

Caro smiled and picked at the tips of her gloves. She'd been increasingly uncomfortable at having withheld from Edie what had happened with Strayeth and Chumsley, and that she now intended to teach them a lesson. But she couldn't begin to explain these developments now—not when she was so close to executing her scheme. She also had to conceal her growing fondness for Adam, and the way his kindness and respectfulness had eroded some of her pessimism regarding marriage.

But only *some* of it.

"You should have seen the crowd at Lady Blick's," Edie continued once they were alone. "I swear, I might like to watch my brother squirm, chatting up all the bucks and fops about my pleasing attributes and such. But even I would've stayed home if I'd known we'd be stuffed into every corner, like some holiday roast."

"That's nice," she answered, distracted.

"Did you hear that awful business with the wager?"

Adam and Toby were still together—thankfully—but had ventured so far off that Caro could no longer make out Adam's expression.

"Caro? Did you hear me?" Edie continued.

"What? Sorry—no."

"I asked if you knew about Chumsley's wager. The one with Strayeth."

"No," Caro replied, turning away so Edie couldn't see her face as she lied.

"No? Well, it's quite the thing." Edie told her all about the wager, which she had heard about from Lady Blick herself, and which she had discussed many times with guests at both of the parties she'd attended in recent days.

"What do you make of that?" Edie asked her.

"I think it's tedious," Caro told her. *At least I can be honest on some points.*

"It is truly low, even for them," Edie replied. "Didn't you say you saw Strayeth at your father's lecture? I'm surprised he didn't mention it."

"He knows I have no patience for his idiocy. Chumsley's, either."

"Indeed," Edie replied. "We must have made it clear long ago that we don't stand for such nonsense."

Caro noticed that Adam had turned in their direction, and appeared to be trying to wrangle Toby their way. Edie took her arm and turned them in the opposite direction.

"I swear, I don't know what is wrong with him lately."

"Edie, wait—could we sit here awhile?" she asked, pointing to a nearby bench. "I apologize; I know you want to evade your brother, but I could stand a quick rest, just the same."

"Of course. Is everything all right?"

"It's just my feet. These half-boots are worthless. One of these days, I'm going to follow through on my threat to get a pair of Hessians, like Mama."

* * *

If nothing else, Adam had succeeded in tiring the dog out a little. He had no idea how a dog with relatively short legs and a barrel for a chest could have so much buoyancy and verve.

If nothing else, Adam saw why the creature was such a good match for Caro.

"Brother. Glad you made it back to us alive," Edie called to him, amusement in her voice.

"No thanks to you," he replied. He dropped the leash and Toby bounded to Caro, landing in her lap on the bench.

"I am sorry, Ca—*Miss Crispin*," he called out, hurrying over.

She was laughing, tilting her head back while the dog swiped at her throat with his tongue.

"It's nothing," she replied. "Off, Toby!" she called out finally. The dog gave her one more lathe across the face before jumping down.

They stood and allowed Toby to lead them back to the pathway that would take them to the street, and then to the intersection where they would turn in opposite ways.

He needed to speak with her before they reached the edge of the Square, but they couldn't do so with Edie there. He risked a quick glance at Caro and then slowed his step, knowing that Edie—who was holding Toby's leash—would have to move ahead of them, to keep up with the dog's frenetic pace.

It worked. Caro slowed too, taking the hint. They had but little time, as they were only a few dozen yards from the edge of the park.

"I invited Strayeth to the launch," she whispered in a rush.

"And?"

"I made it sound as if there would be an opportunity for a tryst of some kind. We spoke only briefly and I ran off, hopefully without much notice."

Adam stiffened. He didn't enjoy asking this at all, but it was essential: "And was he…forward with you?"

They were but yards from the street now, where Edie stood, using all her might to prevent Toby from showering his affection on a servant passing by with a small child. Caro slowed nearly to a stop, and whispered, "Strayeth asked me to slip away from Rotten Row, and when I refused, to let him escort me to my next appointment. When I offered to meet him at the launch instead, he seemed content."

He inhaled sharply, his jaw muted and grinding. "And Chumsley?"

Edie was looking back at them now, so Caro picked up her pace and headed toward her. "You're not going to like it."

He looked at her. "What did the bloody idiot say?"

She sighed.

He stopped walking and put his hand on her elbow—just the slightest touch, gone in an instant. She stopped and backed up a half-step, so they were standing together. "I don't mean to alarm you, Adam—I can handle all of this just fine." She glanced up to check that Edie and Toby were still standing with the servant. "But when he asked if I would go for a ride in his phaeton and I gave him my excuse, he told me that he knew which window was mine, at the house."

Adam bit his lip and looked around, holding back a myriad of vivid oaths.

"But it was nothing, Adam," she said, starting to reach for him but stopping herself. "He would never be so bold as to enter my home uninvited. Besides, I intend to keep a lock on the window, Toby on my bed, and a hairpin under my pillow."

The dog had pulled Edie back to them, and they were no longer alone.

"Ah! Once again, our outing has been too brief," Caro said as she took the leash from Edie and embraced her. "Edie, Adam. I will see you again very soon, I hope."

She turned and headed off. He tried to sort through his jumbled thoughts, wondering if he should call out and attempt to stop her, to better understand her state of mind.

To convince her to let him stand watch by her window.

But he stayed silent. And as they watched her go, Edie turned to him and asked, "Since when does Caro call you Adam?"

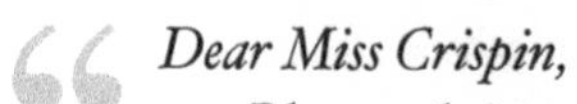

Dear Miss Crispin,

Please advise me as to the status of our project. I should not like to move forward if you are not entirely ready. If something has occurred that gives you pause, or if you have reconsidered the wisdom of our plans, please inform me at once.

Regards,

Lord Ryland

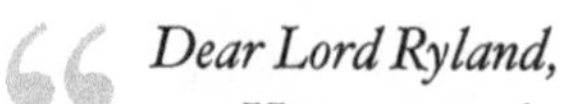

Dear Lord Ryland,

How unsteady you must think us! Of course we are ready to proceed as planned. We are undeterred, and shall pretend you never doubted us.

Regards,

Miss Crispin

Dear Miss Crispin,

I could never call you unsteady. Hurricanes, perhaps. But never you.

I will move forward, then.

Regards,

Lord Ryland

CHAPTER FIFTEEN

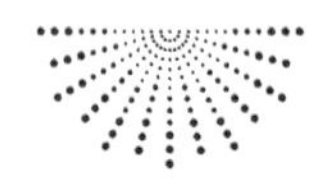

"This way, Lord Strayeth! The balloon is this way, my lord."

Lud, this gentleman has the focus of a gnat. She put her hand through the crook of his arm, trying to guide him. He barely moved.

"Who are all these people, Miss Crispin?" he asked, wide-eyed in spite of the dark, early-morning hour. He looked around in wonder.

"They are called *workers*, my lord."

"And is that Ryland over there, by those carts? What is he doing here?"

"Is it?" she replied, still tugging him along. "I'm sure I couldn't say. He is a new patron of ours, so perhaps my parents invited him."

"Your parents?"

Lawks. Was it truly so hard to imagine? "Yes, my lord. I have a mother, you see, and she *does things*. Now please, come this way. As you can see, the balloon has already been filled with gas, and is ready to go aloft."

He reluctantly trudged along. "Really, Miss Crispin. You are the strangest girl!"

She pulled him to where Mama and Papa were monitoring the final checks to the balloon. A large net held the envelope in place over the wicker car, with ropes tied to iron stakes driven deep into the ground. Two additional ropes—several leagues in length—had been tied to the inside of the car, and would keep the entire apparatus tethered to the earth once the balloon went aloft.

As she'd predicted, Mama and Papa were too distracted with the launch to care that she had gone ahead and invited a couple of aristos.

Strayeth pulled his arm to his side, yanking her close. "I thought we were here to linger in the wood, *chère amie*," he whispered. He slowed his pace and pulled her back.

"But sir! I could not manage it myself."

"Manage what, my dear?"

"Flying, of course. It's too frightening!" She did her best impression of a maiden in distress, her hands on her cheeks and everything.

"Flying? You are going to...*fly?*" The whites of his eyes doubled in size.

"No, *we* are going to fly. But we'll be tethered, of course. What did you think we were going to do?"

He stared at her.

"We'll be alone up there," she whispered, looking at the sky, which was just beginning to lighten into day. "No one will be able to see us, my lord. I thought you might like that."

"Yes, but..."

"Perhaps I should send for Lord Chumsley."

"*No!* No. I am right behind you, *chère amie*. Do...do lead on."

She seethed, but continued along anyway. *Does he think I don't know what he means? I am not your* "chère amie," *you dandified windsucker. I am not your lover, and I never will be.*

* * *

Adam checked a third hitch, then a fourth. He was no stranger to horse-drawn carts; he used them all the time at Ardythe, for his dabbles in earth-moving and landscape-shaping. But as comfortable as he was moving dirt, he wasn't quite sure how to move people in one with any comfort.

He finally found the sturdiest-looking of the bunch and tied three leather straps to a wooden plank on the inside, each one forming a large loop. He hoped it would give his passengers something to hang onto, as it was sure to be a bumpy ride.

He led the mare through the equipment area and past a small huddle of workers who were smoking and chatting, their work filling the balloon now done. They stared at him, perhaps wondering why he would bring an animal and a cart so close to the mysterious balloon and the commotion that surrounded it.

"Can we help ye, my lord?" an elderly man asked.

"No, I'm quite fine." They went quiet, watching him take a horse that wasn't his, leading a cart that wasn't his, toward a scene that was tense and crowded with people.

What a privilege it is to be an earl.

He stopped about twenty feet outside the circle of iron rings that held the balloon in place and stroked the horse's forelock and muzzle. He watched as Mrs. Crispin turned and saw him, doing a double-take and then staring at him.

He tipped his hat and smiled at her.

She cocked her head at him as if puzzled by something (there was a great deal worth puzzling over), but after several seconds she turned back to the work at hand. They needed to check the barometer, Caro had told him, and the bags of sand tied to the side of the car. But Mrs. Crispin also kept looking aside at something, and he followed her gaze to the far side of the circle, where a green windsock fluttered but gently against its wooden post.

There was only the slightest of breezes, just as Caro had hoped.

He then watched as Strayeth entered the circle, leading Caro by the hand. His heart jumped in his chest and banged at his throat as if to get out. The mare tossed her head and pawed at the dirt.

He patted her on the withers and whispered in her ear, trying to calm himself, too. He couldn't hear them, but he kept his eye on Mr. and Mrs. Crispin, the former of whom wrung his hands as they conversed with Strayeth and Caro.

They will not say no to him. They cannot say no to a lord, even an impetuous one, demanding to go up in their balloon.

Thankfully, they also trust their daughter.

Sure enough, they moved aside and Caro opened the door to the car.

She and Strayeth stepped inside while her parents continued speaking to her rather intently, perhaps giving her some final instructions. Then they stepped back and signaled for the men at the iron rings to untie their respective ropes.

The balloon lifted from the ground at once.

* * *

"The funny thing about balloons is that they ascend rather quickly," Caro said cheerfully as the envelope surged skyward, yanking the car from the ground, sending Strayeth to his buttocks on the floor beside her.

She held onto a rope and stayed on her feet.

"Are you all right, sir?"

Strayeth looked up at her, his face pale and moist. "Have you done this before? How high will we go?"

"The tethers will allow us only to the height of St. Paul's Cathedral. And yes, I have done this before."

He nodded briskly, still on the floor. "Good."

As if on cue, the tethers reached their limit and the car lurched violently before stopping its ascent. The breeze pulled them sideways a bit, swaying them gently, to and fro.

Their new stability seemed to embolden Strayeth, and he dug his fingers into the wicker and pulled himself up. She waited until he was standing flush against the wall, peering over the side in childlike wonder, before she reached under her skirt and pulled out the butcher's knife she had strapped to her right calf.

"Let's make this interesting, shall we?" she asked as she brought the blade down on the first tether, then the second.

And just like that, they were free.

* * *

When the first rope came tumbling to the ground, Mr. and Mrs. Crispin scratched their heads. When the second one fell, they grabbed a hold of one another as the rest of crowd—workers, pupils, horses, and earl—froze as one. The balloon was loose.

Within seconds, everyone but Adam and the Crispins turned, shouted, or ran amok—not knowing what to do, not knowing what to say. Chaos ensued.

"Easy, old girl," he whispered to the mare, shaking off his fear and beginning his task. "It's all part of the plan." Then he led her through the crowd, reassuring her in his most soothing tones.

"I need you to come with me," he told the Crispins when he reached them.

Still clutching one another, they turned and stared at him, the worst kind of fear on their faces.

"Miss Crispin is fine, I assure you. Now please—get *in*." He pulled Mrs. Crispin by the hand and led her away from her husband, to the back of the cart. The poor woman seemed in shock. Mr. Crispin was a little better, but Adam had to take his hand, too, and lead him into the cart behind his still-stunned wife.

"Hold on to one of the straps. There you go. Tightly, now."

Then he climbed onto the seat, took the reins, and urged the mare on.

"Your daughter is fine," he repeated, turning his head to check on his passengers, who were now bouncing behind him and likely in great discomfort. He'd never realized how uneven the ground was in that part of the park. "I'll try to find the smoothest path."

Mr. Crispin seemed to have regained some of his composure. "What's this about, Lord Ryland? How do you know what is happening?"

"I've been getting to know your daughter, Mr. Crispin. And I am confident that she will be fine. She has flown in your balloon many times, has she not?"

"Yes, but we've never had a tether break before..."

It didn't break. She cut it. Both of them. "But she has handled other unexpected events with courage and competence, has she not?"

"I suppose," Mr. Crispin replied. "I suppose you are right."

Now Mrs. Crispin spoke up. "Is this as fast as you can go, Lord Ryland?"

"No, Mrs. Crispin. Is this as fast as *you* can go?"

She shook her head.

He turned forward again and saw that the balloon had grown smaller in the sky—it was now half the size it was just a moment ago.

He urged the mare into a trot, and she quickly complied.

* * *

"Miss Crispin! What in blazes have you done?" Strayeth shouted. He had sunk to the floor again and was gripping the wicker behind him as if his life depended on it.

She supposed that it did.

"Whatever do you mean, my lord? We are out for a pleasant ride."

"Have you lost your wits, you crazy chit? How will we land? What can we do?"

"*Ah-ah-ah!* No name-calling, Philip. May I call you Philip? Let's be informal." She flipped the knife so that the handle landed cleanly in her hand again. Mr. McNabbins, the juggler from Sadler Wells, had taught her the trick many years ago. She'd never dreamed she would make such excellent use of it.

"You're mad."

"Am I, Philip? Or am I a whore?" she replied, brandishing the knife at him. "It's unlikely that I am both, or the good people at Bedlam would have locked me up by now. So which is it?"

He stared at her.

"*You* look rather mad, you know. Your hair is whiter than it was a moment ago."

He glanced around the car as if looking for an escape hatch, or a sign that this was all a bad dream. He didn't find either, so he sat back again, shivering.

"Do you know the other funny thing about balloons, Philip?"

He shook his head.

"If we get too high, the valve will freeze shut."

He looked up at the base of the envelope, where the valve was. "What happens then?"

"Then we die."

"Well, *stop* the bloody thing!"

She reached out and grabbed the delicate chain that dangled from the valve, pulling it once, *hard*, so that it released some of the gas with a hiss. The balloon stilled for several seconds before descending a half-dozen feet and leveling out again.

Strayeth looked at her, desperation in his eyes. He scrambled to his feet as if to lunge for the chain.

But she had expected this, so she held out her knife. "Ah-ah-ahhh! *Sit,* Philip."

He slunk to the floor. "What do you want from me, Caro?"

"Ah! Now you are catching on. Now we are getting somewhere."

"Just tell me what you want, and get us down from here."

She clucked her tongue at him. "*Tsk tsk tsk.* So impatient! When you called me a whore—"

He snorted at her. "I did no such thing."

She reared back, shocked at his arrogance. "I heard you, man! When you and Chum made your wager, I *heard* you! In the hall of my own home! And now, you'll make me a few promises, or so help me God I'll tell all of London that you mewled like an infant up here, and vomited on your boots."

"I did no such thing," he repeated.

She reached over the side of the car and sliced a bag of sand clean-through with her knife, then turned and did the same on the other side. They rocked violently and shot skyward.

He shrieked. *And really,* Caro thought, *the resemblance to a mewling infant is remarkable.*

"Firstly," she began, "promise me that you will not tell Chumsley that I know about the wager, or anyone else that I was involved in it."

"I promise."

"And that you will never again speculate about a woman's virtue. These things are not your concern."

"I promise. But you are taking away my favorite subjects of conversation, here."

She reached over and slashed another sand bag, whereupon he sputtered and fell forward. "Find some new subjects, Phil! For all our sakes'!"

"*We are dead,*" he muttered. "We are both of us dead."

"Last thing: You will never again attempt to seduce a woman in bad faith. *Say it*."

His brows had burrowed deep between his eyes, and his famous forelock was slick with perspiration and plastered to his forehead. He gave a longish, primal sort of grunt, the likes of which she had heard only once before, from a rabid dog she'd come upon on a walk. "Both of you," he seethed, "both of you are the worst sort of trollops."

"*I beg your pardon!* 'The worst'? Honestly, Philip. It's difficult to know what makes a good sort of loose woman, and what makes a bad one."

He gripped both sides of the carriage, breathing heavily but quickly.

"And what do you mean, 'both' of us?"

"You and the Ryland chit."

"'*The Ryland chit?*'" She scoffed and huffed and glanced around, as if looking for someone to share in her indignation.

Strayeth took advantage of her apparent inattention and lunged again for the knife.

But she had seen desperate animals before. She knew how their posture, their expressions, and their breathing changed when they felt trapped. So she had already begun slashing several more sandbags, ripping through the burlap as quickly as she could, before Strayeth had even gotten to his feet. He slammed against the side of the car, much harder than before, then the floor. And this time, instead of sitting up he rolled onto his back and moaned—showing her his soft belly.

She also knew a submissive animal when she saw it.

"I promise I will not...seduce a woman in bad faith. Ever again."

At this, she pulled the chain and opened the valve again, causing them to descend a little. She did it again and again, slowly and masterfully, and they gradually made their way closer to the ground—still in Hyde Park, and far from steeples and sword-wielding statues. Soon, the figures below were close enough to recognize, and she could see that Adam had followed her as promised, with Mama and Papa in tow.

"No one will even know I was up here, you know."

"Oh, look! Is that the man from the *Gabster*? How kind of him to accept my invitation to cover our little test launch this morning. I hope he doesn't see what's happened to your breeches."

"Fine. Please, just take us down now."

She brought the car gingerly to the ground, but before the nearly-deflated envelope came down on top of them, she made eye contact with her parents, who looked extremely relieved—and just a tiny bit angry. She also got a quick glance at Adam, who smiled at her. She wanted nothing more right then—at her moment of triumph— than to run over and embrace him.

She was struck by the realization that perhaps, *just perhaps*, working with a partner had its benefits after all.

CHAPTER SIXTEEN

Adam's heart was still racing as he walked into Corinthian Luke's. He was so eager to see Caro, to see her standing with both feet on firm ground, and to touch her and ensure that she was still flesh and bone and breath, that he wasn't quite himself. He was tense and excited, unable to calm down, and unsure how to pass the time until Edie's coming dinner party.

So he had made his way to the boxing gymnasium, for the first time in over a decade.

"Ryland? Funny seeing you here," Quillen said, getting up from a stiff-backed chair along the wall as he entered. His old friend had cherubic, golden curls, trimmed just below his ears. He was a great favorite with the ladies, if Mother was any indication; she had once described his pale blue eyes as the color of "washed-out violets, at the end of the season."

"Quillen—I was hoping you would be here. Let me join you." He took the chair opposite him and before long, fresh coffee appeared on the low table between them.

"I haven't seen you in a fortnight, Ryland. And here I'd thought that with you finally in town, I'd have some conversation for once."

"You didn't see me at Lady Blick's? Playing the matchmaking mama?"

"Sadly, no!" he replied, folding up his newspaper. "It was such a crush that I left for other haunts before midnight." Quillen had cultivated a reputation of some mystery, and had come to be known as a smooth-talking dealmaker who knew everyone worth knowing—in government, the underworld, the aristocracy, and the arts.

Adam glanced around. They were in the coffee room, but with the gymnasium just next door, the shouts and muffled thuds of the sport carried easily into their conversation. A steady stream of young bucks strutted to and from the gym, their boasts and back-slaps further punctuating the salty, sour atmosphere of the place. Adam's leg was pumping up and down before long, and he put his hand on his knee to still it.

"Pardon the intrusion, Ryland. But you don't seem well."

Adam whipped around. "I am fine."

"This place makes you uneasy, still?"

He glanced around again. Tattered old postings hung on every wall, advertising once and future bouts, and the walls themselves seemed deliberately shabby, as if the owner knew that his wealthy patrons would enjoy the sensation of having left their rarefied world for the grit of the underclass—albeit just in their heads, and only for a short time.

"It's odd," Adam began, shaking his head. "This place just seems sort of...sad to me now."

"How so?" Quillen laced his hands together and sat back, looking at him sideways. There was no fooling his old friend. Quillen had never been one to tease him about boxing, or about his interests in the art and engineering of landscapes.

He shrugged. "As a boy, all I wanted to do was to please my father, and that meant practicing athletics much of the day. Mainly boxing. When he died, I turned to the things that *I* liked, but I have always been ashamed of not continuing the things that Father loved."

"And now?"

"Now, I wonder if perhaps the best tribute I could have given him would have been to become a champion in my own way."

"It's not too late, you know," Quillen replied, shifting in his chair. "What's brought about this change of heart, by the bye? Will you be yelling it from the rooftops now, that you're a pacifist who doesn't fight with anything but the brambles on his estate?"

Adam looked at the ceiling. His body still thrummed with the events of the morning—the fear brought about by Caro putting herself in danger, the thrill of witnessing her put her scheme in motion, the anticipation of seeing her again and holding her close. The thrum was all about Caro. His new outlook was all about Caro. Everything was about —and due to—Caro. He was in love with her.

He sighed. "I've been spending my time lately with someone who pursues what she wants, damn the consequences, and damn what anyone thinks of it. I suppose it's rubbed off on me."

The door opened and Chumsley wandered in, his hair looking a little greasier than usual, his clothes a bit more rumpled. Anger flared in Adam, and he was relieved when the idiot turned quickly into another room. He turned back to his friend and changed the subject. "Have you heard this morning's news? Of the events at Hyde Park?" he asked, sipping his coffee. His hand trembled, and he struggled to take the hot liquid without spilling it.

"I heard some talk of it, yes."

"I was there."

Now Quillen sat up. "What were you doing there?"

"I've become a patron of the Crispins. And I was invited to view the testing of their balloon."

Quillen lowered his voice and leaned in close. "They're saying Strayeth looked positively green when he got back to *terra firma*," he said with a chuckle.

Adam laughed and Quillen added, "So—should you be thanking me for introducing you to Miss Crispin, the night of her last ball?"

Adam sat back. Had he been so obvious in his affection for Caro? Already? Before he could answer, Chumsley returned to the room and approached them. He stumbled a little, Adam noticed, and he stank of gin.

"Have you lot heard the news?" he asked.

"You mean your friend's trip to the clouds this morning? We were just discussing it," Quillen replied, looking around. "Where is he now? I expected to be plugging my ears for a week at least, just to avoid his blustering."

"I wouldn't know," Chumsley replied, clenching and unclenching fists.

"The devil's gone and left town. Came right home, his man said, and asked for his horse straightaway."

"'Struth?" Adam could not believe it. Caro must have terrified him! He suppressed a smile.

"Why has he gone?" Quillen asked.

Chumsley shrugged. "I couldn't say. But it looks as if he's forfeited our little wager."

"It doesn't follow that *you* have won it," Adam replied. The grin on Chum's face was the first thing he'd actually wanted to punch in his life, and the very thought made his stomach sour.

Chumsley laughed. He hooked his hands inside the lapels of his coat and thrust back his shoulders with a slight wobble. "Soon enough, Ryland. Soon enough. With the competition gone from town—"

"I wouldn't be so sure," Adam interrupted, his fist landing on the table much harder than he'd intended. The other men looked at him. He put his hand back under the table, and was beginning to feel rather frantic—as if he were about to cast up his accounts, and would soon need to excuse himself and find the nearest chamber pot.

"Well, you're all riled up, aren't you, Ryland! Good! Are you going to the fights, then?" Chumsley asked, nodding to the wall behind them.

Just above their chair backs was a poster that looked newer than the others:

OPEN RING
at the
BEAUTON HARVEST FESTIVAL
October the 1st and 2nd
Celebrate the harvest with some punch!

"That's out near Banmoor," said Quillen, referring to his estate, ten miles beyond London. "The theater people do it every year. It's a casual sort of affair, but they draw serious fighters."

"The Duke of Portson will be there," Chumsley added. "Now's your chance, Ryland."

"Chance for what?" Adam breathed deeply, glancing around for a nearby window he could open.

"To show everyone you've still got it." He chuckled and wandered off.

"Don't mind him," Quillen said once he'd gone. He picked up another paper. "He's a bag of moonshine, that one. Utterly full of it."

Adam leaned back in the chair and took out his pocket-watch. The nausea had not yet abated. "There was no reason for the fight, you know."

"What fight?"

"Mine and Portson's. Back at school."

"You really are rather confessional this morning, Ryland."

"I'd just never had a real bout before," he went on, unable to stop. "I'd only ever sparred. During training, with Father and his friends, and his friends' sons. So when Portson challenged me that day at school, I figured it was time to try out the real thing."

Quillen put down his paper, as if intuiting that this was a sensitive matter. He was a good friend that way.

"And then I broke his arm," Adam continued. "And his nose. And it was all for nothing. *Nothing!* Nothing but stupidity, and a childish desire to prove to my dead father that I wasn't too cowardly to do it."

"You were grieving, Adam. And Portson had quite a hold on you, as I recall. He was choking you."

"Yes, and I panicked. And I wanted to end the thing, because it was all so miserable. A real fight is nothing like sparring, Quill. Nothing. It is terrible."

"I know, Adam. *I know*."

For the first time in many years, talk of his boxing skills wasn't what disturbed Adam the most. What disturbed him most was that he wanted to dust them off and use them.

That, and the fact that there were still several days until he could see Caro again.

CHAPTER SEVENTEEN

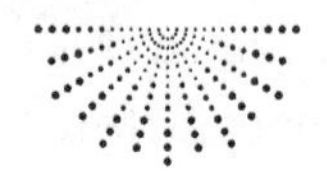

Caro was glad that Mariah Asperton had come to Edie's small dinner.

"Lady Ryland, what an extraordinary dinner this is," Mariah said softly when they had settled into their first course.

"Do not blame this menu on me!" Lady Ryland bellowed between sips of her onion soup. "Tell your grievances to my daughter—it is her party."

Mariah stopped chewing and turned to Caro for explanation.

"Do not be alarmed," Caro said, putting a hand on her arm. "In this family, it's an entertainment of sorts to throw barbs at one another, and to pretend one doesn't care for the others' feelings."

Taking this as her cue, Edie replied, "Mother, you are just sore that Lord Quillen declined to grace us with his flaxen curls this evening."

"Humph," Lady Ryland replied.

"You see?"

Caro was also glad that she hadn't heard or read any more gossip involving Mariah, let alone anything concerning a pregnancy. It seemed that society had not figured out that she was the "lady scientist" from the *Gabster*, though for some reason, she had not embarked to Bombay as planned, either. Perhaps Caro could broach the topic of her travel some other time, in a more private setting.

"I'm curious," Mariah said, taking a bite of her sole. "What do you all miss the most about Mrs. Hellkirk's?"

She and Edie swirled their spoons and thought for several seconds.

"I would have thought it was the radical teachings," Adam offered when no one spoke up. "Or the absence of the male half of the species."

"No, indeed," Caro replied. "We missed your lot terribly. If only because we had no one to dominate." They exchanged smiles over their spoons.

"Caro, is it true you were the youngest-ever pupil at Mrs. Hellkirk's? That you started when you were nine?" Mariah asked.

Caro nearly choked on her soup.

"Is that true?" Edie exclaimed. "The rule is that one must be at least ten!"

Caro took a sip of her wine. "That's almost true," she said finally. "Except I was actually eight when I started."

"However did you manage that?" Adam asked. "I had to beg them to take Edie, and she was eleven."

She frowned at his playful insult. "All I know is that my mother wrote to Mrs. Hellkirk repeatedly, and that she refused to accept my going to any school with a traditional curriculum."

"Now we know whom your stubbornness comes from," Edie added.

"There was a sizable donation involved, too, partly in the form of free building services," Caro continued. She looked to Mariah, eager to shift the conversation to a topic other than herself. "What do *you* miss the most about school, Mariah?"

"I miss the discussions we would have. I've found that spirited, well-meaning debate is extremely difficult to find outside our little school," Mariah said softly.

Caro dropped her spoon with a splash. "You can speak with us any time!" she exclaimed. "We're a bit rusty on our herpetology, but indeed, Mariah—we'll argue with you, any time you like."

Mariah smiled.

"Lawks," Edie added, still staring at her in disbelief. "Even my brother could string together a thought or two on certain subjects."

A wave of dread hit Caro unawares. The idea that another woman might claim Adam's time and attention? That he might partner with her in her schemes? It smashed into her and left her reeling.

A wave of intense guilt hit her next: Mrs. Hellkirk had taught them never to compete with one another, and she adored Mariah. But she knew now how Adam must've felt when he'd come upon her chatting innocently with Mr. Perkins. And she knew, too, that she could not tolerate a future in which Adam was claimed by anyone except her.

She was still struggling to right herself in these roiling seas when she noticed Adam looking at her from across the table, his head cocked, brow furrowed. He was concerned.

And all at once, the heat in her cheeks took on a happier meaning: Adam had already set his cap at her, of course. She needed only admit that she felt the same attachment—the same, dare she think, love—and embrace it. Marriage to Adam would not be a leash; it would not be a hand held over her mouth or an arm that pushed her behind him. It would be a hand held out to her in a storm.

She closed her eyes briefly, feeling foolish, then gave him her silliest smile, feeling the guilt seep from her as she did so.

"I'd like to hear Miss Crispin tell us about her balloon launch the other day. I was there on the ground, and I can tell you it was quite the scene," he said.

"Yes, do!"

"Indeed—tell us everything!"

"No detail is too small!"

She smiled at him, then told them all the harrowing story of how the balloon's tethers had broken in a most unfortunate—and most unexpected—accident.

When she'd finished, she continued, "And I would like to hear Lord Ryland's thoughts on plantings—"

"Well, I would not," Edie interrupted.

"Must we all, though?" Lady Ryland added.

Caro raised her voice over their protests, continuing, "My parents have asked Lord Ryland to offer some ideas for our garden. And I am so excited to hear what he's come up with."

Edie and Lady Ryland looked at her in astonishment. Caro gave them each a pleasant smile then nodded to Adam, who seemed to chew his potatoes with a touch more satisfaction than he had a moment before.

* * *

After dinner, the three younger ladies retired to the drawing room, to work out a dissected puzzle at a candlelit table.

"I have a question for you," Caro began.

"What is it?" Mariah asked.

"Do you study snakes, or just frogs?"

Mariah burst into laughter. Then Edie followed, taking Caro with her. It seemed to strike them all at once as a rather bizarre question for their lot, sitting as they were in one of London's most exclusive drawings rooms, sipping primly from their coffee.

"I don't study snakes *professionally*," Mariah replied when they could finally draw breath again. "I just—"

"You just study them in your closet?" Edie offered, elbowing Caro in the ribs. They both laughed again, but stopped when they noticed Mariah's sly grin.

"Lady Mariah Asperton," Edie continued, "are you telling us you *do* still keep small dead creatures in your closet?"

"Not exactly," she replied, picking up her coffee. "I only have one. And he's neither small nor dead."

Edie went bug-eyed. "What kind is it? You keep it in the country, of course?"

Caro steepled her fingers together and arched a brow. "Precisely how big is this snake?"

Mariah shook her head. "He's called a python. And no, I keep him here in town. At the house."

Edie reached out and smacked her arm, and Mariah let out a shriek followed by the most enthusiastic and cathartic bout of laughter that Caro had heard in some time. "Please do not tell my father," she gasped, clutching her stomach. "Either of you! I would be in terrible trouble if he ever found out."

"And here I thought Toby was a handful," Caro said, picking up her coffee.

"Oh, Frederick isn't a handful," Mariah replied, shaking her head. "He's not fully grown yet, and he's as gentle as a lamb."

"Mariah, he probably *eats* lambs."

"Not since we moved to town," she clarified.

Caro reached over and squeezed her hand.

"It is *so* good to see you both," Mariah added, returning the squeeze. "It's been a difficult few weeks." She looked into the candle as she said it, nodding once before returning her attention to the puzzle.

After a moment of quiet contemplation, Edie sat back and crossed her arms. "Do either of you think I'm...eccentric?"

"What do you mean?" Caro began, careful to keep her tone even.

She didn't know how Edie and Adam had come from the same two parents. Where Adam was a quintessential Englishman—if a bit tall—Edie seemed to have come from another world. With her green eyes and hair like straw that had been dragged through the summer mud, she struck Caro as the likely offspring of the fairest forest nymph and...some other, and far more mischievous, woodland creature.

"I do not care to have a husband," Edie continued. "I've said this many times. But now that I find that no prospective husbands want *me*, I find myself rather put off by it."

Her friends threw their heads back now, unable to contain their laughter. Eventually, Edie joined them.

"Dearest," Caro soothed, taking her hand. "Do be patient. It's going to take an extraordinary man to deserve you. And it's going to take Ad—I mean, your brother—a while to find him."

"Ah-ha!" Edie said as she sat up, raising a finger in accusation. "I caught that, Caro. What's this with you treating my brother like an intimate, all of a sudden?"

She felt herself flush crimson, from her widow's peak to her décolletage. "You know me, Edie. I've never met a gentleman whom I didn't bring to my level, at the earliest opportunity."

Edie lowered her hand. "True. But what does Adam have to say about that? He lets you tease him so?"

"He tolerates me, so far." She looked at her other friend and changed the subject: "Mariah, I have a favor to ask of you."

* * *

Adam said good-night to Mother and dismissed the beefy footman who'd helped him install her safely in her room. He tried not to look too hurried as he descended the main stairs, back to his sister's small party, and back to Caro.

He had to speak with her. It had been entirely too long since the Incident on Caro's Stairs, and while he was keen for an Episode in His Study or Some Such, he also had to discuss with her the strange feelings that had roiled him since the balloon launch. He had to see if she was feeling out of sorts herself.

He went to the drawing room, where Edie and her other friend were sitting at a candlelit table, absorbed in a puzzle.

"Has Miss Crispin gone?" he blurted out. *Damn.* He had meant to be more subtle than that.

And indeed, his sister and Lady Mariah exchanged looks. "She's gone to the kitchen to look for some sweetmeats, brother. Ever the independent lady, she would not wait for a servant."

He bowed quickly and left, hearing them titter behind him.

So now Edie knows for certain, as does her friend.

He would think about that later. He had to find Caro.

Even with a sizable candelabra, the house was very dim. And as he descended the servants' staircase toward the kitchens he cursed—once again—the dark, decades-old paneling, too-skinny passages, and poor fenestration throughout the home.

"Forget renovation," he growled as he bumped his shoulder against the door frame of a workroom. He peeked in and found no one there. "Maybe I should just sell the place."

"But where would you go?" came a smiling voice from across the hall.

He stood still. "Caro? Is that you?"

"It is," she answered, peeking from around the butler's pantry.

"Are you after my claret, then?"

She feigned shock and stepped into the corridor. "I thought if I skulked around long enough, I might overhear one of those gentlemen's wagers I enjoy so much."

He hooked his hand around the small of her back and pulled her hard against him. "*Never.*"

"*Oh!*" she exclaimed as her hands caught between them.

"What is it?" he replied, stepping back.

She giggled and peeled her hands from her gown, where perhaps two dozen delicate jellied candies were now smooshed to bits.

"Oh!" he exclaimed. "Your dress!" But her giggles wouldn't be contained, and soon bubbled up into an effervescent sort of laughter that spread quickly to him.

"Well, you did say you wanted silliness," she eked out between giggles. He guided her into the pitch-dark scullery and when he turned around to her again, the candles illuminated the front side of her—a golden, ghostly apparition, smiling and gesturing grandly with fruity, sticky hands. She gave him the wobbliest of curtsies and said, "My lord, I give you *silliness*."

He froze. What did that mean? That she felt they were a good match?

A *love* match?

He blinked himself back to the present and set his candelabra on a worktable at the center of the room. Then he swept aside everything else, grabbed her by the waist, and lifted her onto it. She laughed and let out a yelp.

"Now then," he whispered as he pressed his waist against her knees. "Let's get you cleaned up. May I have a look?"

She nodded, and he lifted her wrist until her hand was illuminated in the candlelight. The flames reflected back at him from the dark ocher of her eyes as he pulled her hand close and put the entirety of her index finger in his mouth. Her eyes fluttered shut as he closed his lips around it, sucking on it gently before swiping it out again with a guttural sound he had not intended.

As he moved on to her next finger, a sound emerged from her own throat that did not sound entirely voluntary. So he moved on to the next, and the next, and the next.

He had barely finished her first hand when she opened her knees and allowed him to push through them, his waist hitting hard against the table. He let go of her hand and grabbed her bottom with both hands, cupping it roughly and yanking her right up against him, soiled dress and all.

"*Adam,*" she whispered into his ear, putting her newly clean hand at the nape of his neck, drawing her nails across his skin with a pressure he felt in every extremity. "You are getting very dirty."

"My darling, you have no idea," he said before turning his face and putting his lips to hers—lightly at first, opening his own as a cue for her to do the same.

He had been with women, of course, but he had never felt that insatiability he'd read about in novels, in poetry. That feeling of never being full enough, of never being able to slake some new thirst. Not until now, here with Caro, where a deep and inexorable need for her nearly overrode his every faculty.

It frightened him. But still, he kept drinking.

Caro tilted her head to him and ran her fingers through his hair, her nails applying gentle pressure to his scalp, from nape to crown, soothing and inflaming him all at once.

Then slowly, tentatively, she broke from their kiss, and he could tell from the gentle press of her cheek against his own that she was smiling.

He nuzzled her back, then rained kisses on her lips, cheeks, and chin. He forced himself to stop when it came to that irresistible neck of hers, however, as he knew that if he let himself go there tonight, there would likely be Quite an Occurrence in the Scullery.

She went to kiss him again but he leaned back. "What is it?" she asked, looking pained.

"I have something to tell you, and I'm afraid it cannot wait."

"Has something happened?" Her voice went weak as he stepped back and away from her.

"In a moment, love," he said as he opened a cabinet. A moment later he returned to her with two small towels and a pitcher of water.

She wiped her hands, then dabbed as best she could at the bodice of her dress. "Now. *What is it?*" she asked, giving him a quick whip with her towel.

He exhaled and leaned forward, resting his fists on either side of her. "I saw Chumsley at the gymnasium. Strayeth has left town," he said.

"That's wonderful."

"Yes. You've succeeded in making your point to him."

"And?"

"And Chumsley thinks he's all but won the wager."

She snorted. "I figured as much. Is there something else?"

He dropped his chin to his chest and breathed deeply again. "Seeing Chumsley there...listening to his boasts...I wanted to hurt him, Caro."

When he lifted his head, her eyes were darting rapidly to and fro.

"I wanted to stand up and crush him. I—"

"I should never have involved you in this," she said quickly, her voice raspy. She reached out and took his face in her hands. "I am sorry, Adam. You don't have to involve yourself any further."

He wanted to tell her more—about the way he'd been unwell for some days, how he couldn't calm himself no matter what he tried. But it occurred to him that if he told her the extent of his ill feelings, she might abandon her scheme. Or worse, do it on her own.

So he shook his head and yanked her close again. "Don't be silly. I am in this as long as you are. To the end."

She traced his jaw from ear to chin, as if searching his face with her fingertips as well as her eyes. "Are you quite sure, Adam? I—"

"It's not even a question. Now—what is our next step?"

He stood to his full height and took one of her hands from her lap, cradling it gently, enjoying the luxury of her soft, bare skin against his own calloused kind. He wanted more than anything to have this sort of moment every day of their lives, and was more and more confident that she did, too. She had acknowledged their silliness together; she had recognized his distress and tried to release him from her scheme; she was placing his peace of mind first. It was something he could not have said for Father—that many people could not say of their parents or spouses. His heart banged against his ribs, as if it would push out a proclamation of his gratitude to her, of his full feelings for her, right there in his basement scullery.

"A few nights from now, at my party," she began again, "I'll ask Chumsley to go for a carriage ride with me."

"What about the tower, down at the river?" he asked.

She shook her head. "I've changed the scheme. My parents had quite a fright at the balloon launch, so I've found a way that doesn't involve dangling someone from their tallest structure."

"Right. What do you need from me, then?"

"I'd like your help on the morning of the rendezvous. Would you meet me, first thing?"

"Of course." Could it be the right time to tell her what he felt? They were alone, and they were ready for the next part of their scheme. He tightened his hands on hers.

"It's funny," he continued. "I've been trying to be patient, to focus on your scheme and refrain from asking if I can begin courting you in some formal way. But I think we are already courting."

"Indeed," she replied, laughing.

"And we are already getting to know one another."

"In some ways, yes." She cocked her head at him, as if she knew his thoughts were heading somewhere new, and she didn't quite know if she wanted to go there yet.

"And I already know that I love you."

She blinked, her eyes suddenly submerged in a bath of would-be tears. "I love you too, Adam."

"What I already feel for you, Caro," He pursed his lips, concentrating. "What we already feel for each other...do you think...is it too soon—"

"Adam, please," she interrupted, putting her hands on his chest. "There are things I need to know, to—"

"Caro!" called a voice from the top of the stairs. "Are you all right?"

It was Edie.

"Caro?" she called again.

"We must hurry," Caro said as she slid from the table and picked up the candelabra in a single swift motion. "She will be worried about me."

"Caro," he said with a laugh, sifting his hands through his hair. "I'm fairly certain that Edie knows about...*us*. If she didn't, she'd be standing right there in the doorway, looking horrified."

But she was already gone, disappeared into the darkened hallway. It was almost as if she were eager to get away from him.

Or more likely, just from his talk of marriage.

* * *

Caro's thoughts sloshed around her mind with the lurching of the carriage. And no attempt to fix her gaze or to lean out the window for some night air seemed to still them.

If she wasn't mistaken, Adam had not begun to ask if he could *court* her; he had begun to ask if could *marry* her.

And she hadn't wanted to stop it.

She knew, now, that she could not be happy without Adam. It was as clear to her as the raindrops that had begun to fall on her head, her hands, the sides of the carriage.

She hadn't wanted to stop it, but she'd needed to postpone it—to set it safely aside, like a thrilling volume of stories on the table next to her bed, with every intention of returning to it with the attention it deserved, at a point in the not-too-distant future. Because before she could agree to such a future, a few matters needed to be sorted out and agreed upon.

So when the carriage stopped and Edwards opened the door, she scampered into the house and up to her rooms, where she could write Adam a letter. She hoped he would understand that she was not *really* talking about architecture when she wrote:

> *Dear Lord Ryland,*
>
> *We find it is essential to have a clear understanding of a gentleman's hopes and needs for the future before we partner with him in the building of his new home. To this end, we have a few additional questions for you.*
>
> *For instance: What can you tell us of your entertaining habits? Will you be in town much, or continue to live primarily in the country? Also, do you suppose that your future wife will be allowed space in your home for purposes and pursuits that are uniquely her own? And so on.*
>
> *As inspiration, I offer you something of myself: I, for example, entertain a great deal and could not live without my various plans, projects, and schemes. Also, I love town but have never had an opportunity to love the country, so I couldn't say.*

Kind regards,
Miss Caroline Crispin

She had the letter delivered first thing the following morning. And within a couple of hours, she was neglecting the preparations for her upcoming party so that she could read and reply at once to letter after letter from Adam:

> *Dear Miss Crispin,*
> *Of course you need basic information about my habits, needs, and wants. We are collaborating on a new home, after all. It's just good sense.*
> *Forthwith: If I have the good fortune to marry, I fully intend to partner with my wife on such decisions as the use of the rooms in our home, whether we live in town or the country, and how much entertaining we require—and can handle. It is all about compromise and balance, don't you think?*
> *Please feel free to tell me more of yourself. Your "Facts of Caro" was an excellent source of inspiration as I responded to your request.*
> *Regards,*
> *Ryland*

He seemed to understand, thank goodness, that she was not talking about architecture.

> *Dear Lord Ryland,*
> *We would like to hear more of this domestic "balance" you reference. Do you anticipate children? Do you foresee needing accommodations for a medium-sized, yet muscular, dog in future?*
> *Please be as specific as you can.*
> *Regards,*
> *Miss Caroline Crispin*

> *Dear Miss Crispin,*
> *Such excellent questions! Please, allow me to elucidate.*

Firstly, I do not currently have a dog in my life, but I hope to rectify that in the very near future. He or she is to be given every luxury imaginable.

As for a family, I am first and foremost "in want of a wife." The question of children is another I could answer only in conference with said wife. If we do have them, however, they will likely be very spoiled, much like my future medium-sized dog.

Regards,

Ryland

"*Dear Lord Ryland,*

Did you just quote Miss Jane Austen to me? Sir, you have told us everything we need to know.

Regards,

Miss Caroline Crispin

"*Dear Miss Crispin,*

That is a shame, as I had barely begun enumerating my habits and preferences. I have not yet told you what I would like to do, in which rooms. Surely, this is of interest to you?

Regards,

Ryland

CHAPTER EIGHTEEN

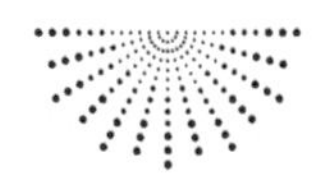

"That wasn't so bad, was it?" Caro asked as she took the wooden box that Adam held out for her. "The people at the workhouse thank you for your generosity."

"Well, candles are much lighter than books," he replied, a shock coursing through him at the quickest brush of their fingers.

One day! In just one day, her scheme would be complete and the season would be over. Very soon after—perhaps the very next day—he would be able to finish his proposal. He could scarcely stand the wait. "So! How will this evening proceed, Miss Crispin?"

"Everyone who has donated a candle will have five minutes with Papa," she replied.

"Are we to form a queue somewhere? There always seems to be a queue in your home."

She shook her head and handed him a small slip of paper. "This is your number. When Barclay calls it out, you can head to the saloon where Papa will be available to speak with you about an architectural issue, or any other topic of your choosing."

Adam opened his paper. He was number forty-three.

"Do I receive some additional perquisite for bringing more than one candle?"

"No. You will have five minutes."

"Not five per *candle*?" he held out his hands. "I brought you ten!"

"Rules are rules, Lord Ryland. I knew people would test my generosity if I allowed otherwise."

"Would you like to test *my* generosity?" he replied in a lowered voice, bending forward to deposit the words in her ear. "Because you are welcome to do so."

"I am sure I would," she whispered in reply, returning his leer but pointing him in the direction of the ballroom with a playful push. "Now go find some refreshment, Number Forty-Three. You are going to be here for some time."

* * *

Adam had just been handed his third glass of the most delicious, amber-colored punch when he saw Quillen approaching. "I didn't realize you were in need of architectural advice, Quill."

"I'm not," he replied. "But it's in my interest to know things about powerful people. And these parties are always full of those."

"I don't understand."

"Miss Crispin's soirees are an excellent place to talk to all manner of people, and to have the most fascinating conversations. It allows me to collect bits of information that might be useful, later on."

Adam turned back toward the line of dancing, searching for Caro. "I don't want to know any more about that."

Quillen laughed and put his hand on his shoulder. "No, I didn't think so. And besides, I think you are too preoccupied to listen to your old classmate, anyway."

Adam turned back to his friend and breathed deeply. He knew he was referring to his fondness for Caro, and he also knew there was little sense in lying to someone as wily and seemingly omniscient as Quillen.

"How do you know such things? *What* do you know?"

"Anyone who looks at you can tell that you care for this lady, Ryland. You don't need to be a sneaky bounder like myself to gather it." He looked around to see whether anyone was standing close to them. Once a young fop made his way out of earshot, Quillen leaned in and gripped

Adam's shoulder more firmly. "Don't fret, old friend—I have no interest in the lady, in my business or otherwise. I do, however, know about the wager."

"Indeed. We talked of it at Corinthian Luke's."

Quillen looked around again. "I mean that I know that your lady is the subject of it."

Adam shrugged his hand from his shoulder. *"How do you know such things?"*

"As I said, Ryland: I collect information."

Adam spotted Caro finally, and watched as she finished a conversation with some friends. She turned away and bumped right into Chumsley, who was waiting directly behind her.

What is that about? Chumsley's pursuit of her had been outside the view of the *ton* up to that point, just as he'd predicted. Perhaps Chum was redoubling his efforts, now that the end of the season was so near.

As they watched him lead Caro to the dance floor, Quillen slapped him on the back. "Don't trouble yourself, man. As we speak, every servant in Mayfair is up in the family attics, dusting off the trunks for the annual exodus to the country. In a matter of days," he added, waving an arm, "these people will all be gone. And you, with any luck, will have your lady."

"Don't call her that."

"Why not?"

"Firstly, because I know several graduates of Mrs. Hellkirk's Seminary for Fiery and Independent Ladies, and I know that none of them would like it. And secondly, because I am superstitious."

Quillen crossed his arms and looked at his boots, smiling through squinted eyes. "Ryland, you are *almost* enough to make a black heart like mine go all romantic again. Almost, but not quite." He put his hands on Adam's shoulders and turned him toward the floor again. "Console yourself with her looks, for now. And be patient."

Adam looked up. On every turn of the quadrille, Caro sought his gaze. Chumsley was not a good dancer, and as he looked down and concentrated on the steps, Caro looked to Adam and rolled her eyes, nodding her head sideways in the direction of her awkward partner.

It warmed him all the way through, and he smiled back at her. He turned to shake hands with Quillen but found that he was nowhere to be seen. He turned every which way, seeking him out, and in doing so he discovered Edie standing nearby. He went over.

"What are your feelings tonight on the topic of matrimony, sister? Are the winds blowing in favor, or against? I need to know if I should round up some slavering suitors for you."

"I don't know anymore, Adam. It's a sad business."

"Marriage?"

"No, not marriage itself. It's this business of *finding* a partner that revolts. Why must it be so...so *transactional*?"

He laughed and she continued, "I wouldn't mind, I don't think, meeting a nice gentleman one day. That could be nice. But I cannot abide the way I have to parade myself here like a prize mare, and for my own brother to have to promote me, on my superficial merits, to assorted strangers. It's...it's—"

"It's not *you*."

"Exactly."

He reached out and put a hand on her shoulder and squeezed. "Then there's no need to go about it this way. Why not just enjoy the evening, and forget about suitors and such? Look! I see Lady Tilbeth there, in the hall—perhaps you should go to her and tell her how much attention the Crispins have been lavishing upon us, as our architects?"

She put her hand on top of his and squeezed it. "Do you know, brother? It's been entirely too long since I've piqued Lady Tilbeth. I think I'll go and do just that."

* * *

"I have never been given such a...such a *gift*," Caro said, gingerly accepting the object Chumsley held out for her.

"Excellent, most excellent. I have long wanted to be the first with you, Miss Crispin."

She had known that she might receive gifts of an unsavory nature from him, but a lock of hair? That was most untoward.

"I believe it is more customary for the lady to—"

"Yes, yes—I know what you will say. But since I am quite known for my fine *coiffure*," he interrupted, patting his fair hair, "I thought I would bestow some on you, as my favorite."

She was perhaps a half-inch taller than Chumsley, and liked to irk him by tilting her head downward in an exaggerated manner when they spoke. "My lord, I cannot dance with...*it*...in my hand," she added.

"No, of course not! I will keep it in this pocket, then—it will give me an excuse to see you before I leave."

"How romantic," she droned.

She raised her hands to begin another dance—a waltz—and regretted at once that she'd included the intimate number in the evening's program. But she consoled herself with the knowledge that in a matter of days, this oaf would be chastened and contrite. What's more, the season would be over, and with it, the wager. She smiled.

Chumsley smiled back at her. "What is it, my love? What thoughts have you smiling at me so prettily just now?"

I am thinking about Adam. I'm wondering when he might try to propose again. I'm wondering when we can be married, and what it will be like when we are. I am imagining ten different ways in which that will be a most pleasing state of affairs.

"My lord, do not ask a lady's thoughts if you are not wholly prepared to hear them. You might find yourself rather shocked. Scandalized, even."

"I can think of nothing I would like so much as to be shocked and scandalized by you, Miss Crispin."

She looked at him again, wondering if she could have a little fun at his expense. The last part of her scheme—his comeuppance—wouldn't take place until the morrow, but there was no reason she couldn't embarrass him a teensy bit on the dance floor.

"My lord, I was just thinking how nice it feels to be in love."

He turned his foot on its side and stumbled, choking a little and coughing spastically before righting himself.

And just like that, she was enjoying her dance a great deal more.

"I can see how you would think that, Miss Crispin," he replied finally, glancing around the ballroom, horrified that she had mistaken his attentions for love and courtship.

"I never thought I would find myself in love with a beau, Lord

Chumsley, but indeed: I find myself most happy, and grateful, and...*excited*, in all senses of the term! If that isn't the beginning of love, I don't know what is." She gave him her most beaming smile. She'd have him believing she'd already named their five children, if the waltz only proved long enough.

"Miss Crispin, many ladies are wont to fancy themselves in love when an eligible gentleman acknowledges them. That is all you are feeling just now—the compliment of my attentions."

"Is that so, my lord? Please, tell me more about how I feel on such matters. I have no other way of knowing." Now he looked sickly *and* confused, so she decided to show him some mercy.

He was hardly an equal adversary, after all.

"Come, come my lord. My thoughts might have been on love just then, but that does not mean I am not up for other adventures. In fact, I want you to join me tomorrow morning, for a ride in my carriage."

The ensemble finished their playing just as they twirled to the edge of the room, not far from the French doors that led to the terrace. Most of the guests clapped fervently for the musicians, but Chumsley went still and studied her face, his arms hanging stiffly at his sides.

"At daybreak, shall we say? Excellent. I'll pick you up in my carriage." She curtsied and began to turn, but Chumsley grabbed her hand and threaded it through his arm, clasping it in the crook of his elbow.

"Why wait, Miss Crispin?" he asked, his tone like acid.

She went cold as he pulled her toward the doors, her mind blank. She looked over her shoulder at the blur of faces behind them, desperate for a name she could call out. But suddenly Chumsley stopped: Mrs. Meary had appeared in front of them, blocking their way. And she was holding onto Toby's leash.

"Begging the intrusion, Miss! But young Tobias here has been *most* ill, all evening. Whining and scratching himself silly. Do you think something might be the matter? I knew he could only be right with *you*, Miss. So sorry for the trouble."

The housekeeper dropped the leash and Toby surged toward her.

She grabbed his collar and looked at Mrs. Meary, deep in the eye for several seconds, trying to convey her gratitude. And if she wasn't mistaken, the housekeeper gave her a taut nod in return. She pulled herself from Chumsley's grip and headed toward Edie, who had just appeared again from the entrance hall.

* * *

As he made his way around the edge of the ballroom, Adam came upon Mrs. Crispin near a cluster of potted trees.

"Mrs. Crispin," he said softly. "How lucky that I have found you here."

She turned to him, wide-eyed, and brushed her hands this way and that on her black gown.

"Don't worry," he added. "I am not very talkative. And if you like, I'll frighten away anyone else who is."

She smiled. "Thank you, Lord Ryland. Is it that obvious?"

"That you would crawl under this table if you could? Yes, I'm afraid that it is."

Now she laughed aloud, but seemed to think better of it and turned serious again. "I suppose I'm in the habit of making myself invisible at large parties."

"May I ask you a question?"

She retreated a bit. "The sketches are underway for your renovation, my lord. They will be ready for your review very soon."

"Oh, no—there is no urgency in that quarter. My mother, sister, and I can continue living in our dank and outdated rooms without much difficulty. We all find that cursing helps a great deal."

"What is it, then?"

"I was wondering what your favorite building was, here in town."

"Among those that my husband has designed, you mean?"

"No, the ones that you and your husband have designed together."

She looked at him like she'd just been caught in the coffers of a bank. She stepped closer. "Did Caro tell you this?" she whispered.

He shrugged, not wanting to get his beloved in trouble. "During one of my visits to your studio, I saw a particularly skillful drawing of a design for a new folly at Carlton House. It bore your initials, and I simply deduced that you and your husband were partners. Am I mistaken?"

"Forty-three! Calling number forty-three!" Barclay called out.

"They're calling my number," he confessed. "Would you care to join me, as I bend your husband's ear? Or should I leave you to your skulking? I would enjoy speaking with you both together, about my renovation."

Mrs. Crispin hesitated, looking at the arm he offered. Then she looked him in the eye and took it, and together they went off to the saloon, to discuss his dank and outdated townhouse with her husband, for no more than five minutes.

CHAPTER NINETEEN

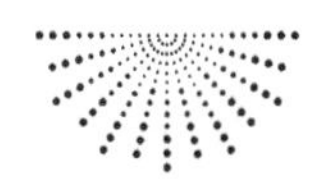

"You'll leave him in the box?"

"I cannot promise you that."

"And you'll leave the box on the floor of the carriage?"

"That I can do."

"He's already been fed today?"

"Yes."

"And you'll stay away from busy streets?"

"Yes."

"You'll come right back?"

"My dear Lord Ryland, the exams at Mrs. Hellkirk's had fewer questions than you. Are you quite certain you wouldn't like to come with me?"

He considered it again. "You are just going for a ride through Mayfair, yes?"

"Yes."

He considered it some more. "Then, no. I suppose not."

"Any more questions?"

"Yes. Just to clarify, one more time: the snake will *stay in the box?*"

"I cannot promise you that." She turned to Mariah. "Now, then—do you have any misgivings about this?"

"Not so long as you follow my instructions, Caro. Frederick is docile, but he is still a python, with all that comes with that. However, he does come out in the carriage with me now and again, as I said. That's why I have the box. He will be fine."

She turned back to Adam and puffed out her chest. "He seemed to like me, too."

"I wouldn't say *that*," Mariah added.

"Lady Mariah, would you mind excusing us, please? I require a word with Miss Crispin."

"Of course. Just promise me, Caro, that one day soon you'll tell me what this is all about."

They embraced, and Mariah left the mews and returned to the house with her butler, who had helped Adam carry the large box, with its small and round holes, down from the house and into the Crispins' carriage. Outside the mews, a thick, dank mist hung low in the air, smudging the brilliant green of the trees and the red-coated silhouette of the Crispins' coachman, who stood smoking his pipe under a lamppost.

It was nearly dawn, and about a quarter-hour from Caro's meeting time with Chumsley.

"I am not comfortable with this," Adam began when they were alone.

"It will be a very short ride. The trick will be saying my piece before Chumsley finds a way out of the carriage."

"I'm more concerned with Frederick finding his way around your waist. Or neck."

"He has never bitten anyone, Mariah said. Nor squeezed anyone."

"And your family had never broken a tether before."

She fixed her bonnet and picked up her reticule. "Fair enough."

"I—" he began, rubbing his jaw roughly, his other hand on his hip. "Caro, you have my unwavering assistance. I will be with you on this until the end, as I promised."

"Excellent."

"But I can't help but think there is something wrong here. That we are allowing the actions and judgments of others—including some who are entirely unworthy—to influence us."

"You said yourself that you wanted to pummel him."

"*Precisely!* And that's what disturbs me the most about all of this." He walked around in a tight circle, kicking at the straw.

Caro looked at the roof of the stable, her eyes moistening. "Do you not recall, Adam, that we are talking about the man who tried to drag me from my home last night?"

He pinched the bridge of his nose. "The issue isn't that you want to do something to thwart him, Caro. I want to as well. It's the manner of it. I despise feeling these intemperate impulses. I feel ill in my stomach. We could wait..."

"I haven't stopped feeling ill to my stomach since the night of the wager, Adam. And this is not an impulse—it is a well-thought-out plan." She took a pocket-watch from her reticule. "I have to go now, or I'll be late."

He offered her his hand as she opened the door to the carriage and climbed in. He gripped hers tightly, clamping onto it as if that might lock it to his, somehow. "I'll wait for you here," he said softly, reluctantly letting her go.

"A half-hour. That's all I need. And Adam?"

"Yes?"

"I love you. I love you so much. Thank you for doing this."

Her words struck him like a mallet on a bell, and their impact reverberated through his chest—loud and strong and pure. "I love you, as well," he replied softly when he'd recovered his wits. "But *please,* Caro. Keep that bloody snake in its box."

* * *

Chumsley bounded into the carriage, clomping with one boot, then the other, on top of the shallow box on the floor.

She cringed as she thought of poor Frederick underneath. Did such clomping irritate a python? She didn't know.

He tipped his hat, the sheen of it worn off in spots. Then he sat *next* to her, on her side of the carriage.

She couldn't help but recoil.

"What's this, Miss Crispin? Did you not invite me here today? Come, sit close. It's bloody cool out there this morning—strange enough, for August."

He closed the door behind him, and they were off.

She decided to get right to the point. "Edmund—may I call you Edmund?"

"You may call me anything you like." He inched closer. He was right up against her, and she struggled not to retch. "What shall I call you?"

"Never mind that. I want to introduce you to a friend of mine."

"Oh?"

"Yes. His name is Frederick." She reached down and lifted the top of the wooden box, its hinges creaking softly, to reveal the creamy-yellow snake, as thick in the middle as a young oak, snoozing contently in an irregular coil.

He leaned forward. "What's this?"

"This is a snake, Edmund. A snake in a carriage."

She'd never seen someone shoot up so quickly. He hit his head on the roof of the carriage as he frantically scraped the heels of his boots against the velvet seat-back, trying to get as high as possible, as far away from the floor as he could manage.

"What the devil is this?" he cried, his voice high, his Adam's apple lurching.

She sighed. "We've already covered this, Edmund. This is a snake. A cousin of yours, perhaps."

"Blazes, Caro. You know what I'm asking you—what's the meaning of this?"

"It's simple, really. I know about your wager, Ed. And I know the terrible things you said about me the night you made it. I also know that you show very little respect for ladies in general, and I wanted to make it clear to you that it will not be tolerated anymore."

He banged furiously on the top of the carriage, as if to alert the driver. But Caro had ordered the coachman—a long-time employee of the family—not to stop on account of any banging or screaming he might hear, so they kept moving. Then Chumsley leaned forward and grabbed the door handle. When it didn't budge, he put his other hand on it and rattled it as if his life depended on it.

She supposed that it did.

At this, Frederick finally popped his head out of the box, to see what all the ruckus was about.

Chumsley shot straight back to the ceiling again. He reached for the small window nearest to him, but when he pulled the curtain back saw that it had been blackened out.

She reached onto the seat next to her and picked up the can of boot polish. She waved it at him and smiled.

"You're mad, you know. Daft. And you *are* a bloody whore, you know that?"

She looked down at Frederick. "Did you hear that, Freddie? Eddie here doesn't believe that we're quite serious today." She reached down and slid each of her hands under his smooth, rubbery belly, preparing to lift him the way that Mariah had taught her.

"*No—no!* All right! All right, Caro! I'll do whatever you say—just put that thing back. Put it back!"

She wanted to lift the snake out, to force Chumsley to shrink back still further, to tease him about being afraid of such an adorable little tongue. That's what she would have done—had this happened to her a month ago, or a year ago. That was the purposeful, stubborn Caro she had been her entire life. But today she heard Adam's voice in her head, and that voice told her that what she'd already done was enough; it warned her that lifting the snake was too risky.

It told her, in wonderfully deep and raspy tones, that the person she had come to love would appreciate it if she left the snake in its box.

So she pulled her arms back out.

"Promise me, Chumsley, that you will never speak recklessly of a woman's virtue, or try to seduce her in bad faith. That you will never tell anyone I was the subject of your wager."

"I promise."

She shut the lid to the box and pulled the key to the door from her reticule.

"Second from the left, fourth floor."

"What?"

"Second from the left, fourth floor! That's your bedroom window, is it not? If you break your promise, Chumsley, you should know that Frederick and I know where it is."

She tossed him the keys and watched him scramble out. Then she rang a hidden bell in the wall of the carriage—the signal for the driver to return her to Mariah's—and sat back, and smiled.

CHAPTER TWENTY

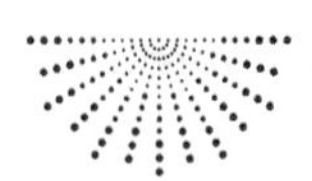

"You might not be aware, Adam," Caro said as they turned from the kitchen door of Mariah's house and headed back to the mews. She wiped her hands together, sending straw and dirt to the ground. "But there are many advantages to having a mother and father who work for a monarch."

"Pray tell," he replied, as she reached out and took his gloved hand in her own. It never ceased to amaze him how a touch from Caro could skip through him, as quickly as a stone on a country pond. They descended the slate steps together, still wet from the morning rain and mist.

"For one, I've procured us a special invitation to Carlton House. And I'm taking you there right now."

"What?"

"Just to the gardens, as I thought you would enjoy seeing them. His Royal Highness isn't there, of course, but one of the stewards has promised to give us a tour."

"Indeed? How very thoughtful." He leaned over and pulled of bit of straw from her hair. "That would be a real pleasure for me, I am sure. But would you mind riding back to your house, instead?"

She looked stricken. "Are you sure? I wanted to thank you for helping me with my scheme."

"You are a treasure, Caro. Truly—I am most appreciative. But there's no need to thank me. And I told your mother and father that I would stop by and see their progress on our drawings today. In truth, I've been dying to see them. Would you mind?"

He watched her chest expand slowly and contract, her brows knit, and her lips purse. "Yes, of course."

His own lips turned upward, into their wickedest smile. "That took strength, didn't it?"

She exhaled. "How could you tell?"

He laughed. "I know you, my darling. And I know that when you've devised a scheme, you fully intend to go through with it."

"I left the snake in the box, sir!"

"Yes, you mentioned that already."

She closed her eyes. "I am trying, Adam. I am trying to listen to more advice. I'm trying to be more...cooperative."

"I know. And I know it is difficult for you, as you are quite used to living by your own rules, and doing things for yourself. I promise I will not try to take all of the stubborn out of you—especially since that is part of why I fell in love with you."

When they reached the carriage, Caro told Edwards to take a couple of hours to himself, and when he'd gone the two of them got to cleaning the boot-black from the windows.

* * *

"Perhaps it's too risky for us to be alone in your carriage in the middle of the day," Adam said when they'd finished their cleaning. "There are many more people up and about now."

"True. But we've earned it, haven't we? Strayeth and Chumsley have received their lesson, and with the families of the *ton* leaving London this afternoon and tomorrow, the season is over and the wager is, too. We've done it."

"*You've* done it, Caro, and I suppose I agree—we do deserve some celebration. What shall it be?"

A proposal, perhaps? Her chest flared; she would welcome it if Adam asked her to marry him, right there in Mariah's mews. Indeed, she wanted it about as much as she wanted him pressed up against her right there in the mews.

Which was quite a great deal.

But they had time for both, she knew. They had time for many things, now; the wager was over.

She climbed into the carriage and pulled a small basket from under the seat. "There must be some burgundy in here, if I know anything of my parents."

He stepped inside and as the carriage took off, he gestured to the space next to her. "May I?"

"You may." She straightened herself up, holding two goblets and a bottle of the wine. "My ideal celebration would simply be spending time with you, you know."

He sat back. "Is it, indeed? You are out in society so much more than I am, I've wondered, at times, if my love of smaller company would be tiresome for you."

She put both goblets in one hand, their stems crossing awkwardly, and grabbed his lapel with the other and pulled him close. "This is not 'smaller' company, Adam. This is the biggest and best company of all." She kissed him then, hard and fast, and he wrapped his arms around her. When they heard the dull *scratch* of crystal coming together against its wishes, he pulled hastily away from her, snatched the goblets, and deposited them at their feet. Then he kneeled on the floor and turned toward her, his fists coming down on either side of her. He lunged forward and pressed between her knees, easing her back against the cushions.

They kissed languidly, savoring the reward—the victory—of this closeness. Several days had passed since Edie's dinner party, and in those days she had recollected and relived, again and again, its wonderful, sundry sensations. She had imagined in vivid detail what it would feel like when she found herself once again in Adam's big, all-encompassing embrace.

She felt sheltered by it, now; enclosed and liberated all at once, as he reached underneath her and scooped his hands under her bottom, lifting her toward him, squeezing her roughly with both hands, sending tendrils of sensation curling through her from below.

She put her hands on his chest, and he reluctantly lifted his head. "What is it?"

"To be clear, I love a good party and always will. And I absolutely need to meet with the girls from Hellkirk's regularly, of course..."

He leaned forward as she spoke, his low chuckle vibrating through her where he pressed his cheek against her neck. "Mmm-hmm."

"This is *most* important to me, Adam."

He took his tongue and pressed it into the indentation at the base of her throat before running it up the length of her neck. "I am well aware of that. Do go on. I want to hear what else is *most* important to you." He opened his mouth and let his teeth rest lightly around her throat.

She let out a soft squeal.

"You were saying?"

"I was about to say that this feels pretty important, too."

"Good." He gave her throat a nip—just a touch of pressure with his teeth—before lifting away to deposit kisses in the rounded rift of it. He let his tongue touch down first each time, before closing his lips around several inches of her skin, sucking it lightly into his mouth until she arched her back, her breasts pressing against him.

"Perhaps this would all feel even *more* important if done with less talking."

He laughed and pulled her waist toward him still further, kissing her neck in the same way, over and over, taking a leisurely path toward her chin. "Don't be so sure, my love. I suspect that with you, talking can be quite nice, too."

Now it was her turn to show him what was important, and she put her hands around his waist and under the tails of his coat, encircling as much of him as she could manage. Then she pulled at the back of his shirt, loosening it from its tuck inside his breeches.

"Careful, love," he said, bringing one hand around his back to still her. "How disheveled are you willing to become here, today? Because if I am to be undone, you are most definitely coming undone with me."

* * *

When Caro didn't immediately answer—staring back at him with a ravenous stare to match his own, he got up and sat on the opposite bench, pulling her with him by the waist. She landed in his lap, her legs off to one side, her soft, gloved hands cradling his head. Her thumbs grazed his cheekbone—a subtle, wifely gesture that pushed pleasure through him like a flood. In response, he gripped her waist still tighter and pressed her onto him.

She leaned into him, tilting her head and putting her warm—and now raw—lips on his own. Her hands left the safety of his jaw and traveled lower, trailing along his throat until they were on his chest, dipping under his lapels and then his waistcoat, too—until only the thinnest of silks separated the skin of her fingers from that of his chest.

"This is unbearable, Adam," she whispered, breaking their kiss. "We cannot disrobe any further here, yet that is all I find myself thinking of."

He laughed again, removing his hands from her waist and resting them on top of hers, still inside his coats. "I am very happy to hear that, love. Although, I must admit, there is something else on my mind at the moment."

She leaned back, removing her hands. "Aren't you supposed to be thinking only of my bosoms, and such?" she teased. "I know you're not exactly a rake, but still—think of my feelings."

"Caro—my lovely, lovely Caro—we men are not all so incapable of controlling our appetites. No more than all young ladies are simpering delicates who think only of marriage."

She blinked at him. "Fair enough."

"But do let me assure you, I find you utterly irresistible—"

"Brilliant," she interrupted, reaching for him again. "*Likewise.*"

"—so irresistible, in fact," Adam continued, grabbing onto her arms and stilling her again, "that I feel I must procure a lasting agreement from you as soon as I possibly can. Something that transcends what is happening between us right here, and yet ensures that it can happen again and again—as often as we should wish it."

She stopped and looked at him. "Is there a particular question you'd like to ask me?"

He let his head go back and laughed. "You are not a sentimentalist, are you?"

She sat back and attempted to look impatient, her lip betraying her amusement. "Go on, then. I'll hear it from you if I must," she teased.

"Thank you for indulging me," he teased back.

She gave him a courtly roll of her hand, suggesting a gentleman's formal bow.

He looked across at his Caro—his beautiful, bold lady—and she looked back at him with a mixture of impatience, insouciance, and hunger. He had been looking forward to this moment for some time, and he found that now it had arrived, he was far more amused than anxious, far more certain than not. Indeed, it was hard not to be subsumed with a deep, enlivening optimism for their future together.

They had come to know each other to an unusual extent, and through unusual circumstances. They had endured the strife of the wager together, and they had done it with laughter, respect, and cooperation. That had to be the basis for something strong when it came to a marriage. And of course, they had their silliness.

All that was left was to ask the question, receive an answer, and secure the blessings of her father and mother.

His spirits soared, higher even than *Bertie II.*

"Miss Caroline Cris—"

He wasn't able to finish, as the carriage came to a stop and someone began knocking on the door and calling for Caro.

"Miss Crispin?"

It was a male voice—a lord, by the sound of it—and both their eyes went wide.

They waited a moment, huddled together, hoping for the voice to go away. Instead, it called out even louder.

"Miss?"

Devil take it. Caro was, pending her answer to his proposal, likely to be his fiancée—and soon. The wager was over, by God, and he needed this. Could he *please* have some time with his bride-to-be? Would whoever it was who had interrupted his proposal please exit his soon-to-be connubial bliss, for good? These seemed like reasonable expectations.

Bang, bang, bang. Now the mysterious lord was knocking with considerable force.

She looked at him with her head cocked, frustration and sympathy written in her brow. She came closer, her lips grazing his ear as she spoke, her breath a bath of steam against his skin: "Get onto the seat as much you can, so that you can't be seen. I'll see to whatever this is, and tell the coachmen to head to Mayfair."

She was right. Nearly engaged or no—it was best not to be seen alone in the carriage together.

When she pulled away—leaving him colder, quieter, and with growing ire at lords of all kinds—he nodded and got up onto the seat. It must have been a comical sight: all six feet and four inches of him, curled up like a conch shell.

* * *

Caro felt as light as air, and as optimistic about the future as she had ever felt.

Mind, she was also quashing all sorts of pleasant new sensations from the carriage ride, and irritated to be doing so. But for the most part she was giddy, and resigned to waiting a little longer to explore them with Adam.

She opened the door and was surprised to see Lord Quillen standing there.

His brow weighed heavily on his face, which was whiter than she remembered it being. He was only a few years older than Adam, but the lines around his features suggested that he had aged considerably more in his three decades. She accepted the hand he offered and stepped down.

"Miss Crispin—please, allow Barclay to escort you inside, where Lady Edith awaits." She looked up and noticed Barclay standing at the top of her steps, looking every bit as grim as Lord Quillen. "And I know this is untoward, but if you have no objection, Miss, I would like to take a ride in your carriage."

"Right now?"

"Yes, Miss Crispin. Right now."

Something was dreadfully wrong. But she knew Lord Quillen through her parents—he had introduced them to a number of new patrons over the years—and she trusted him. "Of course," she replied, curtsying.

"Drive," he commanded the coachmen, who looked to Caro for confirmation. She nodded quickly and Lord Quillen alighted the carriage in a single step, just as the horses were taking off.

* * *

When she entered the house, Edie ran toward her from the top of the stairs. She was breathless.

"Caro—oh, God, Caro," she gasped. "You'll never believe it."

"What is wrong, dearest?" she asked, her thoughts racing.

Edie shook her head and reached for her. She couldn't get her words out, and she clasped Caro by the forearms, putting all her weight on them.

"Breathe, Edie. Just breathe," she soothed. She turned and glanced around. "Barclay, what is going on? What is the meaning of this?"

He wrung his hands and stepped closer. "I don't know, Miss. Should I call a physician?"

"No..." said Edie, shaking her head. "It's the paper...it's...it's *bull*."

She jerked her head back, perplexed. "What paper?"

Edie nodded to a side table. Barclay picked up a newspaper there and brought it over.

Edie let go of her, now that she was no longer heaving and could stand on her own two feet. "What am I looking for?" Caro asked as she took the paper from Barclay.

It was the afternoon edition of the *Gabster*.

Her heart felt weighted all of a sudden, as if a rock had been dropped into the center of her chest.

"They're saying..." Edie said, still struggling for words, "they're saying that Chumsley got into your carriage this morning...and that the windows were blacked out."

She scanned the page, her eyes glistening, unable to make out the words.

"They're saying you're the lady in the wager, Caro! And that's not all. They're suggesting that...that Chumsley *has won it*." She spoke with disbelief—as if it were an outrageous hypothesis that she hoped would be quickly disproved.

Caro swallowed. She'd begun shaking, hard, and when she tried to reach up and untie her bonnet, she found that she couldn't. She returned her trembling hand to the paper.

"Speak to me, Caro. Tell me what happened this morning."

But she couldn't speak. Instead, she slowly handed her the paper, which Edie grabbed and threw onto the floor.

"I cannot believe they mentioned the windows," Caro said finally, her voice devoid of any notes, any temperature.

"You must talk to me, Caro!" Edie grabbed her by the shoulders. "You must help me tell everyone that these claims are egregiously false, or you will be ruined!"

She thought a moment. *This could not be true—could it?* Was she ruined? What was Edie saying? The rock in her chest went lower, sinking and pulling her toward the floor.

"Caro," Edie said, a touch softer. "You must—"

"Stop, Edie. *Please.* I cannot think straight. I cannot..." Words eluded her, and she swayed involuntarily.

Edie's face grew grave. She stepped forward and grabbed her. "Barclay, help me with Miss Crispin."

He came at once and they each took one of her arms.

"I was there, Edie," she whispered as they led her up the stairs. "I put bootblack on the windows—"

"*Shhh,* Caro. Please rest. I shouldn't have pestered you—"

"But he did not win the wager, Edie. They didn't win..."

If she hadn't been so distraught, she would have found it funny that the chaise they placed her on in the drawing room—just as the world began to go black—was affectionately known in their family as the 'swooning chair.'

She had never had a need of it before.

* * *

Adam uncurled himself as his friend stepped into the carriage.

"Ryland?"

"Quillen."

"I am glad to see you!"

"I cannot say the same!" Adam thundered. "What the devil is this about?"

He rubbed a hand all over his face. "Forgive me; I expected to find Chumsley here. But I am supremely glad to find you, instead."

Adam raised a hand and looked sternly back at Quillen. "Listen, man —I don't know what you've heard, or seen. Miss Crispin did go for a ride with Chumsley this morning, but it was part of a scheme to teach him a lesson about his habit of wagering on ladies' virtue."

"'Struth?"

He nodded. "I helped her carry it out, in fact, as she required a twelve-foot snake and could not lift the thing herself. I'm told the lesson was quickly learned."

He expected his friend to be amused at this, or at least impressed, but instead concern tugged at his brow. "Unfortunately, Ryland, I am here because Chumsley had a scheme of his own."

"What do you mean?"

"He invited a man from the *Gabster* to wait outside his home, to witness his getting into the Crispins' carriage."

Adam pawed at the back of his neck. "You're having a joke, right, Quillen? Tell me you are having a joke."

He shook his head. "The man saw the blackened windows, and he claims to have caught a glimpse of Miss Crispin inside the door. Now that I've seen her, I have to admit that he described her attire correctly."

"Please tell me you know this because you've apprehended the man, Quillen, and have him tied in a cellar somewhere."

He shook his head again and pulled a folded paper from his pocket.

Adam took it and opened it—the latest edition of the *Gabster*, printed hastily in cheap, smudged ink. He saw the item in question and bent forward, his head landing in his palm. "They printed her name?"

"Yes, unfortunately. Apparently, Chumsley told the man he would only give them the information he had if they promised to print the lady's name."

Adam looked at the roof of the carriage. "How the devil do you know all these things?"

"Because I've been following Chumsley for some time. He is heavily indebted to a number of people, some of whom I know, and some of whom are rather...well, let's just say they are *unpleasant*."

"Indebted? How much?"

"Ten thousand, or thereabouts."

"Struth?"

He nodded. "He's in quite deep, and I believe that he set Caro up this morning, rather carefully. He needed to make his supposed conquest of her very public, because his goal was to force Strayeth to pay him the hundred pounds from the wager."

"So he believes Strayeth will pay him, if the *ton* believes that he..." He couldn't bring himself to say the words. "...that he's been successful with Caro?"

Quillen nodded. "He's probably hoping Strayeth will see paying out as the honorable thing to do, despite the fact that he didn't abide by the terms of their deal. He has no written acknowledgment from the lady, of course."

Adam leaned onto the cushion next to him.

"One other thing, Ryland. Chumsley set his plan in motion before your lady scared the daylights out of him with her snake. So I wonder, now, what his next move will be. His list of angry enemies—angry, *capable*, enemies—grows more impressive by the day."

Adam wiped his face down with both hands. He couldn't think. And he needed air.

"Out of curiosity," Quillen continued, "what did the rest of Miss Crispin's scheme entail?"

"It entailed taking Strayeth up in her parents' balloon, free of any tethers with the ground, until he was so terrified that he begged her to take him back to Mother Earth."

Quillen tapped his cane against the floor of the carriage and bowed his head, huffing once with amusement. "I thought as much. You have quite a lady there."

"You have some stake in finding Chumsley, then?" he asked.

"Yes. His debtors want me to...find him at once."

"You'll have to beat me to him."

"Shall we do it together?"

He reached out and shook Quillen's hand.

CHAPTER TWENTY-ONE

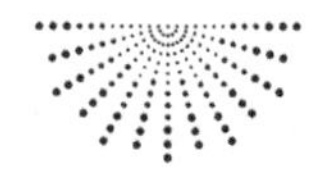

Afternoon sunlight overtook the Crispins' drawing room, an unrelenting and too-cheerful invader. Caro sat on the swooning chair still—it was more a swooning chaise, really—facing the tall front windows and squinting at the bits of dust that tumbled in the air. Edie poured her a cup of chocolate and put another biscuit on her plate.

"Please eat something, Caro. You've been staring at that window for an hour."

"She's right, dearest," Mama added, sitting across from them. Papa leaned on the chair-back behind her.

Still, she said nothing.

"How long have you known?" Edie asked. "And why did you not tell us?"

Caro adjusted her focus—from the dust in the air to the glass of the windows, then from the windows to the building across the street.

She squeezed her eyes tight, letting her chin fall to her chest. Edie moved closer and took her hand.

"I overheard Strayeth and Chumsley when they first made the wager. The morning after our ball—the one with the apples."

Edie sat back. "A whole month ago?"

"I'm sorry I didn't tell you, Edie. I decided that I would teach them both a lesson, and you know how I am about my schemes."

"I certainly do," she replied softly, a thread of hurt in her tone.

"But I eventually realized that I did need some assistance, because I needed a man to go to White's for me."

"Who was it?"

She lifted her head. "His identity shall have to remain a secret."

She couldn't bring herself to tell them of Adam's involvement in the wager. She had to protect him, now—protect him from any association with her and her scandal.

But she supposed she could tell them the rest of the story.

"I am sorry, Caro. I'm sorry you were not able to succeed," Edie said softly, squeezing her hand. "Those men are utter bastards."

"Oh, I succeeded, Edie. Very much so."

All three of them looked at her blankly.

"Well, I ran Strayeth out of town, didn't I?"

"That was your doing, after all?" Papa asked, tossing up his hands and stepping away, infuriated.

She nodded. "I cut the tethers, yes. I'm sorry, Papa. I'm sorry, Mama."

The elder Crispins sighed together. "Please go on," Mama replied, taking a sip of her coffee. "Tell us the rest at once."

She told them how Chumsley had frightened her, mentioning her window and repeatedly attempting to grab her.

Her mother sat back; her father straightened.

"How awful. How...*menacing*," Edie said softly when she had finished. "And you bore all this on your own?"

"I didn't take his threats as seriously as I should have. I see that now."

Then she told them about her morning in the carriage, taking care to omit the name of the person who loaned her the snake, and giving Edie a sharp look to indicate that she mustn't mention Mariah's name, either.

"There's one thing I don't understand," Edie said. "How did the events of the morning make it so quickly into the *Gabster?* Particularly given that Chumsley must have been convinced not to say a word after you frightened him with suffocation and snake-bite."

Barclay entered then, as he always did when he wanted to announce a guest. Caro's heart leaped in her chest, as her thoughts went immediately to Adam.

Had he come to her? What could she say to him, knowing that she was entirely scandalous now, and soon to be cast out of society? Their hopes for being together were impossible now. If they married his entire family would be tainted, and Edie would never be able to marry. She shuddered; she was not an especially spiritual person, but it seemed to her that something was taking leave of her person. Something precious—something life-giving.

"Lady Mariah Asperton to see you, Miss Crispin."

Caro let out the breath she'd been holding. "Please show her in, Barclay. And bring some fresh coffee, when you can."

Mama stood up and took a step forward. Papa came out from behind her chair and followed. "We will leave you alone with your friends, dear."

She looked into their faces, questioning old certainties about the way they had brought her up. What if they had curbed more of her behavior? What if they'd minded when she disappeared behind those curtains and those plants? She'd always thought that their permissiveness had been good for her; it had made her the capable, confident person she was. But perhaps growing up under more watchful sets of eyes would have had its benefits, too.

They approached and kissed her on the cheek. "We'll speak to you later on," they whispered in turn when they squeezed her hand.

* * *

"I'm afraid you're joining us at a difficult time," Caro said when Mariah had settled into the chair previously occupied by her mother.

"I know. That is why I came!" she replied with vigor. She had always been delicate and fair, her eyes two scoops of meringue outside a glossy, hazelnut center. Today, something different was going on behind them, but Caro couldn't say what. "I went for a walk, and was appalled when I overheard someone mention what was in that dreadful paper."

She got up and flew to the swooning chaise to sit on Caro's other side.

"People are already talking of it, then," Caro muttered to no one in particular. She told Mariah what she'd already told Edie and her parents.

"I cannot believe it!" Mariah said. "How brave of you, Caro. I would have suffered in silence. But you took matters into your own hands."

She laughed and took hold of Mariah's hand. "I love you, Mariah, for finding what must be the only positive outlook to all this. But unfortunately, you see where my actions have gotten me. I'm not sure I'm cut out for the revenge business, after all."

"Oh, but it wasn't revenge! Revenge is when you challenge someone to a duel, for honor's sake, or find a way to make someone suffer for a wrong they have done you. But you strove to ensure those gentlemen wouldn't repeat their actions on someone else. And *that* is what is honorable—particularly coming from a woman! Our hands are too often tied when it comes to arranging our own affairs," she added wistfully.

"Indeed," Caro replied, "that was my main motivation. I wanted to show Strayeth and Chumsley that they couldn't trifle with a woman's reputation like that. In fact, that's precisely what I said to..." She stopped abruptly, realizing too late that she was about to mention Adam. If she wanted to conceal his involvement, she needed to stay alert to the way her thoughts—and words, and heart—ran back to him, every time she loosened the reins on them.

"What you said to whom?" Edie asked.

"What I said to Toby," she concluded, laughing nervously. "I confided to Toby that I find it abominable that the word of a man can effectively destroy a woman's life. Whether it be matters of the heart or flesh, a man's word seems always to be deemed believable, while a woman's is cast in suspicion at best, utter contempt at worst."

"On that note," Edie began. "We must take our inspiration from Caro's courageous actions, and think of ways to return her good name—"

She snorted.

"All right. To return her *decent* name to rights."

"Even if both of you went door-to-door in Mayfair, telling everyone that Chumsley lied, I fear it would do little good," she replied. "You could mount a counter-attack the likes of which would make Lord Wellington weep with envy, and it would do little to convince a majority of the truth. People are simply too eager to believe in an illicit affair."

"And besides," Mariah added sadly, "with the season over, most of society has retreated to the country, anyway. We cannot mount a counter-attack when our adversaries will be hiding out the next several months."

Caro chuckled. "I don't know, ladies. Perhaps I was wrong to indulge this need I have to always make things right and fair. Bah! I should have been content with a reputation that was only lightly scandalous. Now it is quite heavily so."

"No!" Mariah exclaimed, taking her dainty fist and hitting it against her own knee, then Caro's. "You were standing up for yourself, and every time a woman does that, it makes it a little easier for the next one to do so. I commend you, Caro! And together, you and Edie and I will find a way to ensure your life is not too changed by this—we must!"

Caro blinked at her. Her friend was but little, but she was fierce.

Barclay entered again, to more furious hoof beats in Caro's chest. "Miss Crispin, a Lord Ryland is here to see you."

"Ah," Edie began. "He might be here to collect me—"

"I don't want to see him," Caro interrupted in a rush.

Edie sat back, surprised. "But you and Adam are so—"

"I *cannot* see him, Edie. Not now. Barclay, please make my apologies to Lord Ryland, and tell him that I am not receiving any more visitors today."

As she spoke, Edie squeezed her hand. "But perhaps he has some news."

"*Please,* Edie. Not today—I cannot bear it." She looked at the ceiling and blinked back the emotions that threatened to breach her cheeks, hoping her friends would not press her further. She could handle the aftermath of Chumsley's horrid actions, but she could not handle discussing her feelings for Adam—and the lost opportunity, the lost life, the lost happiness they contained within them.

Edie nodded, whispering. "Of course, Caro. But I should probably take my leave, for now. Will you be all right, 'til tomorrow?"

She nodded, and Mariah added, "I will come back in the morning, too."

She couldn't yet tell these wonderful women—her wonderful friends—that she couldn't accept what they were offering. That they would, sooner rather than later, need to join Adam in the long, long list of people who could not see her anymore.

* * *

Adam paced the entrance hall. The Crispins' butler lingered near the wall, busying himself with the lighting of candles, to replace the fading, late-afternoon light. He was likely accustomed to dealing with lords and ladies who came into his home with unreasonable demands. Still, Adam did not want to be lumped in with them.

"My sister is inside," he blurted out. "I must wait for her."

"Yes, my lord." He did not look up.

"And, more importantly, I am a friend of Miss Crispin's."

"Yes, my lord."

Adam ached to get some glimpse of Caro's face, to have some sense of her emotions. She was tough, to be sure, but the news that a man had sullied her reputation would flatten even the toughest of women.

It was nearly flattening him.

He stopped pacing, wondering if he had heard something slightly...*off* in the butler's tone earlier. "She is a fine young lady, wouldn't you agree?"

Now the man did look up. "Indeed, my lord. She is a most remarkable young woman."

Aha! Adam knew faint praise when he heard it. Society valued conformity, and 'remarkable' was not always brandished as a compliment. "She is the best kind of woman, Barclay." He didn't know why he felt the need to tell this to someone, but something about stating the words aloud was like a small dose of strength, delivered straight to his heart.

"My lord, I have known Miss Crispin from the cradle. She surprises me every day, and every day I endeavor to make her way in life a little easier." With that, the butler turned and lit another candle.

Adam thought he was finished when he added, "I am more successful on some days than others."

The sound of a door opening upstairs stopped Adam's pacing. He looked up and saw Edie emerge on the landing.

"Barclay, you're needed in the drawing room," she said as she arrived at the ground floor. When she reached Adam, she let out a sigh so forceful it could have lit a fire in an ice storm—certainly with the help of the heated look in her eye.

"What news?" he asked.

She shook her head. "None. Everyone is still quite shocked, and unsure what to do. Caro seems to feel..."

"What? What does she feel?" he asked impatiently.

"Defeated. She seems to feel defeated, and that is not like her at all. And Adam—she has said nothing of you, but it hasn't been difficult to discern that the two of you...have grown close."

"Edie, I intended to propose to Caro today. I had begun to, in fact, when we were interrupted in the carriage."

His sister's face lit up as he'd never seen it, her eyes taking in all the light in the room and shining it back at him. "Oh, Adam! I am so pleased!"

"She has said nothing of me?"

She frowned again. "Adam—today's events have but little to do with you. This is Caro's life we are discussing, so please, let us work together to help her. Now—what news have *you*?"

He told her that Chumsley was bankrupt, and because he desperately needed money, had tried to force Strayeth's hand in the wager.

"Hmm," Edie began, rubbing her chin. "If Chumsley has been running around town racking up debts and hiding much of it, some in society will question his claim about winning the wager."

"That is what I am hoping," he replied. "And if Strayeth can be found, perhaps he can be convinced to spread the word that his old friend is a cheat and a liar. Especially now that he is trying to extort one hundred pounds from him."

"But how is Lord Quillen involved? I was shocked to find him here this morning, even before I had arrived."

"He is the one who knew the full truth of the bankruptcy. He will help me spread word of Chumsley's debts, and find the both of them."

"Good. This is good, Adam! This is a beginning. I will spread the word, too." She put her hand on his sleeve, and he looked up. "And don't worry. It's likely that she just needs time."

"But Edie," he continued. "There is one other thing. If this scandal sticks to Caro, and she and I were to marry, your own hopes for marriage would be—"

"Adam! Do not speak of that! I love Caro."

"But your suitors, Edie—"

She held up a hand and began to walk off. "Honestly. Do not speak at *all*, Adam."

"*Edie*—please consider. The men who will want to marry you do not know Caro as we do. They will have pause when they consider that an alliance with our family, so tainted, would taint their own."

Edie marched to the door, calling back, "I believe I told you to stop speaking."

"Edie, by God, you are the most stubborn sister in all of Britain! I've no less desire to marry Caro than I did this morning. That's not what this is about."

Stinson had already opened the door for her, but she stopped and turned back.

"I suspect that Caro will no longer accept *me*. She will be too concerned about you."

CHAPTER TWENTY-TWO

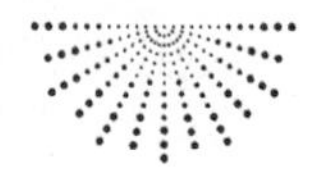

Tick tock, tick tock, tick tock.

How had she never noticed before how very incessant, how very *obnoxious*, the bracket clock on the mantle was? It was *ticking* and *tocking* and *ding-ding-dinging* far more than it had a right to. Caro put down her book and wiggled her bottom from side to side, struggling to claim another inch of the cushion from Toby's haunches.

Tick tock, tick tock, tick tock.

She wrapped her shawl around her shoulders; it had been a month since the carriage incident, and autumn had arrived in London. She picked at the remains of the cake Mrs. Meary had brought her, hours earlier, then got up and shuffled to the table by the door, where a letter from Adam lay unopened. She picked it up and put it in the decorative snuff box where she had placed all the others—all of them still sealed—then closed it with a listless *snap*.

She could not—she *would* not—think of him.

Well...

...perhaps she could think of him just this once.

She hastily removed the letter and tore into it:

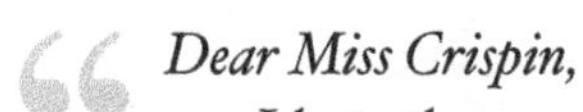

Dear Miss Crispin,

I hope that you are well, and that you have received my recent letters, twenty-seven in total, conveying my eagerness for a meeting on our project. Please advise me at your earliest convenience when I may call on you to discuss our plans.

Regards,
Ryland

She'd just finished reading it when the door opened and Edie entered, Barclay just behind her. She hid the letter behind her back and wiped an errant tear with the back of her hand.

"Any more replies, Barclay? To the dinner?" she asked.

"None, Miss."

"Oh, and Barclay?" she called out as he went to leave. He came back and she handed him the letter from Adam. "Please bring this to my parents, and make sure they read it at once."

He nodded—with a bit of melancholy in his eye, she thought—and left.

She and Edie sat on the daybed, on either side of Toby.

"I haven't had an invitation in days," she said, knowing that if she could feel sorry for herself at any point in the day, it was with Edie.

"I am sorry, Caro."

"What parties are there, coming up?"

"None of interest—"

"Please tell me."

Edie sighed. "There's nothing to speak of—truly. Very few people remain in town. And you know me. I don't care much for parties, unless..." she stopped herself.

"Unless I am there?"

Edie nodded.

"I've had *some* correspondence, actually," Caro continued, picking at a fingernail. "Nearly everyone I invited to your birthday dinner has replied that they cannot attend."

"It's kind of you, but I don't require a dinner, Caro."

"And Mariah will not be in town then, so I suppose it will just be the two of us."

"Again—I am sorry, Caro. But listen! I have some news that might be of interest to you," she said, more chirpily than usual. She laid a newspaper in Caro's lap and pointed to a headline.

"'*Lord --- on the Rocks.*' What does that mean?"

"It's Mrs. Fripp's gossip column. She's written about Chumsley's debts for the third day in a row, and makes no mention of the wager. That's great news, if you ask me. Chumsley's bankruptcy scandal is competing with yours for column inches, and it's winning."

"It's lovely of you to try to cheer me," she replied, her voice low. "But there are a half-dozen such columns, and most of them have not forgotten the wager."

"As a matter of fact," Edie replied, reaching for her reticule, "Tildie and I have made a study of the gossip columns and society pages, and we've noticed a decided shift from talk of the wager to talk of Chumsley's lurid financial affairs."

She sat up and looked at Edie's lap, where rolled-up and folded-over newspapers spilled from her delicate drawstring bag. "His situation really is so bad, then?"

"Oh, it's dire. He hasn't a sixpence to scratch with, Caro, and hasn't for some time. By the end of the *last* London season, he'd already gambled away everything that wasn't entailed. Money, properties, investments. Even his silver, china, art, and wine cellar! So for some time he's had nothing left to sell, save his precious phaeton, to pay off his debtors. And there are some scary fellows among the lot, banging down his door for payment. Or so Adam says."

At the mention of Adam's name she began to perspire, and her breathing became uneven. Since the *Gabster* article appeared, she hadn't been able think of him without sensing that she had been rapidly bled of something—some humor, some plasma—that had become essential to her well-being.

So she did her best not to think of him. She set aside his letters each day, and when he came to call—sometimes with Edie, sometimes on his own—she told Barclay to send him away with the same excuse: *Please give*

Lord Ryland my apologies, and inform him that I am not receiving any more visitors just now.

Perhaps he would stop coming one day soon. From sheer frustration, or from good sense, or some other perfectly understandable reason. She knew that must happen eventually, but she couldn't bear to think of it so she didn't think of him at all, if she could help it. It was as if she could slow the erosion of it all somehow, if she just refused to acknowledge it. She could cling to the shifting sands a little longer.

"I know you haven't wanted to speak of Adam," Edie began softly. "But I thought you might like to tell me why you won't see him. I won't share anything with him, I promise."

Caro crossed her arms and squeezed herself tight, then leaned forward until her forearms rested on her knees.

"He's afraid you've decided against accepting him," Edie continued, "because you believe it will spread scandal into our family. And if that is the case, you should know that I think it's nonsense. And that Adam remains committed to you. Very much so."

"I haven't wanted to say it, Edie," she said in a muffled voice, her head still in her lap.

"I cannot hear you, Caro."

She jerked her head up. "I can't bear to say it, Edie. I can't bear to say it even to you, but *yes*—I wanted to marry Adam, and now I cannot. It is very much out of the question now." She got up and walked to the center of the room, still hugging herself. "Edie, if I became part of your family, it would ruin your prospects for a match! And I cannot allow that."

"Pish."

"No—it's true, and you will have to stop visiting me, too, although I don't know how I shall bear it."

"You will never be rid of me," Edie said, her voice breaking. "You know this."

She closed her eyes and exhaled, spying some newspapers on a table at the center of the room. She went over and rifled through them and, when she found what she was looking for, turned back to Edie. "I've been scrutinizing the papers too, you know. Stinson and Mrs. Meary seem to like this *Mayfair Breeze*—have you read it? Their readers must be quite consumed by the wager, because they still write of it every day."

Edie clucked her tongue. "That rag is the lowest of the low, Caro. It isn't even sold in Mayfair."

"Oh, but it is! All the valets and ladies' maids buy it up in the early hours and leave copies for their employers, who are all too proud to admit they hang on its every word." She pointed to a line and smiled without amusement. "Look at this! They've taken to calling me 'the Teasin' Tart.'"

Edie snorted. "That's almost as many letters as 'Caroline Crispin'."

"I don't think they're trying to save space," she replied. Then she cleared her throat and read:

> *Lords—and indeed, all respectable gentlemen—do not take kindly to low-born ladies who flit about and throw themselves in their path, as if they weren't flinging mud on everyone present with their garish behaviors. One only hopes the Teasin' Tart will take the much-overdue cue from this paper, and from her newly diminished stature, and find a place outside of society that is better suited to her slatternly ways.*

Edie got up, snatched the paper, and went straight to the fireplace. "I've been thinking," she said as she tossed it behind the grate. Caro walked over and joined her, transfixed by the flames. "We took Strayeth and Chumsley to be the bogeymen in all this, but what of these columnists and their publishers, who print such things about women and their worth? What of people like Lady Tilbeth and her gaggle of loose-tongued harpies, all of whom buy them and read them? And what of those of us who don't speak up in protest when we hear such things repeated? There is no one bogeyman. There is only *all of us*."

They watched the fire consume the last of the cheap paper.

"You sound like Mrs. Hellkirk," Caro whispered, her face hinting temporarily at a smile. She turned to Edie. "I'm sorry that I've refused to answer your questions about Adam, Edie. I just haven't known how to understand my feelings in regard to him. I feel...*overturned*. I certainly do not care for him any less—" she said, her voice breaking, "but I fear I must change my ways when it comes to men."

"Caro—"

"No—please listen, Edie. My behavior with men has always been too forward. Not just when we were younger, when I kissed half the gentlemen between here and Yorkshire, but also in my response to Adam when he showed an interest in me."

Edie put her hand on her arm. "Has something happened? Something more…intimate?"

She smiled into the fireplace, shaking her head. "No. But all of these assignations, assignations that I thought were harmless—that I thought I deserved—were really just indulgences on my part. Why did I think I was any different from any other young woman, Edie? I have been selfish. I have made excuses for what was simply a reckless curiosity about men…and about men and women. And I need to take responsibility for it now."

"What are you saying?" Edie asked, taking her hand in both of hers.

"I'm saying that, between you and I, I'm taking a solemn oath right here and now to swear off men for a while." She chuckled. "And ironically, it's more or less the same advice your brother gave me, when all of this started."

* * *

A footman ushered Adam and Quillen into the Curzon Street townhome. The new autumn sunlight was the only décor on the pale walls, a single bench and side table the only furnishings on the black-and-white floors.

"We are only wasting more time," Adam grumbled when the footman left to announce their arrival. "September is nearly gone, and we've made no headway."

"You are losing patience, Ryland, and I can hardly blame you. But Lady Cantemere is worth speaking to. You will see."

"Four weeks, Quill. Four weeks and no word of Strayeth *or* Chumsley."

"And let me guess: Miss Crispin still won't return your letters?"

Adam looked away.

"She just needs—"

"It's been a month!" he snapped. "She will not admit me. And this morning there was this, from her parents." He handed him the letter.

Dear Lord Ryland,

Please accept our deepest apologies for the lull in our correspondence. Miss Crispin requires a respite from her usual role in receiving and responding to our letters, and I'm afraid we have fallen behind in the task. Can you meet with us in two weeks' time, to look over the designs for your renovation?

Regards,
Mrs. Betsy Crispin

"This all seems quite reasonable," Quillen said when he finished reading. He handed back the letter. "Anyone would need a 'respite' after what Caro went through."

"This," Adam replied, shaking the letter, "is a polite way of telling me to shove off."

Just as Quillen put a firm hand on his shoulder, a slight woman with wisps of white hair and a frilly mobcap peeked around the landing above. "Reuben!" she called out. "Where are you, Reuben?"

The footman ran back into the hall, sliding several feet across the tile before coming to a stop, looking stricken. "I thought you were in the garden, my lady."

She made a shooing motion with her hand and the footman scuttled away again.

"Gentlemen, stay where you are. I must speak with you," she said, emerging onto the landing in a bronze gown. She came down the stairs in a slow but steady march, holding onto the railing and putting both feet on every stair, giving no indication that she cared a whit about the noise she made, the time she took, or the space she required.

Quillen called out to her. "My lady, it's been too long—"

"Save your breath, Quillen," she said, making her way down the last few stairs. "And introduce me to your friend."

"Lady Cantemere, may I present to you the Earl of Ryland. He is acquainted with your nephew, Lord Strayeth."

She looked him up and down, her fists on her hips. She looked to have some eighty years, and when she pushed the sleeves of her dress above her elbows, as a scullery maid might do, she exposed her tanned and sinewy forearms. "Well, I never. How do you do, Lord Ryland? Lord Strayeth's grandfather was my brother. I am Philip's favorite aunt."

He stifled his shock. "You aren't his Aunt *Fanny*, by chance?"

"I am indeed. You know of me?"

"I thought you were apocryphal!" he replied, smiling for the first time in what must have been weeks. "Your nephew invokes your need of him whenever he wants to excuse himself from something undesirable. But I'm afraid he is a bit less attached to you, Lady Cantemere, when the shooting is good."

She offered him a half-smile. "Ah, yes. Family myths are ever so tiresome, aren't they, Lord Ryland?"

His skin prickled; he didn't know why she would make such an allusion, and was trying to think of a reply when Quillen stepped in.

"Lady Cantemere, we are so pleased we could see you this morning," he began, his honeyed tones gliding easily off his tongue.

"No you aren't," she replied, flicking a wrist at him.

Adam struggled to contain his amusement. He had never seen Quillen struggle to charm someone before.

"You're here because my nephew is a cad," she continued. "And quite possibly a coward—I'm still unsure. Either way, the only thing that surprises me is that no one else has called here in the past month to complain about him. Not a one!"

"The only thing that surprises me is that no one has been here in twenty-five *years* to complain about him," Adam replied.

She shook a finger at him. "I like you," she replied, her half-smile inching up to perhaps three-quarters. Then she turned and walked to the glossy black chair at the edge of the room, the sunniest spot in the hall. "Forgive the informality, but my back is not what it used to be."

"Would you be more comfortable in your drawing room, Lady Cantemere?" Quillen asked.

She shook her head.

He cleared his throat. "Lady Cantemere, you are right. We are here about Lord Strayeth," he began. "But it's because we are rather desperate to find his friend, Lord Chumsley. And we thought your nephew might know of his whereabouts, or be willing to help us...uncover him."

She stared toward the back of the house, through a window and out to the garden beyond. Her hands rested gently on either side of her. There was dirt beneath her nails and her skin was shiny and impossibly smooth—from a lifetime spent out in the wind, Adam guessed. She was clearly a person who spent time around projects out of doors, though perhaps not as much as she would like. Adam always knew this trait when he saw it in another.

"Chumsley is an even bigger ass than my nephew," she said finally.

He couldn't help it then. He could not remember the last time he had felt amusement, and it was a welcome relief. He laughed heartily and bent forward. "There cannot be many ladies in London who delight in such oaths," he said between laughs, "but I seem to know all of them."

Quillen was undeterred. "We've spent the last few weeks searching for Chumsley, but to no avail. We've discovered that his villa here in town has been closed for some time. And he's not been to the chambers he's let for some weeks."

"Let me guess: He owes them a great deal of money."

"Indeed."

"I have not heard from my nephew, gentlemen. And I've heard nothing of his friend that wasn't printed in the papers. I cannot help you."

"Is there anyone else we might speak to?"

She shrugged. "I am alone in this house. And with the season over, everyone in my circle has left town."

Quillen glanced at Adam. "It seems that most everyone has. We've come to the conclusion ourselves that we'll need to travel more widely if we're to track either man down."

"Tell me—are you only after Chumsley to collect his debts?"

"Yes. Why do you ask?"

She turned from the window and stared at them, and there was something in the heaviness of her posture, the glassiness in her eyes, that infused Adam with great sadness. "I thought you might also be here on behalf of the lady. The Crispin daughter."

Adam was surprised by her bluntness, and didn't know what he could claim anymore when it came to his relationship with Caro. He believed he was searching for Chumsley on her behalf; but if she had pushed him from her life, was that really the case?

He was grateful when Quillen cleared his throat and spoke up. "We are friends of the Crispin family, yes. Do you know something of Miss Crispin's situation, of how it might be improved? I was not aware that you knew her."

She looked down and shook her head. "I do not know her. I haven't found society tolerable for many years—not since my Charles passed. But I know *of* Miss Crispin, of course. She is quite a giant here in town, though even she cannot survive a scandal of this magnitude. And I would like to do something for her."

She pushed down hard on the bench, slowly raising herself up, her elbows shaking. She made her way slowly over to them.

"She does much for charity, I know. Which is her favorite?"

Adam thought a moment. "She talks a great deal about a new group that hopes to improve the situation of animals in town, particularly the dogs that are forced to fight in Westminster Pits."

"Can you provide me with their information?"

"I can get it for you," said Quillen.

"I would like to donate one hundred pounds to them, at the earliest opportunity."

"The same amount as the wager?" Adam asked.

She nodded. "I'll donate it under the name of Strayeth, with the hope it will send a message to society that my nephew's ridiculous wager wasn't won by either party. And also that...that there is remorse regarding this whole business. At least in some quarters."

"That would be a wonderful gesture, Lady Cantemere," Adam replied. He resolved to make a donation to the charity, too, and to get Quillen—and others—to do the same.

But Lady Cantemere flicked her wrist at them again. "It is a trifle, and it is too late." She looked at Adam as she added, "I wish I could do more for your Miss Crispin. But I'm afraid it's too late to raise a man not to behave so."

"I fear she will remain the talk of the *ton* until the next shocking scandal occurs."

She nodded. "She will be under duress. At least until the next giant falls."

"Thank you for seeing us, Lady Cantemere. We won't take up any more of your time."

They bowed and had turned to go when she called out, "Lord Ryland?"

"Yes, Lady Cantemere?"

"Life is so much brighter when you step out from the shadow of others. Do remember that, before it is too late."

When they reached the street, Quillen said, "That was most interesting. I've almost developed a smidgeon of respect for Strayeth, knowing that he has such an aunt as his favorite."

Adam glared at him. "Let's not give her nephew any credit for her good character."

"I think is she is right, by the bye; we've exhausted all our leads in town. It's time to look elsewhere for Chumsley."

"Past time, I'd say."

"And Ryland?" He put a hand on Adam's shoulder. "Let this be my fight, now. You have no stake in Chumsley's financial affairs. And Lady Cantemere's charity donation will be a capstone of sorts to all this wager business. Go—be with your lady."

"I confess, those were my thoughts exactly," he replied, exhaling. "But do get that information to Lady Cantemere soon, about the charity."

"I'll send it today, before I leave for the festival."

"The festival?"

"You know the one. The Harvest Festival, from the poster at Luke's. It's quite the to-do."

"Yes, I remember. But I didn't know you were an enthusiast."

He shrugged. "I'm hoping to see some men there, on business related to Chumsley's debts. But don't worry—I shan't embarrass myself by getting into the ring. The last thing I want is to be the subject of scurrilous chatter in drawing rooms across all of England next week."

CHAPTER TWENTY-THREE

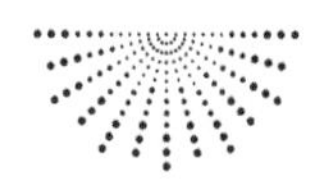

"Why aren't you seeing Edie and Lord Ryland at their house?" Caro asked.

"Lord Ryland insisted on coming to the studio," Mama replied. "He said—or wrote, rather—something about his mother, and not wishing to disturb her. You saw his note, Caro. And it's fine; we do not mind hosting them here."

"But...wouldn't it be helpful to discuss your designs *in situ*? To make it easier for everyone to imagine what you're proposing?"

Mama stopped shuffling through her drawings and turned to her, taking her chin firmly in her hand. "Caroline Crispin, you know that we host patrons here in the studio. And we've had two tours of Lord Ryland's home already. Now, what is going on with you? If I didn't know better, I would think you were trying to avoid them."

You haven't seen Adam come every day to the house, and every day refused. You haven't considered that Edie will suffer if she continues to be my friend. Such things always pass under your and Papa's notice.

"Since you do not need me, Mama, I'll be in my—"

She didn't get to finish her sentence, because Barclay opened the door to announce someone's arrival. She froze in place; she was going to have to see him.

* * *

Adam nearly stumbled as Toby bolted around his legs, squeezing between him and the door frame. He hadn't thought it possible for another being to be in more of a hurry to see Caro than he was.

She was the first person—the first anything—he saw when he entered the room, a dark silhouette standing stock-still near a table that appeared to have been set up with papers and drawing tools for their use.

"Lord Ryland," Mrs. Crispin said warmly, curtsying and coming toward him with her arms raised. "Please, come in and have a seat by the window. I need to see to something downstairs, but Mr. Crispin and I will be in directly. Pray—where is Edie?"

"She could not be here today, Mrs. Crispin. I'm afraid I am the only Wexley on the premises."

He looked at Caro as he spoke, and she looked directly at him, her hands clasped in front of her. He suspected from her wide-eyed expression that he'd caught her unawares. He'd arrived a few minutes early, which was impolite, but he was not above rudeness and trickery if it meant seeing his Caro.

And now her mother had given him an unexpected gift: She was leaving them alone together.

God bless the Crispins and their unconsidered, unconventional ways.

When the door closed behind him, he let his eyes leave Caro for the first time. Scattered thoughts and torrents of barely contained emotion swirled through him—pain, anger, excitement, guilt, confusion, hope. He wished he'd kept his hat or cane to fiddle with, because despite having had nearly a month and a half to dwell on matters, he still wasn't certain what he wanted to say to Caro first.

"I want to thank you for your contribution to the society for the Prevention of Cruelty to Animals," she said finally, her voice raspy and uneven. "It was wonderful of you."

"I feel responsibility for what has happened, Caro. For not foreseeing Chumsley's desperation. For not trying harder to persuade you to find another course of action—for all of it. I am responsible."

She shook her head at him slowly, and closed her eyes. And that was when he saw a single tear slide down her cheek, crashing into the ridge of her lip while another followed directly on its course. He was to her in an instant.

Family be damned, propriety be damned—all of society and tradition could go to Hell in a proper handbasket for all he cared in that moment. He did not care about any of it anymore. He put his arms around her and felt he might crush her with the intensity he'd accumulated in six weeks' time, that she might be smothered with the release of so many sensations at once. But she withstood it; she softened in his arms, in fact, and it gave him an unexpected pleasure, a pleasure he felt he didn't deserve.

"Caro..." She was shaking then—although no longer crying—and he knew he must get her out of the room. "Where can we go?" he whispered, his breath visible in the movement of her hair. "Where can we have a few moments to ourselves, before your mother and father return?"

She pulled away and took his hand, leading him to the end of the room where a door opened onto a servants' staircase. It was pitch dark, and with Caro leading, they descended to a tiny landing, where a single door likely led to another corridor. In his haste, Adam had forgotten to pull the studio door shut behind him. However through that opening came their only light—a slash of sunlight, about three inches in width.

"Careful," Caro advised as she turned to face him. It was much warmer than in the studio—uncomfortably so. "There's scarcely enough room for the both of us."

That was all the permission he needed to pull her to him again, and she put her arms around his neck. He pressed her against the wall. He had no inkling of how to soothe her fears, or how to convince her to accept his visits—or his imminent proposal. But he could certainly envelop her in a dark stairwell. That much he could do.

* * *

Caro curled her arms around Adam's neck, savoring the warmth of his breath on her face, her neck, her arms, her hair. They stood like that a second or two, just breathing, adjusting to the darkness. His own arms had slid out from behind her back and were now resting heavily—and wonderfully—on her hips.

She had refused to see Adam because a love at arm's length was preferable to a love wrenched cleanly away from her. And if they did not meet, how could they say good-bye? But here, in the blackness, away from the clucking tongues and prying eyes of the tastemakers and the gossips, did their meeting really count? If they enjoyed each other here, would the clock keep standing still for them?

"Your breathing," she began. "Are you quite well?"

"No, dammit. I am *not* well. Caro, I am really bloody put out," he growled, giving her hips a light shake.

"You are not used to being denied what you want."

"That is true, Caro. But can you not believe that I have also been worried sick over you?"

She nodded—pointless in the dark, she knew—before adding, "Yes, Adam. I know that, too. I am sorry."

"Why wouldn't you see me?"

"I suppose that in a completely irrational way, I thought that in refusing to see you, I could delay the day when I could no longer see you at all—at least not in the way I've grown accustomed to. Not like this. Not as if I were still your..."

"Say it," he said gruffly.

And at the sound of his commanding her, she gave in—gave in to the myriad sensations coursing through her, to the voice in her heart that screamed at her to stop pushing this man away, to allow it to enjoy being backed up against a wall, being the object of this heady mixture of love and lust.

"As if I were still your *intended,* Adam. I do not wish to stop feeling like your intended."

He slid his hands up to her waist and clamped down hard—pulling her to him, bringing his forehead flush against hers. "Caro—I am not going anywhere. *I am not going anywhere.*"

Yes, she decided. Time could definitely be allowed to stand still, here and now. At least for a moment.

She pushed her hips against him then, as hard as she could. And something about the dark, the proximity of others, and the possibility of a servant stumbling upon them at any moment, drove her to signal to him as clearly as possible that, like him, she was primed for more than an exchange of promises.

Adam responded to her boldness with a surprised growl, and leaned over her until his mouth found hers in the dark. He went for her lips with such force that her head hit the wall behind her, but when he pulled back and caressed her crown, she did not care for the pause; indeed, she grabbed his hair and pulled him roughly back to her mouth. She was glad for the wall; it gave her the ability to receive the full pressure of the kiss. She opened her mouth wide to him and he responded in kind, kissing all of her, with all of him.

He gripped her waist and slid her up the wall, so that her head was closer in height to his own. She thrashed with her legs, trying to free them from beneath her long skirts so that she could wrap them around his waist. Soon, she felt Adam's fingertips grabbing fistfuls of fabric at the top of her thighs, tugging them upward and, eventually, after a slight ripping sound from God knew where, her legs were freed just enough for her to encircle him as she wished.

She gripped him with all her might, stilling him exactly where she wanted him.

This was the sort of reckless intimacy she had imagined, a hundred times or more, in the nights—and some of the days—since she and Adam had first met, in the portrait gallery. And now that it was happening she found it did not disappoint. She had read every tome on intimacy and relations that Mrs. Hellkirk's small library had to offer, and her expectations were high. And even so, these seconds with Adam in the flesh—oh, God, the *flesh*—exceeded those oft-imagined rewards. And again, that screaming voice inside her said, *Do not let this end. Make this go on and on and on. You need this, like you need nothing else.*

Adam's hands had gone back on her waist, and his thumbs, which had been resting low on her tummy, curved downward now, and engraved a sweeping arc in the seam where her thigh met her torso. When she had first kissed Adam, she had mistaken the feeling that occurred in her extremities for tingling or numbness, but now she knew it was not the absence of feeling; it was the opposite. His touches filled her with sensation, as if everything inside her were rushing all at once to the place where his hands had most recently traveled. It left the rest of her feeling emptied and dizzy.

He continued his agonizing exploration of her groin with one hand, and the other he brought slowly upward, along her side, grazing her breast with his thumb.

"You know, none of my books dwelled much on the erotic properties of thumbs," she said as she broke away from his kiss, thrilled to her bones when she felt the deep vibrato of his laughter as he pressed his cheek against her neck.

"God, I have missed you." The higher of his hands abandoned the side of her breast in favor of tracing, with several roughened fingertips, the bare skin along the top of her gown.

She lifted her chin, allowing him all the skin he could wish. "I have missed you, too—you have no idea how much. I am sorry I could not see you these past weeks."

"But you *can* see me. You could see me all the time, if you wanted to. My feelings have not changed. If you will have me, Caro, I would—"

"Stop! *Please,* Adam—you must stop. Do not say it," she interrupted, the frissons between them abating quickly as she slid her hands from his neck and rested them on top of his shoulders.

"I know what you will say," he murmured, his lips resting on, and still heating her skin. "You worry about Edie's marital prospects, if we should marry. And a general...lowering in society for our family."

Pleasure and gratitude gripped her like a vise; he had referred to all of them—Edie, his mother, himself, and her—as a family. But she wrenched herself free of it at once; such things couldn't be.

"I refuse to abandon this happiness," he continued, "for a future that may not come to pass. And as for how society might treat me? They can go hang for all I care. I love you, Caro."

They heard sounds from the studio above—a door closing, several sets of footsteps on the hardwoods, and muffled voices.

"You must go back, Adam. I will duck out this door." She wriggled, trying to undo her legs from around him, but with his arms tangled in her skirts and no light to guide them, she struggled.

"Tell me you do not want this, Caro. Tell me you do not want this for all time."

"Of course I want this!"

"If you want this, then do not push me away—"

"You must *let me go*," she said more urgently as she pushed at his arms, trying to remove them from her legs so that she could come off the wall. She felt herself becoming panicked. It was too dark, too small and stuffy and hot, and the memory of Chumsley grabbing her and touching her against her wishes too fresh in her mind.

They finally untangled themselves, and Adam moved his hands to her waist again to support her while she regained her footing.

"Don't you see?" she said, her voice breaking. She was frantic, now, from the inability to free herself, yes, but also because she was irritated beyond all reason at having to deny her own feelings —at having to push Adam away, both in that moment and as a suitor, when all she wanted was to pull him close and accept him. Her blood ran hot at these uncertainties and contradictions, and from the helplessness that seemed to govern her new life. She pushed some damp hair back from her forehead, and decided right then and there that she must sever her ties with Adam in as permanent a way as possible. She had to force him to leave her—for his own sake, and for Edie's. And she would have to be cruel to do it.

At least then, one of her uncertainties and contradictions would be over with. "Don't you see, Adam? I want your hands on me because I *am* a whore. I cannot help myself around gentlemen, just as Strayeth and Chumsley said. And that's the only reason I am here on this landing with you. I am flawed, and fallen, and weak."

As soon as she was steady on her feet, Adam stepped back, and the sliver of light coming from above made a diagonal slash across his face. She could make out all of his features, now, from the fine lines around his furrowed right brow to the downturned left corner of his mouth. All of him looked still, and forsaken.

"That's not true, Caro. I am not just any gentleman. And this is not just any assignation."

"It is going to have to be," she snapped back at him. "There can be no more." She wiped the back of her hand across her face and let herself into the cooler air of the corridor, leaving Adam to return upstairs on his own, and to explain his mysterious foray into the servants' stairwell for himself.

* * *

One of the many advantages to being an earl was that people, especially those outside the *ton*, rarely questioned your behavior. So when Adam emerged from the back stairwell looking hurt and flummoxed and disheveled, he murmured something about getting lost on the way to the water closet, and no one raised an eyebrow. It helped that Mr. and Mrs. Crispin needed extra time to gather their materials and, if anything, seemed to appreciate his extended absence.

They did not seem to miss their daughter, either, which he had come to realize was the normal way of things in this family. But who was he to judge? Heaven knew his own family was chockablock with flaws and foibles; and if Caro adored her mother and father, they were good enough for him, too.

There he went again: thinking of her as his "intended."

If she wanted to push him away, she was going to have to do more than brand herself a whore and him just another assignation.

He knew her refusal was about Edie's prospects, and nothing more.

As the Crispins continued to move about the studio, gathering rolls of paper and directing the one pupil who had joined them, he took the seat they offered him and rested an elbow on the table, then his forehead in his hand. His knee pumped furiously under the table, trying to keep pace with his thoughts.

He had been stupid—utterly stupid. He had been so damned excited to kiss Caro that he'd missed the opportunity to have a proper conversation with her—and didn't know when he'd have one again. He'd forgotten to tell her, among other things, that he believed the damage to her reputation was reparable. And it was because there had been four or five things on her person that he found more pressing, or at least *worth* pressing. And caressing, and biting, and generally lavishing the better part of his attention on.

And the distress she'd shown, when she tried to pull away from him? It had pained his heart, quite literally, and now sat heavily on his mind.

He closed his eyes and ran his fingers through his hair, shaking his head slowly. He had done his best to help her free herself, but they'd been tangled up like a pair of abandoned fishermen's nets.

"Are you unwell, Lord Ryland?"

He looked up at Mrs. Crispin, who was standing at the table, just around the corner from him. He had not noticed her there, clutching sheets of tracing paper to her chest.

"How is your daughter, Mrs. Crispin? Is *she* unwell?" he replied.

"She is..." she began before stopping herself. She peered into his face, as if checking in its corners and crevices for any insincerity that might be hidden there. Apparently, she did not find any. "Miss Crispin is not quite herself, my lord."

Her lack of surprise at his question led him to believe that she had some inkling of his relationship with—or at least interest in—her daughter. His earlier disappearance, his lagging with Caro on their first tour of his home, their cheerful and excessive letters to one another regarding his renovation? They had done little to conceal their affection from their families.

"I miss seeing her, Mrs. Crispin. And I want more than anything to help her."

Her lips parted, then—whether in surprise or concern, he couldn't say. She looked over her shoulder where her husband and Mr. Davies approached, the latter with a tray of refreshments.

By the time she turned back, he had decided to continue down the path of naked honesty. "I've spent these past weeks trying to devise a way—or many ways—to help Caro," he whispered. "I am at her service. But without knowing her mind, it is impossible to know how to act."

"What do you mean by that, Lord Ryland?"

"I mean that I will do whatever is in my power to restore her spirits, and to give back to her the opportunity to do as she wishes."

"My lord—"

"Please, call me Ryland."

"—Ryland, I will speak with her." She shook her head, and for the first time, he read not only sadness but worry in every line of her face. "I cannot imagine what it must be like for her. To be the subject of gossip columns? To be talked of so widely, and so scurrilously, in drawing rooms across all of England? It is quite beyond me."

His head snapped up, just as the others arrived at their table with a clatter, dropping armfuls of rolled-up drawings and boxes of writing implements. And after clearing a space amidst this new detritus, Mrs. Crispin unrolled the most evocative set of drawings he had ever seen.

But he could not focus on them at all, because he had just realized what he needed to do. It was as if the pieces of a broken mechanism he had struggled to make out had suddenly come together on their own, right before his eyes.

"Forgive me, but I must leave you at once." He flew out the door and barreled down the stairs, as fast as he could go.

As he recalled, the last day of the Harvest Festival was coming up soon—it was either the very next day or the day after. Thankfully, it was just a ten-mile ride to the Village of Beauton, and about the same to Quillen's beloved Banmoor.

CHAPTER TWENTY-FOUR

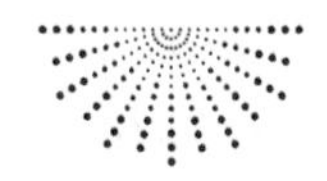

Caro was looking down and putting on her gloves when she nearly crashed into a darkened figure in the entrance hall, standing just inside the front door.

It was her mother.

"Mama? What are you doing here?"

She looked at the door, then back at Caro. "This is the way to the street, is it not?" She gave her a sly smile.

Caro squinted back at her. Betsy Crispin did not linger in doorways—or give sly smiles. She was entirely too busy for such things. "What is going on here, Mother? Are you feverish? Do you need me to write a letter to the Prince Regent, explaining once more why you cannot build him an underwater drawing room?"

Mama finished putting on her gloves. "Can't a mother wish to join her daughter on a stroll to the work site?"

"She can *wish* it. But will she *do* it?"

"She will indeed. Now—where do you keep Toby's leash?"

Caro held it up.

"Perfect. Let's go, then."

"How have you been these past few days?" Mama asked when they stopped to wait for Toby to sniff at a tall, flowering weed in the middle of the sidewalk.

"What can I say?" Caro sighed. "I've had to cancel Edie's birthday party, which makes me despondent, but I also find myself feeling sorry for Chumsley, if you can believe that. I'm glad that the newspapers have begun reporting on his debts and the lies he's told about them, but it remains to be seen whether these facts will serve to repair *my* situation at all. My heart is everywhere all at once, and I can't make sense of any of it."

Mama put her arm around Caro's shoulder and gave her a squeeze. "Would you like to know what I've been doing?"

"Of course."

"Do you recall how the owner of White's wrote to Papa last month, to commission a series of paintings for the entrance hall of his club?"

"Of course."

"Well, I now have two of the loveliest oil paintings you've ever seen, well underway."

"That's wonderful, Mama. What are they of?"

"Recall, if you will, that he did not specify what the paintings should be of..."

Caro turned and looked her in the eye. "*Mama?* What are they of?"

"One is of a balloon, and the other is of a snake."

She nearly doubled over, hooting with laughter.

"So Strayeth and Chumsley will be reminded of their promises to you, each and every time they go into their favorite haunt."

They both laughed heartily for several moments, and when they'd finally caught their breath, Caro said, "Edie said something not long ago that I thought was very interesting. She said that Chumsley and Strayeth were never the real villains in all this; she said I've been up against something bigger—something that harms women all throughout England. It's certainly consistent with Mrs. Hellkirk's teachings, but what do *you* make of it, Mama?"

Her mother walked with her arms crossed in front of her, pinning the corners of her shawl against her chest.

"The whole thing makes me feel hopeless," Caro continued. "The entire English way of life doesn't seem like something I can work on."

"You've taught Strayeth and Chumsley their lesson, Caro. An important—and rare—one, and you've done it in memorable fashion. I believe they will remember it, and even impart it one day to their sons. By teaching them to respect the ladies all around them."

"Or by telling their daughters they can stand up for themselves when they've been wronged."

"Precisely. And that, my dear, is how you change a way of life."

Her mother looked up then, the early-morning light setting her bourbon-colored eyes aglow. It occurred to Caro how little she took notice of such things about her mother: her extraordinary eyes; how slight her shoulders appeared, wrapped in her black lace shawl; the elegance of her long neck. The two of them seldom lingered like this over a personal matter, or out in the fresh air, or without Papa. And they never lingered without the presence of their fourth family member—their never-ending work.

Caro closed her eyes and savored the feeling. "Speaking of standing up for oneself, I have sometimes wondered: Looking back, would you take a different course, if you could?"

Mama tucked a curl behind her ear, and Caro saw herself in the gesture. "What do you mean? Would I decline the opportunity to learn architecture?"

"No, Mama. I'm asking if you would decline Papa's proposal."

"Heavens, *no!* Marrying your father was...well, it was my escape. Twice over, in fact."

"How so?" She shielded her eyes from the blinding sun as she watched her mother step carefully around Toby, who had stopped again, this time to stare down an insect.

"My mother was a lady's maid, as you know, to a very generous lady who paid for my schooling. I was fortunate that my school taught drawing, and that I had a knack for it. But the road to becoming a painter goes through the Royal Academy, and that institution does not admit women.

"My accomplishments would have ended there, Caro, had I not fallen in love with a man who was about to become an architecture pupil. So marrying your father kept me from going into service, and it gave me an opportunity to take up a profession that I never would've dreamed of pursuing otherwise."

They continued their walk, Caro staring at the ground. "But he receives all of the accolades, Mama, whilst you've been hidden and silenced. If you were able to pursue your artistic talents as your own, with or without public acclaim, then perhaps you wouldn't be sad so often."

She was quiet for several seconds as they walked. "I suppose it's been rather obvious to you that my situation pains me, at times."

"I don't desire to be ignorant of it, Mama. I've often wished I could help you, and have taken some comfort in the fact that I am able to carve out a life with greater freedom—and a louder voice—as a result of your lessons and your efforts."

"Is that true, though? I've been worried that my peculiar mothering has caused you more harm than benefit."

Caro's mouth became a tight line. "Undoubtedly, there are those in society who believe that my freedom and my tongue are to blame for my current predicament. There was a moment or two when I believed that, too. But no—I wouldn't trade the trust and confidence you and Papa have always given me, for a better reputation. I wouldn't trade them for anything."

Mama took her hand and kept it.

Caro sighed. "I might have lost my ability to move so highly in society," she continued, "but at least I will have my own home my whole life."

"Why do you say that, Caro?"

"You've heard me say many times that I would never marry."

"Yes, but I've always assumed you would change your mind for the right person."

She scoffed. "Mama—I'd have to give over the control of my inheritance if I married. I'd have to tailor my views and activities to those of another, and *that* is anathema to me."

"It's no secret," Mama replied, putting her arm around her with a laugh, "that you feel thwarted and wronged when you are asked to make a compromise."

"I am being quite serious," Caro replied as she stopped walking. She braced herself, trying to stop the tears from rushing onto her cheeks, though they hit her with all the force of a flash flood. "We are not talking about the likelihood of marital spats, Mama. We are talking about the likelihood of losing everything I love to do. And it is my worst fear."

"*Oh*—dearest. I am sorry. Come here." Mama turned and reached out for her, putting both her hands on her shoulders and massaging them gently. "I do not mean to mock you, dear Caro."

"I—I only want to lead the life that you could not."

Mama stepped back and let her hands fall to her sides. "I do not wish you to live your life for me, Caro. I have never wished for that."

Caro stopped sniffling and looked at her through bloodshot eyes.

"Although I see now how you might have concluded that," Mama continued, looking at the ground and wringing her hands. "My sadness must have seemed like regret all these years. Then I sent you to a strange school—"

"—under somewhat dubious circumstances," Caro finished, smiling despite her tears.

"And I am the one who has cheered every one of your schemes. Even the harebrained ones." Mama chuckled and reached out to her, rubbing her arm.

Caro put her arm around her mother's waist, and turned them onto their path again.

"And you're right that marriage is a risk for a woman," Mama continued. "But my own situation should serve as proof, Caro, that you needn't avoid it entirely! Our marriage was not the cause of my pain."

"But it could very easily become the cause of my own."

"Then you are very fortunate, my sweet Caroline, that Lord Ryland will support you in whatever you want to do with your talents, regardless of what the law allows."

"I beg your pardon?" she sniffed.

"Do not play coy with me, young lady," Mama replied. "It's obvious to anyone with eyeballs or earlobes that that gentleman cares for you, a great deal."

"Lord Ryland may have...concern for me, but my scandal makes a union with him impossible." She tightened Toby's leash around her hand. Two days had passed since she had pushed Adam away—since she'd implied to him that he was no different from any other suitor, or any other man she might kiss. The mere recollection of her dismissive words stung her.

"He seems like a good man, Caro. And well suited to you. I believe your attachment to him shows good judgment."

"Mama—you are ahead of yourself. Please consider that any formal association with me would ruin Edie's prospects for marriage." She let go a great, shuddering sigh and added, "He may not wish to have me anymore, at any rate."

"I haven't kept up with the nitty-gritty of society's rules, so I cannot guess what the future holds. But you and Edie and Ryland—"

"Oh, he's *Ryland*, now?"

She smirked. "I do beg your pardon, daughter. I was just going say that the three of you would not lack for money, and have a circle of family and close friends who will stay by you."

They walked slowly the rest of the way to Carlton House, indulging Toby in stops over rubbish and unexplained stains on the sidewalk. They talked of too-light shawls and muddied gloves and compared remedies for both; they talked to small children and encouraged them to pet Toby and gave them a sweet from Caro's pocket. And they arrived at the work site hand in hand.

CHAPTER TWENTY-FIVE

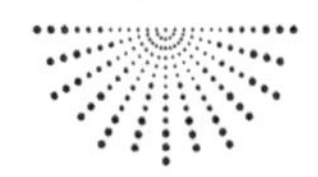

"How about accounting, then? I could keep the books," Caro said, accepting a growler of ale from Mama, who was sitting beside Papa and removing pies and cheeses from a large basket.

"Dearest, you do not *like* numbers. You run everything in our household *except* for the books, and yet you wish to do so for the business?" Papa replied. He was seated on the opposite corner of a wool blanket that Caro had laid for the three of them, on the smoothest patch of ground she could find. All around them, workers bustled to and fro, wheeling carts, mixing mortar, climbing ladders, consulting drawings, and arguing over the work ethic of some person or another. They were erecting an especially tricky part of the Prince Regent's new folly—a faux "ruin" of sorts—and Papa and Mama felt they should remain close, even during their luncheon.

"How about managing the building supplies? I could help you order materials, and—"

"The pupils take turns doing that," Mama added. "It's part of their education. You know this."

"How about managing one of the project sites? You must agree I am quite adept at ordering people around."

"The pupils do that, too."

"Cleaning and organizing the studio?"

"You wish to take over some of Mrs. Meary's fiefdom? Good luck to you."

"Research, then. I could find precedents from antiquity that could inspire your designs—"

"Pupils, again."

"What then?" she sighed over a bite of bread. "What do you propose I do with my time now that my charity schemes are no more?"

"Your charity schemes are not over, Caro," Papa replied. Behind him, a bedraggled stonemason, his clothes covered in mud and some other crusted-over substance, lingered over a cart of bricks. "They are simply on hiatus until society becomes bored with this...with this *incident*."

"Now that the other newspapers have reported that Lord Chumsley paid the *Gabster's* man to be there, and to print your name," said Mama, "I believe that society will begin to put the clues together. That he was in debt and desperate for money, that he claimed to have won the wager despite not heeding the real terms of it."

The workman behind Papa stopped and rested his forearms on the edge of his cart. When he tipped his hat at them, a familiar, faded tattoo became visible on the underside of his forearm.

"Can we help you, Georgie?" Caro asked.

Her parents turned around.

"Beggin' your pardon, Miss. But I couldn't help overhearin' you talking about them bastards. Them ones who made the bet."

"Sir—" Papa began, starting to get up.

"Please, Papa," Caro interjected. "It's all right. Let him speak."

He tipped his hat again, shifting from foot to foot, perhaps reconsidering speaking to the architect—the only person who stood between himself and the Prince Regent—on a topic of such sensitivity.

"Please. Go on," Caro added when he still didn't speak.

"I don't know if you've heard, but that lord—the one who said them things? He's gone now."

"I beg your pardon?"

"I heard it this morning, over an Old Tom with a bloke at the Hound and Hare," he replied.

"Where has the gentleman gone, do you know?" Caro asked, her heartbeat picking up.

"All I heard was that he ran out of the country, like a rat in the night."

"France!" shouted another workman, passing by with a bag of something slung over his shoulder. "And good riddance, I say. Let the bloody frogs have the bounder."

Georgie turned back to her and nodded his approval. "Like he said, Miss, France." Then he went back to rummaging in his cart.

"Lud!" she cried, grabbing the growler from her mother again. She took a long and pensive swig. "France! Edie was right—Chumsley's scandal really *is* worse than mine."

"His reputation is dead now, for sure," Mama added, taking the growler for another sip before wiping her mouth with the back of her hand. "Mark my words, Caro. This will all turn out in the end."

"The truth may out, Mama. But even so, society isn't likely to welcome me back with open arms. Two lords deemed me likely enough to become their lover that they bet a hundred pounds on it. And for many, being that sort of woman is bad enough."

"Even so," Papa added, wiping his brow. "To some extent, the tide of opinion will turn in your favor. You needn't resign yourself to the bookkeeping circle of Hell, just yet. And speaking of Hell, where do things stand for Edie's birthday extravaganza this year? Should we anticipate damage to the terrace again?"

She scratched her forehead, embarrassment and disappointment dueling bitterly for the larger portion of her expression. "No, Papa. I've had to cancel Edie's dinner. Out of a hundred invitations, not a single person said they would come."

"That's too bad."

"You know what you should do, Miss," said the stonemason, popping his head out of the cart again.

"What is that, Georgie?"

"You should go to them fights tonight. That would be right entertaining, and take your mind off things."

Papa's mouth opened, but Caro spoke up before he could reprimand the poor man. "Thank you for the suggestion, Georgie, but I am not a fighting enthusiast."

"All right, then. Truth be told, we was hoping you would go and then tell us about it."

"You don't say," she replied as she began gathering the linens and utensils to return to the basket.

"'Struth. The lot of us are right vexed to be missing the big rematch."

Her hands stilled. "What rematch is that, Georgie?"

"The one with that Lord Ryland bloke. He's to fight the Duke of Portson for the first time in over a decade. It'll be a crush, I'm sure."

Her heart flared. "You must be mistaken, Georgie. Where did you hear of this?"

"'S'right over there," he said, nodding to a small lean-to where some of the men took a mid-day meal. She jumped up and ran over and sure enough, a newish-looking poster had been pasted over an older one, both of them related to the Harvest Festival. The one on top read:

Get here earl-y and put up your dukes!
Rematch of the century!

She gasped.

"What is it, dear?" Papa called to her.

Why would Adam do this? Fighting makes him ill. He hasn't trained in years, and he doesn't like the atten—

Her heart skidded to a stop: Adam was *hoping* for attention. Of course he was. Win or lose, the Earl of Ryland getting into a ring with the duke he once walloped was going to be a *sensation*. And a new sensation would draw society's attention away from her old one; the gossips would parse *his* triumphs, *his* humiliations—and soon enough, they would leave her be.

But at what cost to Adam? She could not allow this to go forward.

She hiked up her skirts and turned toward home, without even stopping to say goodbye. Mama and Papa shouted after her, Toby chased her, and Georgie could be heard saying, "See? Now that's what I would call an enthusiast."

CHAPTER TWENTY-SIX

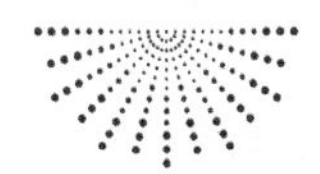

"S*tinson!* The carriage—I need the carriage at once."

"Yes, Miss. Edwards is already coming 'round with it."

"I need it now, Stinson. Please—go and tell him to hurry. *Go!*"

Caro smoothed at her dress to stop her hands from shaking. She spotted a laundry maid turning to come down the stairs and called up to her, "Louisa, I need you to pack something for me. Just a small overnight bag, but I need it immediately." The girl turned and scampered back up.

"If I may, Miss," said a voice behind her.

She turned and found Mrs. Meary wringing her hands. "What are you hoping to accomplish, running off to this festival?"

"I want to stop Lord Ryland from participating in this bout."

"But you can't ask a man to back out of a fight, Miss."

"Of course I can."

"And you cannot go unaccompanied to such a place. A raucous festival, with lots of...of *theater* people," she added, her voice curdling with distaste.

"I haven't anyone to ask, Mrs. Meary. I haven't a lady's maid, and I haven't...well, I haven't any friends anymore, either."

"Then I'll go with you."

Caro noticed, now, the rumpled and threadbare bag at her feet. She looked back up and smiled weakly. "Do you have money on this bout, Mrs. Meary?"

"You've never been to a fight, Miss. I have. I know what they're about, and I can help keep you safe."

"That's a lovely offer," Caro replied, reaching out and taking her hand. "But my lack of experience doesn't signify—"

"And I'm coming too."

She whipped around and saw Stinson drop a bag of his own at his feet.

"What is this, a family holiday?"

"Please listen, Miss," Barclay added as he strode into the hall, holding his hands behind him. "This isn't the time to exercise your...independent streak."

She threw up her hands. "All right, family holiday it is." She was too fluttery, too distracted, too worried to mount a protest. And they were right. Going anywhere without a chaperone—or two—was highly improper, especially to a prizefight, and especially given her current predicament.

"There'll be no place to stay the night," said Mrs. Meary. "The inns will be overfull, so we'll have to sleep in the carriage tonight." She nodded to Stinson. "You'll go on top."

"No," Barclay added. "There's no reason you cannot turn 'round and make your way back here tonight. It's just twenty miles all together, and the horses will be plenty rested. Just be on your way again, as soon as it's all done."

Mrs. Meary nodded. "Let's take our bags, just the same."

Barclay pulled something from behind his back. "And take this, Miss."

He held out a thick wooden stick. It was a foot and a half long and tapered to a ball on one end, studded with something metal.

"What *is* that, Barclay?"

"A cudgel, Miss. Take it." He gave it a light shake.

"What are these?" she asked, touching a finger to one of the sharp metal points.

"Spikes, Miss. Small ones."

"We are going to Beauton, Barclay. Not the Middle Ages."

"*Ohhhh!* Just give me the thing," Mrs. Meary snapped, reaching out and snatching it. "Louisa! Get down here at once. Stinson—get those bags stowed, and get up with Edwards. And don't you just stand there, Miss. I thought you was in a hurry."

Caro saluted her and smiled, surprised at her ease. The three of them were insisting that she compromise—that she allow them to guide and even join her—and she didn't mind it a bit. She was glad for their input, in fact, and relieved to have their help and their counsel. She watched as Mrs. Meary unzipped her bag, wrapped the cudgel in a cloth of some kind, and packed it away.

* * *

Quillen set his chin in his hand and peered at him through half-shut eyes. Then he walked all around him and when he arrived back in front announced, "I think it's short enough already."

"What are you talking about?" Adam asked.

"Your hair, Ryland. We don't want you getting dragged around the ring by your scalp."

"*Ah.* Understood."

They were standing on a terrace at Banmoor, the sun just beginning its descent toward the western horizon, toward the very grounds where the Harvest Festival was underway.

A servant approached with a tray. "Here. Drink this," Quillen commanded as Adam picked up a glass and peered into it.

"What is it?"

"Eggs. Three of them."

"No, thank you." He set it back down. It wasn't that he feared vomiting; indeed, he felt oddly calm, as if in some respects, his body still knew how to prepare itself for sparring.

Although this time, the fight would be real.

"You've already declined a brandy," Quillen replied, gesturing to the tray on a nearby table.

"It's best if I stay sharp, Quillen. I haven't done this in many years."

"In an hour or so, you might wish your senses were a bit dulled."

"I'll take that risk."

Quillen grabbed the brandy and sucked it down himself. "We'll need at least two more," he called out to the servant as he reentered the house. "And see if you can find some oranges!"

"Aside from the hair-pulling, Quillen, what else can you tell me about the fancy these days?"

He shrugged. "The rules haven't changed: No hitting below the belt. A round ends whenever a man goes down on one knee, and that man has thirty seconds to get back to the scratch line, or he'll be pronounced the loser. There'll be a referee, although given the role of the Sadler Wells folk in this festival, he may be more clown than umpire." He picked up the glass of eggs and after a quick shrug, drank them down himself. "So what's your strategy, Ryland?"

He ignored the question. "You'll be my second?" he asked instead.

"Of course. And my friend here will be your bottle man."

Adam turned to the grizzled fellow lounging drunkenly on a nearby chaise. He'd been sunning his belly on that same terrace ever since Adam arrived, two days prior. His face was nearly as ruddy as a cherry tart, and a pair of missing teeth punctuated his cheerful grin.

Adam extended his hand. "And what is your name, sir?"

"Never you mind it," Quillen interjected. "You needn't know."

"I see. Another of your acquaintances from...outside Mayfair?"

"He's a navy man, Ryland. That's all you need to know."

Navy Man winked at him.

"A quiet one, at that."

"You're sure I can't talk you out of this?" Quillen asked, shifting from foot to foot. "We could say you've been called back to town—"

"No. Let's just get on with it."

"All right, then," he replied as he scooped up another brandy, then another, drinking each in a single draft. "Let's walk."

The three of them put on their greatcoats and set out on a lane near the rear of the house. It led through a wood to the village of Beauton and the heart of the festival. From Banmoor to the ring was a walk of about a quarter-hour, Quillen had told him.

When they emerged from his property and onto the road, they saw a veritable stream of humanity, young and old, man and woman, rich and poor, all making their way into Beauton, shoulder-to-shoulder and laugh-to-laugh. No one appeared to take much notice of their entrance into the lively parade.

"No one is heading *away*," said Adam. "Every single person is going toward the festival."

"Of course they are, Ryland. You're the main draw," Quillen replied. "They've made you the last fight of the day. Of the entire festival, in fact."

"People will be quite drunk."

"Aye. And I hope to join them, as soon as possible."

Adam sighed, trying to ignore his accelerating heartbeat. He changed the subject. "What is Portson's style of fighting, these days?"

"Oh, he's quite preoccupied with what the fancy calls 'the science of boxing.' He's smart, as you know, and I suspect he'll try to be especially quick today as he doesn't have the advantage of size."

"He's not a small man."

"No," Quillen replied with a snort. "And from what I hear, he trains obsessively. But he is no giant." He nodded over Adam's shoulder. "Be easy, Ryland—don't look. But I believe you've been recognized."

Adam scoffed. "Anyone glancing this way is just admiring your curls."

"Nay, Ryland. The postings they put up around the village included a rather nice description of you."

He groaned.

"'Raven-haired,' I believe they called you."

Adam glanced around and saw that several people were indeed looking his way and whispering to their companions. The heady buzz in the air, and the thick flow of people—all heading in the same direction for once—seemed to have created a rare camaraderie among the swarm of them.

"You get him, Lord Ryland," a man in farmer's attire said before glancing around, perhaps fearful of being heard speaking against a duke. "I've got a guinea on you."

"Make 'im bleed, my lord," whispered a middle-aged woman with a babe in her arms, walking alongside him.

"What are the odds on the bout?" Quillen asked her quietly.

She nodded at Adam. "This gentleman is favored quite heavily, I believe."

"And is that on account of his reputation? Or is there something people have against the duke?"

She pulled her child tighter against her, her eyes whiter suddenly. "I'm sure I couldn't say, my lord," she replied. She curtsied and headed into the crowd with two or three looks over her shoulder.

"It puts one in an awkward position, betting against a duke," Quillen said brightly.

"It puts one in an awkward position, *fighting* against a duke," he replied.

Quillen grabbed his shoulder and squeezed. "It's not too late to come up lame, you know. Or to invent some charming but urgent emergency, back in town."

He looked straight ahead. They had reached the festival and their fellow pilgrims spread out among the dozens of tents, carts, stands, and the occasional cluster of musicians, jugglers, and magicians. The smell of pies, of burning wood, and of sweat and stale ale hung heavily in the air.

"What's your strategy, Ryland?" Quillen asked, his tone sharper now.

Adam exhaled and picked up his pace, trying to match the runaway gallop of his heartbeat. "To get the damned thing over with."

* * *

Caro leaned out the window of the carriage. She could not believe the mass of carriages, carts, animals, and people on the road, all of them moving just feet at a time. The sun was sinking fast, with no regard for her being stuck in traffic, still well away from Adam. She drew back into the carriage and took her watch from her reticule. It was nearing five o'clock, and the bout was to begin at half-past.

"We'll never get there in time to speak with Lord Ryland before the match."

"We're getting close, Miss."

She untied and re-tied the silk strings of her bag. "And I don't understand all the pretense to secrecy around this thing."

"Prize fights are illegal, Miss. You know this."

She scowled. "Take a look outside, Mrs. Meary! There are thousands of people on this road. And any magistrate who can't discern the reason for it should be stripped of his title at once."

Mrs. Meary smiled at her and pulled the curtain aside. "Miss Crispin, I understand you are worried for your...for Lord Ryland. But he is rumored to be a very capable fighter. And many people are rather excited to see him in the ring after all these years."

Caro's scowl hardened into a tight knot, and she leaned out the window and whistled up to Stinson and Edwards, each of them reclining with a tall blade of grass in his mouth. "Hullo, you two! Can't you find a way through this mess?"

"No, Miss. There's no other way," the coachman called back to her. "Why not try to enjoy the country drive?"

She scowled at them, too, then looked down and saw a trio of men coming toward them. They stood out in part because they were the only people heading *away* from the festival, and also because two of the gentlemen were holding up the one in the middle, and he appeared to have been badly beaten.

What violence is this? Her first thought was to wonder what sort of crime the poor man had been a victim of, what terrible assault had happened upon him. But then she remembered where she was: some quarter-mile from a "harvest festival" that was little more than a pretext for two days of fighting spectacles.

This man is a boxer, of course. Perhaps a participant from the most recent bout? To begin with, his nose looked...wrong. Not in the wrong place, exactly, but crooked in the middle somehow. Bent. Jointed. Broken. His face was covered in tiger-stripes of grit then blood, grit then blood, and he held one hand cupped tightly over his right eye. As they got closer, he lowered it a moment and she could see that his eyeball had come loose from its socket, and was dangling about two inches below it.

Caro reached inside and grabbed Mrs. Meary's arm. "What *is* this place?" she hissed. "This can't be right. We cannot be in the right place." She felt weak suddenly, as if she hadn't eaten in a month. Everywhere she looked, figures and objects appeared to be dissolving in stars, all around the edges.

"We are most definitely in the right place," Mrs. Meary replied calmly.

She took a deep and clarifying breath and leaned outside again. "Sir! You, there! I am sorry for your loss. You must be very brave."

Another of the men looked up at her. "Beggin' your pardon, Miss! But you're looking at the winner!"

"Stop!" she called out, rapping hard on the side of the carriage. "Stop if you please—*stop.* We'll go the rest of the way on foot, thank you."

Edwards complied, and Stinson jumped down to assist the women as they descended the steps. Mrs. Meary took Caro's hand and gripped it tightly before plunging into the crowd, making no apologies.

No one seemed to expect any. Everyone they passed was having a right jolly time, in fact, and their merriment made Caro even more despondent. *Don't they know what is to happen? Don't they care about these men? About their blood, their bruised torsos, their eyes and their vision?* Stinson followed behind her, having relayed a message to Edwards about where he should wait for them.

It quickly became clear that even on foot, even with Mrs. Meary plowing steadily forward, they would not reach the ring in time to speak with Adam. But Caro could see the thing, at least—the patch of flattened grass surrounded by two ropes and a set of stakes. A dozen or so feet outside these was another set of ropes and stakes that held back the swelling, straining crowd.

She could see figures inside the ropes, too, but knew they were too far off to hear anything she might yell. It was time for a new scheme.

Mrs. Meary glanced back at her. "Are you well, Miss?"

She nodded.

"You are quite pale."

"I am fine," she lied. Her head felt full of gauze, and stars still flickered at the edge of her vision as she struggled to put each foot in front of the other. Thank Heavens for Mrs. Meary and Stinson, who pulled and pushed her forward. She was going to need her strength, for the only thing she could think to do that might stop this madness was to make a scene of some kind.

And that was going to take some doing.

* * *

Adam had to stoop low and bend his knees to make it through the ropes. Portson was already inside, at the opposite corner of the ring, and Adam couldn't help looking over.

His opponent was facing away and jumping up and down, cocking his head from side-to-side. Then he stopped and walked in a broad circle, swinging his arms in unison.

"Stop that!" Quillen hissed, pulling Adam around. "He *wants* you to look at him. He's trying to intimidate you."

Adam felt heavier on his feet than ever, as if lead had been poured all through him, starting at the top of his skull. His head felt foggy, and he swayed slightly. Quillen and Navy Man each took one of his arms and pulled him closer, into their corner.

But after a moment, they turned away to discuss something and Adam couldn't help but turn back again to look at the duke.

He had been curious about his old competitor. He knew that Portson had become a successful fighter, but nothing of what had become of his temperament since their schoolyard bout.

Portson had already disrobed, down to his breeches. He was wearing an unusual pair of boots, probably the special ones that Quillen had told him about—the ones with the spikes on the sole. The rules of the fancy allowed fighters to wear such things, and they were certainly sensible for someone who had invested as much in the sport as Portson apparently had.

The duke was a few inches shorter than he, and seemed compact in comparison—muscular but still swift. *Just as a man ought to be*, Adam thought, smiling at a line from a favorite novel. He looked down at himself, recalling how Father had cocked his head at him when he was just fourteen, mumbled something about his being too slim, and instructed him to begin spending his mornings with the workmen building a stone wall around the park. It required a great deal of heavy lifting, and he knew it was meant to build up his physique for boxing. But Adam didn't mind it; indeed, it helped him discover just how much he preferred such projects to the sparring, jumping, and running in circles Father often demanded of him.

When Adam looked up, the duke drank something his second had just handed him, and it looked suspiciously like a multitude of yellowy egg yolks.

Devil take it. He should've known to listen to Quillen.

Portson looked up and caught Adam staring at him. He smiled, stopped his incessant jumping, and swaggered over—his hand extended in greeting. It was not the smile of a man who had been broken, in bone or in spirit. But neither was it a friendly one.

* * *

The first blow landed immediately, a second into the fight.

Caro yelped and jumped back, but her cry was lost amid the shouts of the crowd.

Adam staggered backward, and her heart felt like it went with him.

She could not watch this.

She turned to Mrs. Meary, her face still. They were still holding hands, their knuckles forming the palest of spines. "I cannot do this," Caro yelled to her, trying to be heard over the crowd. But Mrs. Meary didn't answer.

She looked back at the ring. The Duke of Portson looked like he was dancing as he came hard at Adam again. Adam went down on one knee, and the referee called for the end of the round. Lord Quillen and a man she did not recognize came out and grabbed him and brought him swiftly to their corner.

Good. Lord Quillen will know what to do. He will do whatever it takes to get Adam out of there alive. With both eyes intact. And, she hoped, *in their proper place.*

There were perhaps three or four rows of people between them and the first rope. She could barely shift from foot to foot, so tightly were they packed together. The roar of the thousands assembled around them was shocking in its volume and intensity and it seemed as if everyone in Beauton was itching for a fight—starved for it, even—and would soon become livid if they did not get it.

"Get him back out there!" hollered a man directly behind her, his voice coarse, his breath terrible. She turned and smiled sweetly at him, blinking innocently as she asked, "Pray, Mrs. Meary—where is my cudgel? I may have found a need for it."

The man shrunk back, and she turned slowly around again as others in the crowd continued their jeers and whistles.

She had never felt so small and vulnerable, and it was clear that she could faint or pretend to birth a baby and no one around her, *no* one, save perhaps her housekeeper, and maybe not even her, would care a whit or even notice.

She wouldn't be able to create much of a scene; the bout was already the scene of the day, and it was a good one.

Adam and His Grace returned to the center of the ring. Both were standing tall. She took a deep breath.

They went at each other again, arms raised, moving around, covering the entire area. Whenever they got near to her side of the ring, she yearned to call out to Adam, and nearly did so twice before stopping herself.

She did not want to distract him and create a danger for him, for one thing. And she had no idea what she would say—all she knew was that she wanted this to be over with at once, and for Adam to be safe.

His Grace took a number of swings at him, but his reach came up short, and he could not get his fists past the guard Adam put up with his own. But he didn't seem to tire, even after many long minutes of his dizzying dance. He jabbed and swung at Adam, again and again, moving and easily ducking the few punches Adam did throw.

"Is this what it's always like?" she asked Mrs. Meary.

She shook her head. "It's only like this when the gentlemen know their craft. Usually, it's an ugly, two-man brawl. This...this is *beauty*."

His Grace landed a fist on Adam's side, but he appeared to absorb it without breaking his stance or concentration. Then there was more dancing, more of the untiring Duke of Portson swinging, and more of Adam's long wingspan and skilled guarding. Then once again, His Grace landed another hit on his side. He absorbed it again, and the cycle started over. Indeed, it repeated with no apparent end in sight: dance, swing, dance, swing, dance, swing, *hit*.

She glanced at her watch: The round had gone on a full half-hour. She flinched every time Adam was hit, wondering why he didn't attempt more strikes himself, wondering how many blows a person could take. Perhaps it was her anxiety for Adam, but more and more of His Grace's blows seemed to be landing, and she imagined that she saw more bending, more slouching in Adam with every successful hit. And then, to the shock of everyone assembled, Adam swung wide and struck His Grace with so much force that he literally flew off his feet and into the air—landing flat on his back as if hit by a runaway team of four.

The crowd fell into a hush, and the referee called for the end of the round. His Grace's men ran out to where he lay still on the ground, and Caro looked at her watch again, praying this would be the end of the damned thing. *Thirty, twenty-nine, twenty-eight, twenty-seven.* The crowd remained quiet, rapt, watching the fallen man for any sign of movement —of life, even. That blow had come as if from a bear, and the Duke of Portson was but a bumblebee who'd buzzed a little too long around some honey that had already been claimed.

She glanced toward Adam, too, but Lord Quillen and the other man hovered over him in their corner, and she couldn't see him at all. *Eighteen, seventeen, sixteen.* She thought she might be able to go to him soon, and her heart strained and jabbed at her rib cage in anticipation.

She wished no harm on His Grace, of course; she wanted to see him move as much as anyone. Just not too much, and not for the next several seconds.

Ten, nine, eight.

His foot moved, and the crowd gasped. There were claps and cheers, too, as His Grace sat up and shook his head as if trying to clear off some dust. *Five, four, three.* His men lifted him roughly to his feet and pushed him to the scratch line where Adam stood calmly by, as if waiting to cross the street at Picadilly. The crowd cheered for more fighting.

The referee signaled the start of another round and His Grace sprung from the line, flying at Adam with his fists churning. He got through Adam's guard before the latter seemed to know what was happening.

"It was a ruse," Mrs. Meary shouted to her. "His Grace got himself a rest, and in doing, set up a fine trick!"

Indeed, he pummeled Adam into the ropes as if he hadn't just been knocked silly by a powerful blow, as if he hadn't already spent nearly an hour at fisticuffs. Adam turned away and His Grace hit him again and again in the back as the crowd became ever more frenzied. Caro hugged herself and looked into the faces of the people around her, uncertain if their grunts and blood-curdling whoops were because they wanted to win money, or because they wanted to see a gentleman—either one would do, it seemed—get trounced beyond all recognition.

* * *

Damn fool! He'd hit Portson harder than he'd intended, but not *that* hard. He should have known the duke's fall (and awkward splay on the ground) was just play-acting.

Time seemed to slow as Adam curled away from the duke, protecting his face as best he could, taking a great deal of pummeling on his back and side.

He wondered, not for the first time, if he should just give in. Make a dramatic show of it, perhaps. The words of Lady Cantemere knocked around his head: *She will continue to suffer, until the next giant falls.* Well, it was in his power to make the next giant fall. It could all be over now—Caro's position at the top of the gossip pages, this fight, his reputation as a great fighter.

How freeing it would all be.

But as much as he loathed every second that passed and dreaded every one that was to come, he could not bring himself to lose the fight intentionally. He would be indulging his own unhappiness, he would be cheating the assembled crowd, and he would be disappointing the stern, and ever-present, ghost of his father. He pivoted away when the duke took a little too long positioning his next punch, and danced away. The crowed whooped again.

He wondered where Caro was, and what he would say to her when he saw her next. Would she—oh my God—that tousled hair, that minxy stance, that angry glare! *There she is!* Three-deep in the crowd, to his right! He wanted to look again but knew the duke would punish him for such a folly, so he continued to dance around, hoping to orient himself for another look. Realizing it would never happen, he took a knee and went quickly to his corner, to scattered applause from the crowd, who would probably have preferred to see him continue to take a beating on the ropes.

"That round was another twenty minutes," said Quillen.

"Please stop shouting at me." Every word was like a stake being driven into his skull.

"I'm not shouting."

He ignored him and turned to where he had seen Caro. They made eye contact and he yelled out to her at once. "Let her through! Let the lady through!"

Slowly, after much jostling and disgruntled elbowing, enough people moved aside to allow her through, with two others whom he recognized as her housekeeper and a footman. Caro was still glaring at him, and although the sun had sunk well behind the trees, there was still a glow of sorts in her eyes.

It probably wasn't the kind he wanted, but he would take it.

"Has it occurred to you," she asked, "that if you win today, there will only be more pressure on you to fight?"

He gave her a lopsided grin as Navy Man dumped a pail of water on his head. "Thank you for your faith in my abilities, dearest. It's one of the many things I love about you."

She didn't appear to be amused.

"Win or lose, my love, the newspapermen will be only too glad to report it. Or the newspaper*women*, of course."

That last bit made her smile, as he'd hoped. "I appreciate what you are trying to do, Lord Ryland, but you've made your point. I just want you out of there. Unhurt, and as soon as possible."

"What will you do with me when you get me?" But before she could answer, Navy Man pulled him up and shoved him toward the scratch line.

He went on the attack this time, and the Duke matched him, blow for blow, block for block. They were both invested now, as seeing Caro had made Adam realize just how much he wanted to be done with the thing. It gave him the energy he had lacked to that point, igniting the memory in his muscles, bringing back to vivid life the lessons Father had taught him all those years ago. He and Portson slipped into some known rhythm—part primal, part studied—and suddenly he was back to his boyhood again, practicing with Father.

He had never been a competitive boy, and bloodlust was a mystery to him. So Adam had taught himself—over many years of training—to take and throw punches that were *just* enough to keep an opponent working hard and feeling frustrated. He'd developed his own style of sparring, and it was as free of punishment as possible: it limited the pain of his opponent, without requiring him to intentionally lose. He just fought (and fought and fought and fought) until he reached that happy point when Father called the whole miserable affair a draw, and he could race back to his garden and his books.

That was what he had been in it for, all those years ago: as a means to avoid disappointing Father without revealing his cowardice.

Or at least, what he'd *thought* had been cowardice.

Father had never used that word, of course; he'd come to the conclusion himself that he lacked something important when it came to being a gentleman. He had his legendary father's encouragement, advice, and cheers. He was big, strong, and well-trained. But even as a boy, he knew he would avoid the real ring his whole life if he could help it—and this was curiously at odds with every one of his schoolmate's wishes to become champion one day.

It isn't cowardice, Caro had said, *to be wary of hurting another*. He hadn't allowed himself to believe it until now, but she'd been right: His aversion to the ring was not cowardice; it was a bone-deep revulsion to violence. That was the only thing about fighting that had always come naturally to him, and had only multiplied when he'd injured the duke back at school.

But he had volunteered for the soonest, nearest fight the very moment he'd realized it could be a boon for Caro. He was no less repulsed by the potential violence of it, mind, but in going, he'd proven to himself that he could surmount his old reluctance when it was truly required. And that, he supposed, was bravery of a sort.

It was also bravery to show one's true self to society, as Caro had always done, and as he intended to do from here on out.

He realized all this now, just as he noticed the sweat on Portson's brow, his wrinkled forehead, his bloodshot eyes. Was the duke tired, too? What was *he* in this for? His own purpose in entering that ring—to create a sensation that London's gossips would chew on for weeks —was done.

"What are you in this for, Portson?" he asked during a step back.

The duke's eyes widened, his brows raised. "To win, of course."

He thinks this is part of my strategy. Adam reached out and put his hands around Portson's neck and yanked him into a hold. The duke immediately reciprocated the gesture, as if he, too, was desperate for a rest.

"I want to be done, Portson. That's all I want. But I am not beaten, and neither do I want to do what it takes to win."

"Spare me your claim that you can't hurt a fly, Ryland. I know better."

"I can't do it, Portson. I haven't thrown a punch since our school days. I detest this business."

"Are you saying you want to throw this thing? Which did you have in mind to be, the winner or the loser? I daresay it's not the latter."

"Let's both put a knee down. Together. We'll say we can't go on, and it will end a draw."

"There will be a mob!"

"We've given them nearly two hours! Two hours of the best boxing many of these folks will have seen."

After a few more seconds—and a few boos—Portson replied, "Let me bloody you up a bit more, and I'll do it."

Adam stepped back and took an immediate punch, then another, to the temple then the jaw. His eye stung, and he tasted the metal of blood. "All right, then," he laughed.

But Portson hit him again, right in the stomach and he bent forward with an *ooof!* He was beginning to think Portson had played him again when he heard him rasp, "Your turn. Make it good."

He grinned and took a swipe at Portson, who ducked and grinned—his teeth covered in blood. Adam came at him again and this time he landed the thing. Blood spurted from the duke's mouth. He barreled into him, grabbing him above the waist and tackling him into the ropes. The crowd whooped in delight. He held him there some minutes before allowing him to wrestle free, then danced around as they traded a few more showy punches, each one eliciting a new *"Ah!"* or *"Oh!"* from the crowd.

By the time they came into another hold, Adam was deeply, truly weary. *"Ready?"* he whispered. *"One, two, three,* down." They went to their knees, simultaneously as agreed, and were swarmed by their men as if it were just the end of another hard-fought round.

"I'm done," they announced in unison. "I cannot go on."

The referee raised his hand and called the draw, eliciting shock from their seconds and a roar from the crowd that seemed mostly approving, albeit with a few scattered jeers. Their men pulled them up and they shook hands, exchanging just the hint of a smile.

Quillen and Navy Man helped him to the corner, where he saw Caro just beyond the ropes, looking as pale and grim as a gravedigger. "What is the matter, darling? Are you quite well?"

"Me?" she asked, her voice breaking.

Her reaching for him was the last thing he saw before passing out.

CHAPTER TWENTY-SEVEN

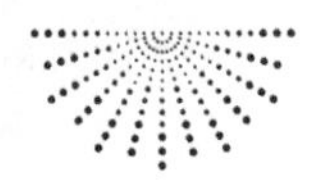

Adam came to in a quiet Banmoor bedroom. Dark curtains alternated with columns of hazy autumn sunlight, and a fire brewed its woody aromas from the far wall.

He tried to sit up, but pain shot through his back. So he laid down again and went still, grimacing in discomfort.

Why was his eyesight foggy? His head felt dull, so perhaps it was from that. He felt weak, too, utterly knackered, and looked for the cord at the bedside, which he knew would summon a servant. He wasn't sure he could reach it without feeling the wrath of God upon him, via long angry fingers reaching deep into his back.

"Do you need something?" said a voice. He tilted his head toward it and spied a figure curled in a chair by the window, and though his vision was too fuzzy to confirm it by the features of her face or the curl of her hair, he knew it was Caro.

"Are we alone?" His voice sounded dry and strained. "How scandalous."

Her blurry form rose from the chair and came over. "How are you feeling? What can I get you?" she asked as she sat gently on the edge of the bed.

"Caro," he said.

"Yes?"

"Come here."

"You are injured, Adam. And I suspect in a lot of pain."

"I am not asking for a tumble. Not yet, anyway."

"And I am offering far less than that," she replied. She'd attempted to sound irritated, though he could hear the smile in her voice. "Not yet, anyway."

He smiled and reached for her, and she took the hand he offered. "I'm not sure yet how cross I should be with you," she continued. Her voice carried with it the promise of tears, and he squeezed her hand.

"Just wait, Caro. Wait until we see what the newspapers have to say about what I did."

"I already know what they have to say."

"That was fast."

"Not really. We've had two mornings—"

"What?"

She laughed. "You've been sleeping for a day and a half. And I can report that you've successfully commandeered the headlines in all the gossip columns and society pages. All they can talk about is your bout. Although, if you ask me, it's hardly a scandal for a man to have fought like a champion against one of the winningest fighters in all of England."

"See? How can you be cross with me, when I am quite your hero?" he teased.

"Yes," she replied. "Indeed, you are. Although I never wanted you to do something that you hate for me, especially something you revile so much as fighting. And to risk..."

"Risk what?"

"Adam..." she sighed. "Never mind. You should rest."

"I—"

"Please try to rest." She got up and leaned over him, kissing him on the forehead. She lingered for several seconds, and the heat of her lips stayed long in his skin, long after she'd gotten up and promised to return to him with soup for his belly and salve for his muscles, some hours hence.

* * *

"Turn over."

He grinned at her, still chewing a bit of his lunch. "Can you demonstrate?"

"Do you want more of Lord Quillen's salve on your back, or do you want to stay in bed—alone—for the foreseeable future?"

Caro lifted the tray of dishes from his bed and put it aside. He turned over and she closed her eyes, preparing for the sight of his back. She removed the lid from the glass jar and inhaled deeply of the lavender and peppermint, then opened her eyes again.

They'd been at Banmoor four nights now, but the bruises were still thunderclouds across Adam's skin: purple and blue and angry as all get-out. When she exhaled a bit too loudly he asked, "That bad, as yet?" He had crossed his bare arms atop his pillow, and was resting his head on them.

"I don't know how you can smile like that through all of this." At least he could move comfortably, now.

"I don't have to see it."

She scooped some of the salve into her hands and began spreading it across his skin, as softly as she could. "Actually, this has improved some, over yesterday. More yellow, and very little black."

He closed his eyes and moaned a little. "I don't know what that is, but it makes a pleasant sort of tingling on the skin."

"I believe it's peppermint," she replied. "Though Lord Quillen told me not to ask too much about it, or where it came from."

"He says that a lot."

She laughed.

"What do you think of the country?" he continued.

She stopped rubbing. "What do you mean?"

"You said once that you loved town, but hadn't had much chance to spend time in the country. I want to know what you think of it now."

She scooped more of the salve and went back to making broad circles across the expanse of his nearest shoulder. She imagined this sort of touch in better circumstances, but quickly cursed herself for such selfish, trivial thoughts. "We're but ten miles from Charing Cross, Adam. It's hardly the hinterlands."

"Ardythe is only twenty. I wonder how you would like it."

Now her chest felt like her salve-covered hands—a curious, hot-cold tingling that couldn't be controlled. She had to speak up; she had to thank Adam for the brave, selfless gesture he had made in entering the boxing ring for her, and she had to apologize for what she had said in the servants' staircase of her house. She had to say all these things before she could hear any more talk of the future.

But he spoke up before she could assemble the words. "You are tired, I think."

"No, I am fine," she replied, sitting up straighter and trying to brighten herself.

Like any accomplished flirt, she knew how to widen her eyes for effect and smile effortlessly. But in truth, she *was* exhausted. She had slept but a few hours each of the nights she'd been there, and all of them had been in the chair by the window, within steps of Adam's bed. The surgeon who had seen him upon his return to Banmoor had said he was in no real danger, that he only needed rest, but she'd heard stories of men who had died a few days—or even weeks—after a particularly bruising fight. She couldn't bear to think of Adam's discomfort either, and if he woke and needed something she wanted to be there. Her nerves had begun to fray from too little rest, and too great a worry.

"What do your parents think of your being here? I'm loathe to complain, but this *is* a bit scandalous."

"Stinson and Edwards informed them of my whereabouts when they took the carriage back to town. Mama and Papa have since written twice, urging me to come home as soon as I can; and now that you're on the mend," she said, pausing, "Lord Quillen has offered me his carriage so that I can go back to them tomorrow."

He fidgeted.

"But Mrs. Meary has stayed on, as my chaperone," she continued. "She seems happy to have nothing to do but rehash the fight with anyone who will listen. All of the maids and footmen are now exceedingly familiar with your tendency to favor your left side."

He laughed. "She's an aficionado, then? What other assessment did she have of my performance?"

"She'll be sure to tell you once you're on your feet again."

"Well, now that I can roll over without shrieking like a lamb at slaughter, I think that will be quite soon. And with any luck, I'll be able to see clearly by then."

Her chin hit her chest. She couldn't take it anymore. Her shoulders shuddered as she tried but failed to suppress the sob that came barreling up from her chest. She tried to cover her face with her hand and squeeze back the tears, but Adam's fingers closed around her wrist and pulled it gently away.

"Come here," he said softly. When she shook her head no, he pulled her out of her chair and onto the bed, first on top of him and then next to him.

"You'll hurt yourself—"

His arms encircled her easily, and he pulled her to his chest. "I am fine," he whispered.

They lay like that for some minutes, her hand swiping messily at her tears, Adam tightening his grip now and again and murmuring soft susurrations into her crown. His heartbeat provided a steady example for her own more erratic, more worried one; and soon, she was breathing normally again.

"I wanted to thank you, Adam, for what you did."

"Shhh."

"Thank you, Adam."

He was silent.

"And I want to apologize for what I said the last time I saw you, in town. You are, as should be rather obvious by now, not just any assignation."

"I knew you wanted to push me away, for Edie's sake."

She nodded her head, then turned and pressed her cheek against his chest, her arms bent in front of her.

"I hated hurting you."

"You didn't. I dismissed it at once."

She chuckled. "You've always had a talent for sorting through my bluster."

He chuckled too, and the vibrations traveled through him and into her, and lulled her to sleep.

* * *

It was night when Adam awoke again. He got up slowly, pausing twice to stretch his stiff limbs, and lit a candle on the bedside table. He was a nighttime reader, by long habit, and having slept for nearly three days, he couldn't keep his eyes closed a minute more. He longed for a book and luckily, he had a good one—and his spectacles—in the pocket of his greatcoat.

He climbed back into bed, next to Caro, smiling at her hair tumbling onto the pillow and her frock fanned out across his bed. Her body curled toward him. She looked worried, however, even in slumber.

He sighed. He did not know what the morning would bring, but it was blissful to be there with her, even if it was just to lie next to her awhile, like the contented and long-married husband he already was in his imagination. He hadn't left his room since the bout, and didn't know what Quillen and Mrs. Meary thought of Caro being in his room, but guessed they were deliberately keeping their distance and giving them the time to be alone that they would not have upon returning to town.

They might even presume they were already engaged.

Would there be awkwardness when Caro awoke and they had to contend with being in bed together like this? He was unsure. They loved one another, and before Chumsley's lies had gone public, they were on the verge of becoming engaged. Had they come back to that point?

Or was his precocious lady simply comfortable lying with him outside of marriage?

She stirred. Her eyelids parted, and he laughed aloud at the skeptical, confused look on her face.

"Hello there," he said, laying his book on his lap.

She raised herself onto her elbows, hair mussed, eyes squinting, and assessed her surroundings. When understanding dawned she said, simply, *"Lud."*

He laughed again. He was sitting up against some pillows, bare to the waist. But she was looking only at his face, quizzically, as if she was trying not to look terribly pleased about something.

"What is it, darling?"

"Your spectacles."

"What of them?"

"I have missed them."

He threw his head back. "They are your old friends, now?"

She started to crawl toward him, innocent but cat-like, and his entire world seemed to turn, a ship keeling helplessly on some tropical reef.

And here I was concerned things might be awkward for her.

She tucked her skirts beneath her and kneeled next to him, then reached up and brushed a bit of hair from his temple.

He brought his fingertips to the spot, brushing softly against hers. "The stitches?"

She nodded. "They're healing nicely." Her warm breath was a tonic; who needed a salve or a surgeon, when there was Caro?

She leaned over him and put a fist on his other side, then kissed him once, gently. "I love you, Adam."

He brushed an unruly lock of hair from her face. "I love you, Caro." Did he say her breath was a tonic? It was nothing to her lips; those were what could cure—what *would* cure—his every ailment.

Then she turned her head to the side and looked down at his lap.

"*That* is most interesting."

"I beg your—" He stopped, and looked down.

"'*Hardwoods of Northern England?*'" She grabbed the book and tried to move away but he caught her and turned her onto her back, shrieking happily.

"How did you know that was a subject of great fascination to me, my lord?" she asked, laughing heartily with her head thrown back, her eyes closed, her hair falling into her mouth.

"I'll show you fascination," he said as he kissed the lovely spot of neck that was now wide open to him. He covered her body entirely, his knees on either side of hers, his hands pinning hers against the pillow, near her head.

When she'd finished laughing he raised his head, but instead of kissing her at once, looked into her eyes. "I want for every night to be like this, Miss Caroline Crispin."

She lifted her head and kissed him. He freed her hands and she brought them to his face, guiding him lower, so she could rest against the pillow.

They opened their mouths in unison and he lowered himself still further, resting some of his weight on her. When she moaned softly he broke the kiss and asked, "Is that too much?"

"Not at all, I adore it. What of you, though? Are you in any pain?"

Now it was his turn to laugh. "I am very much in the opposite of pain."

He looked at her; her expression had turned serious. "Can we have this night, without talk of the future?"

"Caro—"

She had reached under him and was stroking the front of his breeches. He closed his eyes and a guttural sound escaped his throat. Having lost all trace of his previous thought, he plunged his lips back onto hers. He was finished contemplating matters.

They kissed ferociously now, and pressed their bodies together sometimes urgently, sometimes clumsily—seeking friction and heat, yes, but also closeness, unity, peace. There was a sweet torture to it all, and when he thought he might crush her with his need to press the whole of himself against the whole of her, he crooked an arm underneath her and flipped her over, rolling her on top of him.

She sat up and grasped at the fabric of her dress. He saw that she was trying to remove her clothing and sat up to assist her; it was a job that was best done, apparently, with a great many giggles and whispers from not one eager party, but two. There was another shriek as well, followed quickly by a half-hearted *shush*, as items of the finest silks were pulled over her head, untied around her back, and slipped agonizingly along her legs. By the time she was naked, he was overwhelmed with the thrill, the adoration, the trust of it all.

He was also practically quivering from want.

She sat beautifully on his lap and smiled at him, with as little modesty in her manner as there were threads on her person. He pulled her close. The exquisite softness of her skin seemed impossible; she was cool where he was nearly afire, and he brushed his palms and fingers gently, tentatively, down her back as if wary of singeing her. She cradled his chin in her hands and continued to kiss him with such eagerness—such triumph, in a way—that he once or twice felt close to tears.

He was a romantic, after all. And he was with the woman he hoped to spend the rest of his life with, for the very first time. He pushed aside questions of whether she would indeed marry him, of why she was resistant to discussing the future, and savored every precious second, instead.

* * *

Lud! Did this ever live up to her expectations!

She could barely contain her excitement as Adam ran his hands up and down her back, tickling and soothing her, then travelled up her neck and into her hair, removing the few pins that remained there. He pulled her head to him, kissing her deeper than ever. Then he suddenly pulled away.

"There is one caveat to my agreement to spend this night with no talk of the future."

"Yes?"

He hooked a muscled forearm—oh, how she loved his forearms!—around her waist and flipped her over again, back onto her back. Lying underneath him, she traced a fingertip along the front edge of his breeches, dipping and exploring underneath the fabric, delighting in the heat of his skin. He nuzzled her neck and made sounds that magically, miraculously, she felt everywhere from her shoulders to her toes.

"We must discuss whether to take certain precautions..."

She hesitated. She thought it best if they did, but was wary of offending him. "I don't know about you, but I am hoping this is not the only time we do this..."

He laughed. "Meaning?"

"It seems to me there is no harm in...in taking precautions at times. At *this* time."

"That's all I need to know, love."

She thought he might guide her hands then, as they were already nearly pulling down his breeches, but instead he resumed his adulation of her body, which he performed mainly with his lips but occasionally conducted with one or both of his mighty hands. There were kisses and nips, tight grips and feather-light brushes, and she was stunned by the variety of it all. He had begun with her neck—oh, how he seemed to love her neck!—and made his way to her shoulders and down the rest of her, ministering to every bit of her in equal measure.

Until, at least, he arrived between her legs, where he dawdled at length.

Did she say earlier that she'd been stunned? *Ha!* What a fool she had been! She hadn't known what it was to be stunned until that moment, when Adam made her feel things—there and through the whole of her—that she could never have imagined. Her previous encounters pressed up against men, her own explorations, her perusal of the most salacious books in Mrs. Hellkirk's library—none of these things had prepared her for such sensations. She arched her back and grasped futilely at the sheets, and when he brought her to the brink he seemed to sense it, giving her everything she needed to cross over—to pain, to pleasure, to poetry, to satiation.

Did she say that this had lived up to her expectations? Nay, this surpassed them. It thundered over and crushed them, and everything else in its path.

He moved gently up her body, measuring the distance in slow kisses, then positioned himself above her. He brought himself lightly against her as he whispered in her ear.

She wanted to reach around his back and pull him to her, but knew he would be in great pain if she touched him where he was so bruised. So she reached lower and grabbed him by the buttocks instead.

"Easy, love," he replied after a quick groan. He held still, in spite of her attempts to encourage him to greater urgency.

So she stilled herself, and waited, and tried to admire his derriere with her hands. It would not have been a difficult thing to do, had she not been so distracted by the desire to have—*oh*.

Oh.

Now she understood the need to go slow.

He kissed and bit her bottom lip, then sucked it gently into his mouth. Before she knew what was happening, he was guiding one of her legs up and around his waist, moving gently against her, picking up speed, keeping her lip between his teeth. By the time he released it, she had adjusted to his presence, his size, his rhythm. She arched against him until she had more of that exquisite pressure from earlier, and she explored him by hand and mouth, matching him in mounting intensity as he approached his own release, withdrawing just beforehand and spending himself on the bedclothes.

She pulled him gently back toward her, then down onto his side, and they lay like that with their foreheads touching, their contented exhalations their only conversation. She ran her hands over the muscles of his arms and his back, slick with salty perspiration, and he traced her lips with a callused finger and smiled at her. She felt strange and magnificent, spent and replete all at once, and very much in love with the man lying next to her.

But when he fell asleep, she got up and dressed and called for a servant to alert Mrs. Meary to do the same. It was dawn, and she had to leave. After she had packed her bag, she wrote a note and folded it and placed it next to him.

Dearest—

I will see you soon, in town. Rest and recover and come back to me.

—Yours

She did not want to leave, but she had her parents to think of. And she had another scheme to conduct.

CHAPTER TWENTY-EIGHT

"You haven't stopped smiling since I arrived," said Edie. "And that was a full hour ago."

"Haven't I?"

"No. You must be rather thrilled with Adam's new prominence in all the gossip pages."

Caro nodded meekly.

"Or perhaps you are pleased with something else of Adam's doing."

"*Tea?* Let's have some tea," she announced as she jumped up and rang for Barclay.

She didn't need any prodding to think about Adam's doings. Indeed, she'd been able to think of little else on the carriage ride home that morning, or when she'd written her note to Edie just afterwards, or when she'd sat in the morning room pushing food around her plate, smiling stupidly at her toast.

"Tell me about the event that you're planning," she asked as she stood before the fireplace, surprised at the chill that had invaded London in her absence.

"It was my brother's idea, really. He wrote to me from Banmoor, and provided the names of some friends of his and Lord Quillen's that he felt I should invite. I added some of our neighbors and such." She shrugged.

"I guess he wanted to show off the drawings that your parents have prepared for the house."

"An exhibition? Oh, how wonderful. Papa often gives a talk at such things."

"That is what I understand. He and your mother have agreed to come, of course."

"Edie, do you hope to marry?" she asked, turning suddenly from the fire.

Edie sat back and looked around, perhaps surprised at the sudden change in topic. "I have always told you that I'm not terribly keen on getting married."

"You have stated any number of opinions on marriage, depending on the season and how you were feeling at the moment."

Edie flopped her wrist at her. "Nuance," she scoffed. "Who has a need for it?"

Caro smiled. "As you seem to have figured out, Edie, I may find myself in...in a new position one day soon. A position that affords me an even greater interest in your desire to marry."

Edie smirked at her. "I *knew* it."

Caro went over and sat down next to her, taking her hand. "I need to know, dearest. What would you say to my marrying Adam? He has not asked yet—not in full, anyway—but he seems very much on that course. I cannot accept him, though, without your blessing."

Edie's eyes glistened. "I want nothing more than to have you as a sister, Caro. And if I do decide to marry one day, I'll have the best schemer in London to help me find a match."

"Even though this particular schemer is still whispered about, by some?"

"*Especially* because she is whispered about."

They embraced and they cried a little, and then they laughed like the schoolchildren they had once been together. They sipped tea by the fire, talked of the gossip regarding the fight, and disagreed vehemently as to whether Adam had been fairly described in the papers as "being known, rightly, for his impressive presence and intellect."

Even when they'd stopped talking of Adam, Caro's thoughts found their way back to him, as if tethered. But apart from feeling guilty for daydreaming when she was meant to be conversing with her friend, she did not mind this new reflex. She had already concluded that she would be thrilled to marry Adam—and had only needed Edie's blessing on the matter. She knew that she could trust him not to ask her to be silent on her accomplishments or her ideas. Marriage to him would *not* be a tether; in fact, it would be a buttress, capable of withstanding great pulls and pushes, rains and windstorms, and the passage of a great many years.

But if she knew Adam at all, he would be worried that she had refused, the night before, to talk of their future. He had done so much for her; the least she could do was offer him that conversation—and the chance to ask his question, and to receive an answer.

Even if she had to come up with a new scheme to make it the special sort of occasion he likely hoped for.

* * *

When Adam entered the front hall he was shocked to find Mother there—and standing on two feet. Three, if you counted the sturdy cane that she rested her hands upon.

"I am glad to find you in one piece," she said as she approached him, getting close enough to take his chin in her hands and peer closely at his still-bruised face. "There isn't room enough in this house for two curmudgeons with canes and limps."

"Lovely to see you too, Mother," he replied.

She gave his chin a wag before letting go and smiling. "Come, come."

They settled in the saloon, where she sat with a foot propped up on several pillows.

"How does the leg feel, now that you are walking?"

"My *leg*? Pish! Tell me about that gash on your temple."

"I thought you'd have heard all about the fight by now."

"Indeed. Your sister and I were most taken aback, Adam," she replied, sitting forward and frowning at him.

"What criticism could you have, Mother? Your own husband was the most enthusiastic fighter I've ever known."

"Precisely, Adam!" Now she raised her voice, surprising him. "He enjoyed a good fight. You, on the other hand, do not!"

"How do you know that, when we haven't spoken of it in years? Nay, we've barely spoken of it at all, in fact."

She snorted at him and sat back. "I am your mother, Adam. I know what troubles my boy."

"If that were true, then you would have known that I hated it all those years ago. Why did you not say anything, then? Not even when Father required me to spar with him every day, all those years?" He had not meant to raise his voice to her, and was startled when she shifted in her chair and avoided his eyes.

"We did speak of it, Adam," she replied, more softly now. "On occasion. I would ask how your training went, and you answered that it was fine. I thought you were figuring things out, learning how to stand up to Father. I didn't think it my place to figure it out for you."

"Did you ever speak to Father of my unhappiness?"

"Yes. But you must understand, Adam. Your father's own father—your grandfather—was a gloomy, capricious man. And he was about your height, but bigger—much heavier. You did not know him, thank Heavens. But he was strict and prone to outbursts, and I'm afraid that when your father was a child, those outbursts were sometimes violent. He threw a chair at him, just before he went away to school—"

"Struth?"

"—indeed. And so your father took up fighting, to learn to protect himself. He came home from school a grown man, and having never been defeated in the ring. And wouldn't you know it? He never had a chair thrown at him again. Perhaps it was coincidence, or perhaps having a reputation as a bruiser made your grandfather respect him, finally. I couldn't say. I just know that it became more and more of an obsession for him over the years, and that by passing his obsession on to you, he thought he'd be doing you a favor in this world."

"Why did you not tell me this?"

"Since when does anyone in this family speak seriously about things?"

Adam huffed in agreement.

"Or ill of the dead, for that matter? And I will admit, I did not realize the extent of the misery that his training caused you. You were my firstborn, and I was unsure about so many things. I stood back too much."

He looked into the fire. They had never spoken like this. The rapport they had with each other—and with Edie—was so bound up in teasing that they struggled when an earnest declaration was called for.

"I was miserable twice over, Mother. Firstly because I loathed fighting. And secondly because I hated the idea that I might disappoint Father. It increased tenfold when he died believing his only son and heir was a coward."

He looked up and found her staring at him, gripping both armrests.

"*He did not think that, Adam*," she said in a stern whisper. "*Never*. And neither have I. That does remind me, however, of one other thing that I very much regret."

"What is that?"

"I do not agree with the belief, which so many others seem to carry through life, that fighting is somehow part and parcel of manhood. That a willingness to go at another person with one's fists—or a weapon—is by definition a brave act. I should have insisted on digging that out of you, long, *long* ago."

He stared at her. "Please be easy, Mother. I should not place the blame at your feet because I did not stand up to Father. And besides, I seem to have dug it out of myself, at long last."

"Truly?"

"Truly. I have struggled with it, but I am done. I no longer believe myself lacking in bravery—"

"I am thrilled to hear it."

"—and am officially retired from boxing."

She nodded. "After your father died, I was bitter for many years. I eventually turned that bitterness inside out, doused it with humor, and began spooning it out to the world. I knew I would not keep my wits about me—and keep this family together—if I kept such ill humor inside of me."

He went to her and kneeled next to her. "But I should not have teased you so much about the things you *do* love," she continued, brushing the sides of his short hair as if to tuck it behind his ears.

He squeezed and kissed her hand. "Be easy, Mother. I want you to know that I have good memories of Father, too. I have missed him, too."

She covered his hand with her own and gave it one quick pat before drawing it back again. "Now, tell me about this event that you and Edie are having."

He sighed and stood. "It's going to be rather wonderful, I think. We're going to exhibit the drawings the Crispins have done for the house."

"Are they really so magnificent?"

"You will see," he replied as he walked to the window.

He considered telling her that he intended to propose to Caro. But two days had passed since he had woken up alone, and doubts still nagged him as to whether she would accept him. He had not been sore that she had left; she had explained that she needed to leave and in truth, he sympathized with her long-suffering parents' desire to see her safely home. And their night together had been a clarion declaration of their affection for one another—in words and in gesture, and in every quiet moment in between.

But her refusal to talk of the future had left him bothered and restless. Having her love and her desire was a magnificent gift, but it would not be enough.

Not having her at all would be devastating.

How many times now, had he tried to ask her to marry him and been interrupted? It had become almost ludicrous. The first time he'd tried was in his scullery, at Edie's dinner party; then he'd nearly done so in her carriage, after the infamous ride with Chumsley and that other snake. And then, of course, he'd tried to broach the topic when they'd lain in bed together.

When he saw her at the exhibition, he would invite her to spend time with him alone. To take a walk, perhaps. He could not take this uncertainty much longer.

CHAPTER TWENTY-NINE

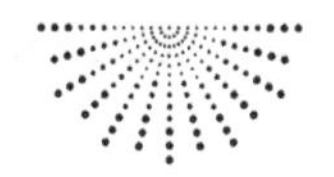

"Miss Crispin?"

"Lady Tilbeth!" Caro replied, smirking openly. She was standing with Edie in the entrance hall of Adam's townhome, welcoming guests to the exhibition. "What a lovely shade of red your cheeks have become just now."

"Indeed," Edie added with an impish smile. "Tell us, Lady Tilbeth: how do you accomplish such a natural flush?"

Lady Tilbeth's mouth opened and closed like the fish that inhabited her pond. "You must excuse me, I...I believe..."

"Please, come inside," Edie replied. "Have a seat. Or a brandy, perhaps."

When she'd gone, Edie turned back to Caro. "I can greet everyone on my own, you know. There's no need for you to suffer this."

"Thank you, dearest. But I want to face everyone and be done with it," she replied. "In fact, I'm feeling a little better already."

Edie squeezed her arm. "Then I'm going ask everyone to be seated. Just whistle if you need rescuing."

"Depending on the offending party," she said as she watched Edie walk away and into the saloon, "I might just throw my slipper at them."

While she waited for another guest to arrive she bounced on her toes, facing away from the door, trying to see past the crowds of admirers who were jostling for a look at the drawings the pupils had set up in the saloon. And as she strained to see, she spotted Adam standing near the large wooden easels, talking with Mama and Papa. Suddenly he looked up at her and they exchanged smiles. She resisted the urge to wave at him.

"I am exceedingly happy for you both," said a voice from behind her.

She turned and found Lord Quillen waiting to greet her. She had left his estate without saying goodbye, and they hadn't spoken since she had passed him there—worried and distracted—in a dark corridor, on her way to procure something or other for Adam.

"Please let me know when I may congratulate you more publicly," he continued.

She curtsied. "I am not flirtatious anymore, Lord Quillen. So I won't pretend that I don't know what you mean."

He frowned at her. "My dear Miss Crispin. I have known you many years, and have only ever known you to be an outgoing, clever, generous woman. If others have given less pleasant descriptions of your manners, it is a sign of their own insecurity and nothing more. Please do not change your nature—not a whit."

She smiled and shook his hand. "I only meant that I will be saving my more flirtatious energies for one gentleman in particular. Rest assured that I will continue to speak my mind to the rest of you lot. Someone must keep you all in line."

"Ah, good. I fear that task must fall to you now, since you have demonstrated yourself so capable of running a man out of the country when necessary."

He bowed and headed toward the saloon.

She bounced on her toes again. It had been surprisingly pleasant greeting the guests with Edie; no one had made her feel unwelcome, although a few—like the Tilbeths—had done little to conceal their shock upon seeing her. But she was impatient for everyone to arrive so that she could have a private word with Adam.

She needed to begin her scheme.

As Edie finished herding the last of the guests to their seats, Adam came into the entrance hall and grinned at her in a most peculiar way. Did he feel the same queerness she felt? That delicious anticipation, overlaid with the agony of having to wait still longer to realize their hopes?

And to hop into bed again?

"Please, Miss Crispin. If you would allow me to escort you, I have saved you the very best seat." He extended his arm for her to take and she took it. Eagerly, and without a care as to who might be looking. They had an understanding now.

Almost.

"Is the seat next to you, by chance?"

"Indeed. But that is not why it is the best."

"Why, then?"

"Come, and you will see."

* * *

Caro took his arm and drew close; so close, in fact, that they jostled against one another, gently, as they walked into the saloon. She looked up at him every so often, too, as they passed the rows of chairs and strode together to the front of the room.

This was not the behavior of a lover. This was a proclamation of her attachment to him, and of his to her. It was the behavior of two people who had an understanding.

She must feel as he did. She *must*. And he had never been happier.

He led her to her seat in the middle of the first row, and when she sat, bowed deeply. She reached out with her other hand and pressed something into his palm—a small letter of some kind.

He pretended to gasp. *"Shocking!"* he whispered before stepping away. He slipped it into his pocket and went to stand before the drawings.

And what drawings they were! The Crispins had outdone themselves: there was an elevation and two sections in pen and sepia, a series of plans in pencil and colorful washes, and even a watercolor perspective that showed not just their own home but the ones on either side, an assortment of trees (that did not yet exist!), and the street out front. A few exuberant-looking pedestrians had been drawn in, too, all of them wearing the latest fashions. When he had expressed his astonishment over the piece, Mrs. Crispin had simply told him, "I couldn't help myself. It was so diverting!"

As a set, the drawings illustrated in great detail the Crispins' proposal for a restoration of the home's façade, including more—and taller—windows; the addition of a fourth and fifth floor to the house, and a third floor to the mews; the removal of a wall to enlarge the dining room and create a single, large entertaining space; a trellis in the front for Adam's greenery; and a terrace built out over the grooms' area in the back, where additional planting could occur. Together with other, smaller improvements, these changes had the potential to ameliorate the inconveniences of their current living quarters, and to help the house become the spacious, light-filled family home he had hoped it could be. The drawings were gorgeous to behold, too, and the crowd was still *oohing* and *ahhing* and debating some detail or other from their seats.

"My friends," Adam began after he turned and faced the crowd, "welcome to our home. My mother, sister, and I have great affection for this old place—many memories of laughing here over our Christmas goose, of setting out for ices at Gunter's, of sitting quietly by the fire while my late father read aloud from a book of verse." He looked toward Mother as he said it, and watched as she closed her eyes and allowed sadness and happiness to dance together on her face awhile as he spoke. It was a rare display of unguardedness, and it warmed him.

"But I am thrilled to open a new chapter on this nearly century-old home," he continued, "and on behalf of our entire family I would like to say how honored we are to have Mrs. Betsy Crispin as the architect for our renovation."

Caro's jaw fell open as if on a well-oiled hinge, and there were audible gasps from the crowd. He began applauding at once, however, and after several seconds of what appeared to be utter shock, Caro lifted her hands and joined him.

Gradually, other members of the crowd did, too.

"Many of you have already told me today how magnificent these drawings are. How inspired the ideas are. How they move you. So I'm sure you will join me in enthusiastically welcoming Mrs. Crispin to the front of the room, to address us all today on the origins of her ideas, and the process she has used to develop them into what you see before you."

He and Caro clapped again and this time, the greater portion of the crowd joined them. Caro was struggling to remain composed, he could tell; her eyes shone and her lip trembled. He waited as her mother walked to the front of the room, the corners of her eyes and mouth crinkling as she turned and faced a few dozen of society's most prominent members. As far as he could tell, not a one of them continued to whisper as Mrs. Betsy Crispin, Architect, shook his hand and began her presentation, her voice strong and clear and true.

He took his seat and looked at Caro, who clamped onto his arm and squeezed it. She mouthed the words *thank you* before turning back to listen, dabbing absently at her tears with the handkerchief in her spare hand.

* * *

The letter Caro had given him had requested that he meet her at Covent Garden, at nine o'clock the next morning.

He chuckled at the appropriateness of rendezvousing with her there. He had developed a fondness for the place since sparring with her over the fruits and vegetables, three months earlier.

He just wasn't sure *where* in the market he was meant to find her. The apples, perhaps? They seemed like a good choice, given the role they had played in their first meeting. Or maybe the cucumbers? Or turnips? Those were the most salacious vegetables they had teased over. On the other hand, it was over strawberries where she had first made him laugh so hard that he nearly choked.

He smiled at the special attachments he had to these foods, and speculated fondly over what other things—whether animal, vegetable, or mineral—he would eventually imbue with memories of time spent with Caro, laughing and talking and yes, flirting.

He recognized the costermonger tending the cucumbers, but before he could ask if he had seen Caro, the man reached out and handed him one of his wares.

The man smiled and leaned back. When Adam tried to hand him some coin, he shook his head and wagged a knobby finger at him, then turned with a warm smile to his next customer.

So Adam was left to move on to the strawberries, and once there, the woman overseeing the cart handed him a sack of the tiny red fruits without so much as a "How do you do?"

"Pray, madam," he said, "Why are you handing me these strawberries?"

She waved him off with a chapped, red hand. "You will see, my lord. You'll see."

The same thing happened at the apples. And the turnips. At the persimmons, the man gave him an empty bushel to carry all of his items. He tipped his hat and when he turned away, spotted Caro standing nearby, her features nearly bursting with that peculiar blend of pride and mischief that he'd come to recognize as one of her hallmarks. At her feet, Toby rolled and contorted himself in the dirt, as if trying to work out an itch.

"Why, Lord Ryland!" she called out, sounding not so much like herself as one of her friends from the theater troupe. In a ruby-red frock he'd never seen before, she came toward him with one hand held aloft, unable to contain her ebullient grin. "How thoughtful of you to bring me a basket of all our favorite produce. It is almost...romantic." The dog shook himself out and followed.

"Mmm. Most thoughtful of me, indeed." He set down the bushel and held out his hands for her to take. "What is all this, Caro?"

"This is the only place in town I could think of," she began, placing her hands in his, "where none of our acquaintances would come upon us and interrupt your proposal."

He tilted his head at her.

"At least not in the morning hours, before the working ladies are up and about. So let's have it, then. Out with it."

He released her hands and rubbed at his jaw, feigning confusion. "Is this my proposal, or *yours*?"

"Whichever you would prefer, my lord. This is your day. Your chance. Your time."

He put his hands on his hips and tried to look serious. Ebullient grins were contagious, it turned out. "It would be most interesting to hear *your* proposal, though I do appreciate you offering me the opportunity to finish my own. Very generous of you."

"You are quite welcome. Please, continue."

He rubbed at his jaw. "Miss Caroline Cris—"

"Wait!"

"What is it?"

"A question: Would we live in town, or in the country?"

"Which would you prefer? I've come to like both."

"Toby and I would like to try the country, but I also require time in town. So good, yes, that will be fine."

"May I continue?"

"Yes."

"Caro, I love you. You leave me in pieces every time I see you. Would you do me the honor—"

"Wait!"

"*Blazes,* Caro! Devil take it!"

She laughed and threw herself into his arms, scaring a kit of pigeons into flight. He lifted her off the ground and brought her face to his. It was a highly untoward display of affection, but it scarcely mattered—they were each other's now. And there were far more untoward things going on at Covent Garden than the two of them embracing and kissing.

"Are we engaged or not?" she asked when they paused, their noses still touching.

"I hope so. I certainly feel engaged," he replied.

"That was quite possibly the strangest proposal in history."

"Strangely romantic, I think."

"Indeed? That's too bad. I was aiming for *silly*."

He laughed. "Sometimes, my dear, they are one and the same."

THE END

Thank you for reading! For more from Willa Ramsey, check out her website and find her across social media.

Twitter: https://twitter.com/WRamsey_Author

Pinterest: https://www.pinterest.com/willa_ramsey/

Instagram: https://www.instagram.com/willaramsey_author/

Facebook: https://www.facebook.com/willaramseyauthorpage/

Website: www.willaramsey.com

* * *

ACKNOWLEDGMENTS

I owe a lot, to a lot of people. That's especially true when it came to publishing this book.

I want to thank the team at City Owl Press, particularly my editor Heather McCorkle and company co-founders Tina Moss and Yelena Casale, for believing in this story and in me. The other City Owl authors have also been welcoming and helpful at every opportunity.

The publishing world is a heartening, supportive place, especially where there are Romance-genre people, and especially where there are aspiring and debut authors. The expertise and generosity of the Rose City Romance Writers and the Authors '18 Facebook Group have been indispensable. I also learned a tremendous amount from freelance editor Wylie O'Sullivan and writers Gretchen Grey-Hatton, Felicia Grossman, MJ Marshall, Lisa Leoni. Author Christy Carlyle has been a helpful guide and friend, and author Tessa Dare gave me lovely encouragement when I first started writing. Dozens of contest judges and mentors helped shape this book, too.

I'm extremely fortunate to have friends, old and new, silver and gold, who encouraged me to write for publication. Christine Teike Hewitt, Chelsa Bailey, and Mary Coelho-Carroll. Nicole Henderson and

Stephanie Carmel. Jasmin Ashley Wright. Kezia King and Katyna Smith. My expanding, RISD-based crew.

I have my friend Jon Fernandez to thank for answers to my boxing questions. I've tried to do right by his expertise, and any errors are my own.

Then there is my family. I hit the proverbial lottery when it comes to family, and I know it. I have inordinately giving, loving parents in Kathy and Dave; hilarious, supportive siblings in Jenn and Davy; a pair of beloved, generous aunts in Dorothy and Trishy; a late grandmother who was as spirited and creative as she was kind; legions of extended family and family-members-by-marriage, who inquire about my writing at every opportunity; a husband whose expansive love and support defy all my attempts to lasso them with words; and two lively, curious kids who understand that Mommy likes books with a lot of words in them, sometimes puts the words in them herself, and that that is an important, and worthy, thing to do.

I'm so lucky to have you all.

Lastly, a number of written sources helped deepen and expand my knowledge of Regency England. Giles Worsley's ARCHITECTURAL DRAWINGS OF THE REGENCY PERIOD, Fraser Simons's THE EARLY HISTORY OF BALLOONING: THE AGE OF THE AERONAUT, and Emily Eerdmans's CLASSIC ENGLISH DESIGN AND ANTIQUES: PERIOD STYLES AND FURNITURE greatly enriched this story. The chapters devoted herein to Adam's boxing match are an homage to William Hazlitt's iconic 1822 essay "The Fight." These were all treasure troves to me.

ABOUT THE AUTHOR

Before becoming a novelist, Willa Ramsey wrote meeting minutes. And web copy. And planning reports. She doesn't miss those jobs, but appreciates how much they taught her: Transcribing all those conversations? Developed her ear for dialogue. Web writing? Taught her pith. Years of city planning? Gave her a fresh take on Regency London. So her road to becoming an author was full of wrong-turns and unexpected stops. But sometimes, those are just what you didn't know you needed!

Image by Kate Kelly Photography

Twitter: https://twitter.com/WRamsey_Author

Pinterest: https://www.pinterest.com/willa_ramsey/

Instagram: https://www.instagram.com/willaramsey_author/

Facebook: https://www.facebook.com/willaramseyauthorpage/

Website: www.willaramsey.com

ABOUT THE PUBLISHER

Please sign up for the City Owl Press newsletter for chances to win special subscriber-only contests and giveaways as well as receiving information on upcoming releases and special excerpts.

All reviews are **welcome** and **appreciated**. Please consider leaving one on your favorite social media and book buying sites.

For books in the world of romance and speculative fiction that embody Innovation, Creativity, and Affordability, check out City Owl Press.

www.cityowlpress.com